Kate's Return

Kate's Return

A Novel

Cheri J. Crane

Covenant Communications, Inc.

For my mother, Genevieve S. Jackson, a woman of remarkable
faith and courage.

Published by Covenant Communications, Inc.
American Fork, Utah

Printed in the United States of America
First Printing: August 1996

01 00 99   10 9 8 7 6 5 4

ISBN 1-55503-982-0

ACKNOWLEDGMENTS

Several people contributed to the creation of this novel. Their time, talents, and willingness to help are greatly appreciated. Thanks again to the wonderful staff at Covenant Communications, including two dedicated editors, JoAnn Jolley and Valerie Holladay.

Again, my hat is off to the Burdick Bunch of Bennington, especially Shelley and Melissa who spent untold hours proofreading.

Special thanks goes out to Trisha Crane of Bennington, and her mother, Betty Donaghy of Dumbarton, Scotland, for the maps, books, and materials that provided colorful background information on Scotland.

I would also like to express gratitude to my sister-in-law, Shar Jackson, who guided me through the Family History Library in Salt Lake City and showed me the ins and outs of genealogical research.

A big thank you to her husband, my favorite (and only) brother, Tom Jackson, the Funding Specialist for UCAT (Utah Center for Assistive Technology). The information and demonstration of equipment available for the physically challenged contributed crucial facts for the character of Ian Campbell. May UCAT be allowed to continue in its quest to offer assistance— touching lives in a significant way!

Thanks to my sisters, Heather Littell and Trudi Jackson, for the loan of several reference books.

My appreciation is also extended to the terrific ladies who work at the Bear Lake County Library, especially Mary, Carolan, and June. Thank you for your assistance in gathering research material.

Finally, a tremendous round of applause for my husband, Kennon, and my three sons, Kris, Derek, and Devin. Thanks once again for your patience, help, and support.

AUTHOR'S NOTE

A few years ago, I thumbed through a family history book and came across an account of sacrifice, pain, and love—the life story of William Stewart and Sarah Thompson, set in the mid-1800s.

William came from a wealthy Scottish clan, but Sarah was born into a poor Irish family. Sarah worked as a servant in William's household and the two fell in love. In an effort to separate the couple, William's mother transported Sarah to a dressmaking school in a distant town, unaware that Sarah and William had been secretly married. Nearly a year passed before William found his new bride. When he learned of his mother's role in Sarah's disappearance, William turned his back on the Stewart family, and the couple lived for several years in Ireland near Sarah's relatives.

Five children were born before William and Sarah returned to Scotland. With the passage of time, grievances were forgiven and family ties were restored with the Stewarts. A proud man, William refused financial support from the Stewarts and moved his family to Glasgow, Scotland, to seek work. While there, they came in contact with the Mormon missionaries, and the family of William and Sarah Stewart joined the Church. Bitter persecution convinced Sarah that her family needed to move to Zion to live among the Saints. When her health failed and it became apparent she would not live to make the journey to Utah, Sarah asked her husband and eight children to promise they would go without her and have the family sealed together.

After her death, the family made every effort to keep that promise and when enough money was secured, came to America. Times were difficult and years passed before Sarah's desire to have the family sealed became a reality. Finally, in 1946, all of the temple work was completed, and the William Stewart family was united with eternal bonds.

The journal entries contained in the latter portion of this book are loosely based on the history of William and Sarah Stewart. (This particular account was taken from *The Descendants of James George Crane & Sarah Jane Butterfield,* compiled by Wayne and Ginger Swensen.) Names, dates, and events were altered to fit the story line.

C. Crane

P.S. Dear readers, when you come to the conclusion of this novel, consider the advice frequently offered by my *good* brother-in-law, Jeffery Crane: *"Don't you fret!"* I am already working on the next book in this series. Until then, *au revoir!*

CHAPTER ONE

K ate blinked in stunned surprise, the accusations made by Sandi Kearns still ringing in her ears. Then, as feeling and the ability to move returned, she glanced around the deserted restroom. Leaning against a nearby sink, she gripped the sides for support. She took a deep breath and stared at her reflection in the mirror. Losing control wouldn't help. Chasing Sandi down the hall wouldn't help. *Linda.* Finding Linda would help.

Kate's eyes narrowed as determination replaced the defeated expression on her face. "You're wrong, Sandi," she murmured. "I had nothing to do with this. Nothing at all."

Several minutes later, Kate burst out of the high school and hurried to the parking lot. Glancing around, she could tell that Linda had already left; there was no sign of her former friend. Too angry to notice the beautiful fall afternoon, Kate began the long walk to Linda's house, adrenaline giving her the strength to walk nearly two miles before she tired and slowed her pace. Her left leg ached slightly, reminding her of the fracture that had recently healed.

In frustration, she ran her hand through her long hair, its slight red cast more apparent in the sun. She had never imagined her return to Bozeman would be like this. If she had known, she would have begged to stay in Salt Lake. Aunt Paige and Uncle Stan had made the offer while she had convalesced in their Murray home. It had been tempting to take them up on it, but this was her senior year, and she wanted to spend as much time at home as possible. Only recently had she realized how much her family meant to her. The accident had opened her eyes to a lot of things she hadn't noticed before.

The accident. That's how everyone referred to the event that had drastically altered her life. Linda had thrown it in her face whenever possible.

"You can't remember who you are because of the accident!" Sandi had accused this afternoon. "You haven't really changed, it's the accident." But both Linda and Sandi were wrong. Kate Erickson was *very* much aware of who she was. The *accident* had changed things, but in Kate's opinion, for the better.

Kate moved onto a leaf-covered lawn to walk around the giggling junior high girls who were blocking her way. She didn't have the patience or the time to remain behind them. Picking up speed, she hurried down the sidewalk. Finally spotting the tall blonde, Kate ran through a pile of dry leaves, oblivious to the pleasant crackling sounds and smells of autumn.

"Linda, wait up. Linda . . ."

Linda glanced over her shoulder. Lifting an eyebrow, she waited as Kate hurried forward.

"We need to talk," Kate panted, slightly out of breath.

"Something I've been saying for weeks," Linda replied, crossing the street. She motioned toward her house.

"I've been talking, you just haven't been listening," Kate muttered under her breath.

"What?" Linda called back.

"I said, we need to talk about something I overheard at school this afternoon," Kate said, heading across the road. "I thought I'd better check it out." She stopped in front of the garage, noticing the Mustang that was pulled off to the side. That would explain why Linda had walked home today. "Is something wrong with your car?" she asked, stalling. The anger was fading to nervousness. This wasn't going to be easy.

Linda shook her head. "Mom was off today. She wanted to change the oil in both outfits," she replied, nodding her head toward her mother's car, a tiny Geo Metro.

"Oh." Kate set her book bag down on the sidewalk near the

driveway. "She's becoming quite the mechanic."

"Costs too much to take 'em in. We only do that when we're really desperate." Linda studied the look on Kate's face. She was certain her friend hadn't come by to discuss car maintenance. "Okay, let's hear it. What's up?" she asked, leaning against her mother's car.

"That's what I'd like to know," Kate replied. "What's this about a party tomorrow night?"

Linda frowned. How had Kate found out?

"One in my honor?" Kate pressed, watching Linda closely.

"What are you talking about?" Linda responded, feigning innocence.

"Don't give me that—I know you're behind it."

Linda returned Kate's unwavering gaze. "Who have you been talking to?"

"Linda, I know, okay?! Give it a rest."

"Fine," Linda snapped. "There *is* a party in the works. Happy now?"

"No," Kate retorted. "What were you thinking?"

Linda grabbed her by the shoulders. "Don't you understand, this party is for you! We're trying to help you," she said, releasing Kate. She scowled. "Do you have any idea how hard it was this summer, thinking you were going to die? Then I hear you're going to be all right. That you've snapped out of the coma. You come home and I think things are going to be fine. Instead, you're like a stranger. You're my best friend and I don't even know you anymore!" she exclaimed. "I thought maybe a party would jar you back to reality!"

"Linda, I don't want—"

"I've heard that line for weeks, Kate. How about what I want for a change? Not that it matters to you, you stubborn—"

"I didn't come here to fight with you," Kate said, cutting her off, hoping to avoid a string of off-colored words.

"So why did you come?"

"To find out why you're throwing this party—and to let you know I won't be there. So you might as well cancel . . ."

"What a surprise," Linda sniffed. "That's why we were keeping it a secret. We figured once you were there, you'd give in and have a little fun. It was supposed to be your welcome home party."

"Why now?" Kate asked. She had expected something like this weeks ago, not now, just as she was starting to convince people she was sincere about turning her life around.

"We kept waiting for you to recover . . . to return to your senses," Linda replied. "We finally gave up and decided a good party is what you need."

"I'm not into that kind of thing anymore."

"I think you're into some kind of weird trip."

"I'm a different person . . ."

"I'll say," Linda said with a smirk. "Quit fooling yourself, Kate, you'll never be one of them," she added, pointing across the street to a sophomore who was considered beneath contempt because of her high standards. "Come with me tomorrow night. It'll be great, I promise." Linda paused hopefully, but Kate remained silent. "If you care about me at all, you'll come."

"I care, but I can't . . ." Kate closed her eyes. "Why are you doing this to me?"

"Why are you acting like a jerk?" Linda countered, flipping her hair over her shoulder. "You are such an ingrate! You have no idea how much trouble we've gone to!"

Kate shook her head. "I don't need this kind of trouble in my life."

"Look, Molly Moron—"

"That's *Mormon,*" Kate stressed, her green eyes flashing.

"Whatever . . . we put this thing together for you! Everyone will be there!"

"Not everyone," Kate said firmly. "I don't need those parties anymore."

"Like you don't need me?"

"Linda . . . you've been a good friend," Kate said, softening. "But things aren't the same . . ."

"Tell me about it! Now that you've had this *miraculous* recovery, you're too good for the rest of us!"

"I didn't say that."

"You don't need to," Linda exclaimed. "It's coming across loud and clear. The way you ignore us. The way you try to fit in with those twits from your branch. And I can't believe how you've acted around Jace. That guy worships the ground you walk on, and you've done nothing but treat him like dirt since you came home!"

Kate sighed. "What is it going to take to get you to realize my life has changed? That dream I had—"

"I am so sick of you and your dreams! I don't want to hear anymore of that garbage! You live in a dream world! When you decide to come back to earth, give me a call. Until then, keep your distance. I don't need this and I don't need you!"

"Linda—"

"Go hang with those religious creeps, if they'll have anything to do with you. I don't care what you do. I never did. You mean absolutely nothing to me."

"Linda!"

"You're like some stray mutt begging for attention. Well, you're not getting it from me anymore!" Whirling around, Linda ran off. Ignoring Kate's pleas to listen, she stormed inside the house, banging the screen door against the aluminum siding. She headed down the hall, entered her bedroom, and slammed the door. Knocking off the piles of magazines, clothes, and CD's, she threw herself onto the bed, pounded a fist into a pillow, and refused to cry.

Only losers cry, she reminded herself. It was ironic she had once shared that wisdom with Kate. A couple of years ago, Kate had come to her, upset after a terrible argument she'd had with her mother. Of course, that was before she had sustained brain damage. Now Kate and her mother got along so well, it was nauseating.

Linda rolled over and glared at the poster attached to her ceiling. A half-dressed metal rocker leered at her. Taking her anger out on him, she uttered several obscenities.

Someone knocked softly at the door. Convinced that it was Kate, begging for another chance, Linda refused to acknowledge the sound. *Let her beg—she deserves the silent treatment!*

The knock sounded again. Linda grinned. The blow-up had been worth it. She should have set her straight weeks ago. Now it would be like old times. Kate—coming to her. Coming for advice, for comfort when her parents overstepped parental boundaries.

Things were finally getting back to normal.

"Linda?"

Linda scowled at the sound of her mother's voice.

"Are you all right?" Marie asked. She had heard Linda slam into her bedroom. That was normal. What wasn't normal was the silence. By now, thundering drum beats and wailing guitars should have been giving her a headache. The noise grated on her nerves, but Marie preferred the strained squealing to the silence that often meant her daughter was getting stoned.

The past couple of years, Marie had turned her back to the alcohol and drug use, fearing it would only get worse if she said anything. She told herself comforting things to rationalize what Linda was doing. *Kids always try that stuff. It's part of growing up.* She knew she was more permissive with Linda than she should be, but guilt nagged at her; she was a single parent, trying to make up for a father who existed in name only. Dwight Sikes—a man who had deserted them both years ago, leaving a legacy of scarring heart wounds.

Dwight had left when Linda was seven, and he had vowed to never return. Aside from the court proceedings, he had kept his word. He had never sought custody of their daughter and had never bothered to ask for visitation rights. It was his way of striking back; his way of evening the score.

Dwight had never wanted to be a father. He had often accused Marie of trapping him into marriage. It wasn't true, but he wouldn't listen. Too late, Marie realized he had used her love to satisfy his selfish needs. He'd had no intention of developing a serious relationship. In every way, he had fallen far short of the man she had thought him to be.

Marie still remembered her devastation when she had realized she was pregnant with Dwight's child. Her father's reaction hadn't helped. Furious, he had insisted Dwight make things "right" by marrying her. Dwight's parents had agreed. But the marriage, based on a mutual lack of respect, had been a mistake. And in the end, Dwight had walked away, not caring that he had shattered two hearts with a single slam of the door.

Marie knocked a third time. "Linda . . . I heard what happened with you and Kate. I think we should talk about it." As she had hunted for an oil filter in the mess that was their garage, Marie had overheard the heated argument between the two girls. She had stepped out of the garage in time to see her daughter run inside the house.

"Marie . . . Mrs. Sikes," Kate had stammered. "I didn't mean . . . I didn't want . . . She won't listen—"

"Give her time to cool down," Marie had gently suggested. "I'll try to talk to her. Maybe later you two can work things out." Kate had nodded before slowly walking away.

Marie knocked again at the bedroom door. When there was no answer, she gripped the doorknob and tried to turn it. As she had feared, it was locked.

"Linda," she called again. "Let me in. We need to talk."

"Go away!" Linda yelled. "Leave me alone!"

Marie stared at the door that separated her from her daughter and realized she had never felt so helpless in her entire life.

CHAPTER TWO

Kate angrily wiped at her eyes, but the tears continued to fall, stubbornly sliding down her face. Leaning against a large maple tree, she tried to calm down. A cooling breeze stirred the multi-colored leaves at her feet, then played with her hair. She slid down to sit against the tree, mulling over what had led to today's disaster.

The trouble had actually started years ago, in junior high. Kate had grown bored with her friends from the Bozeman LDS branch and had started running around with Linda Sikes and her crowd. Drifting from standards taught by her parents and the Church, Kate had been drawn to Linda's carefree lifestyle. Through the years, a bond of friendship had grown, despite the lectures from Kate's parents and several Young Women leaders. Repeated warnings had been ignored, especially after Kate had become obsessed with Jace Sloan, a young man with an unsavory reputation. Appalled by what they were sure was happening, Sue and Greg Erickson tried to put distance between their daughter and Jace by insisting that Kate accompany them on the annual Erickson family summer vacation. Kate had finally agreed to go, promising herself she would make it an adventure in misery.

Plagued by accusations and contention, that vacation had led to a series of mishaps that would forever change Kate's life. After an intense argument with her mother, Kate had decided she'd had enough. She had stormed from the visitors' center at Temple

Square in Salt Lake City, unaware that her mother wasn't the only one following. Her sister, Sabrina, had stepped into the busy street, shrieking with fear as traffic tried to swerve around the frightened five-year-old. Sensing the danger, Kate had hurried back to push Sabrina out of the way of an oncoming car. Sabrina had been shoved to safety, leaving Kate to absorb the impact that had thrown her across the street and into a coma.

The dream she'd had during the coma had influenced her in ways she was still trying to understand. In her dream, she had been forced to travel with pioneer ancestors as they had walked across the plains to what would later be known as Salt Lake City. That journey had offered a fresh perspective and given life new meaning. The hardships that were suffered had transformed Kate as she had painfully cut herself loose from a web of sin and selfish anger. Now she burned with a desire to live the gospel principles taught by her beloved fourth great-grandmother, Colleen Mahoney.

Sighing at the memory of her grandmother, Kate continued to walk home. She kicked at a rock that had the misfortune of being in the way. It bounced once on the sidewalk, then spiraled into the street, connecting with the tire of a parked car.

"At least it didn't hit a window," she muttered, imagining the reaction of the owner. Since her return, she'd had to be so careful of everything she said or did, it was like living in a glass bubble. Sharpened stones surrounded her, waiting for the chance to be thrown. Self-pity seeped in as she relived the misery of the past six weeks.

In the beginning, everyone had seemed glad to see her. On her seventeenth birthday, the last week of August, flowers and cards had littered the house. Several people had come by to visit, including the young women from her branch. But the forced smiles had revealed it was a token gesture only, led by the new Young Women's president, Lori Blanchard. Acceptance by these girls wouldn't happen overnight. They were keeping their distance, still convinced she was having fun with them at their expense.

That barrier had gained strength from the continuing problem of Linda and Jace. Jace was constantly trying to weasel his way back into her life. It wouldn't work, but he refused to admit defeat. It didn't help that during the first weeks of school, her hands had been tied up with the crutches. It had taken several weeks for her broken leg to fully heal. Jace had taken full advantage, approaching her in the hall during school, draping his arm around her shoulders, sending out the message that she was still his property. She had made it clear several times that they were through, but the more she protested, the more interest he showed in her. A couple of days ago, she had overheard Jace bragging to a group of boys that she had become a challenge, a new frontier he would conquer. She had responded by telling him what she thought of him, adding that she never wanted to see him again. Jace had merely laughed and then bowed in an exaggerated fashion, causing everyone around him to burst into laughter.

Jace and Linda had refused to accept the changes Kate was trying to make. She no longer cared about Jace, but Linda had been her closest friend. They had once shared so much and had always been able to talk things out. If today was any indication, the ties between them were now severed.

On the way home from Salt Lake, Kate had daydreamed about helping Linda turn her life around. Instead, Linda had laughed at her attempts to share her experience, telling Kate she was suffering from acute brain damage. Linda almost seemed to enjoy baiting Kate, in an attempt to draw out the side of her that no longer existed. The final straw had been the party Linda was planning for this weekend. A party Kate had known nothing about until Sandi Kearns, a former friend from her branch, had thrown it in her face.

Following her mother's advice, Kate had tried to invite Sandi over to the house Saturday night to watch videos and eat pizza. When Kate mentioned getting together, Sandi had made it perfectly clear she wasn't about to attend one of her wild parties. Then she had hurried down the hall, heading into the girls' rest room.

"What in the world are you talking about?" Kate had asked, following her. "Wait a second."

The petite brunette had turned around to face her in the rest room. "You know perfectly well, you two-faced hypocrite," Sandi said coldly. "That party Linda's planning." Giving Kate a dirty look, Sandi had bolted out of the rest room and disappeared down the hall.

Remembering the disdain on Sandi's face and the disgust on Linda's, Kate frowned. "You won't even try to understand," she muttered, walking through a small pile of dry leaves. "No one will."

When she finally reached her house, she ran through the garage and into the back yard. Leaning against the fence, she clung to it for support. *I'm trying to do the right thing,* she silently pleaded. *Why isn't it working?*

CHAPTER THREE

Linda gazed around the crowded room. The party was a success—even without the guest of honor. They had decided to go ahead, renaming it "Kate's Wake." It was Linda's idea. Everyone had loved it; they were all sick to death of Kate's new attitude. The Kate they had known was gone, replaced by a new, horribly improved version. It was only right that they should take time to mourn.

It had cracked everyone up when a somber-looking Jace had offered a toast to their dearly departed friend. "To Kate, a true party animal who will be sorely missed. And now, a moment of silence in her honor." Jace had dramatically bowed his head, then guzzled an entire can of beer. Grinning, he had belched the final tribute. He was now in the corner seeking what he called "solace" from one of the girls who had come. Lily was her name. Another in the series of girls Jace would use and discard. Kate had been the exception—she had never given in to Jace's demands. In a way, Linda had admired her for it; Kate had managed to keep Jace's interest, which was probably why he was hounding her now. He couldn't accept defeat.

Linda swallowed the rest of the vodka in her cup. She knew Kate was no longer a part of their lives. Forcing the thought from her mind, she moved across the room, searching for something that would ease what she was feeling inside.

* * *

Sue Erickson retreated from the family room and exchanged a look of concern with her husband, Greg. Sandi was here, which was a start, but only because Lori Blanchard had insisted. After Kate had tearfully revealed what had been happening at school and at church, Sue had talked to the Young Women's president. Sue was afraid that if the girls in their small branch didn't start accepting her daughter, Kate would slip back into familiar patterns.

After Sue's phone call, Lori had talked to Sandi and her mother, pleading for their cooperation and help. Sandi had grudgingly called earlier this afternoon to see if Kate still wanted to get together to watch a video. A surprised Kate had agreed. Now, Sandi was here, sitting beside Kate on the couch in the family room, reluctantly eating pizza. Neither girl had spoken more than two or three sentences, but Sue decided not to hover. She had done everything she could think of—the rest was up to Sandi and Kate.

Sandi bit into the piece of pepperoni pizza in her hand and wondered again why she had let Sister Blanchard talk her into coming here. She had never felt this uncomfortable in her entire life. And the movie was anything but entertaining, an outdated Disney movie about a car coming to life. One she had seen about a hundred times. *Oh, well,* she thought silently, *this night can't last forever. It'll just seem that way.* One thing she was sure of, she wasn't about to befriend Kate again. She had never forgiven Kate for walking out of her life during junior high when Kate had chosen Linda and her wild crowd as friends. No matter what anyone said, Sandi was certain that when the shock of Kate's accident finally dissipated, Kate would return to them.

"So, do you like accelerated English?" Kate hesitantly asked.

"It's okay," Sandi answered, reaching for another slice of pizza. If she kept eating, she wouldn't be expected to talk.

"How do you like being president of our Young Women class?"

Sandi shrugged and continued to chew.

Kate tried again. "I'm sorry this movie is so lame. Mom picked it out. I should've gone with her, but I was trying to finish the biology assignment Coach Passey gave us yesterday."

Sandi nearly choked on a mouthful of pizza. Kate actually *did* homework?

"Are you still going out with Bill Swanson?" Kate asked, finally selecting a slice of pizza.

Sandi frowned and braced herself for the insults she was sure would follow. Kate had despised Bill in the past, claiming he was a mama's boy who needed to cut the apron strings. Sandi knew better. Bill's father had passed away three years ago, a victim of cancer. As a result, Bill worked part-time at a service station to help his mother make ends meet. With four children still at home, it was tough. Bill's meager contributions kept the family going.

"I'm sorry for the things I said about him," Kate said softly. "I was wrong. Bill's a neat guy."

This time, Sandi did choke, coughing up bits of pizza while Kate hurriedly poured a glass of water for her. Nodding her thanks, Sandi sipped at the water until the coughing subsided.

Kate watched her in concern. "Are you okay?" she asked.

Sandi nodded again and drained the water from the glass in her hand.

Kate took a deep breath. "I know you're not thrilled to be here, but I'm glad you came. It gives me a chance to talk to you . . . to apologize."

Sandi stared at Kate.

"I've done a lot of things I'm not very proud of, including hurting you."

Sandi set the glass down on the end table. She didn't want to hear any more excuses—Kate had been pumping them out for weeks. "Sorry" didn't fix everything.

A nagging inner voice reminded her of the lesson Sister Blanchard had taught before Kate had returned home. A lesson on forgiveness that the entire Young Women's organization had been subjected to. They had been painfully aware they were being asked to forgive Kate. The plea had fallen on deaf ears. They had been humiliated once too often. None of them trusted Kate, and none of them wanted her as a friend—not with her reputation.

"Please, Sandi. I don't know what more I can do," Kate pleaded, nervously twisting the napkin in her hands.

Tears began streaming down Kate's face. Sandi blinked. She had never seen Kate cry before. Now what? Sister Blanchard had said the greater sin rested with the party that refused to forgive. But how could Sandi possibly forgive her when she had repeatedly been the butt of Kate's jokes? How could she forget the insults, the sneers, the humiliation she had suffered each time Kate had used a secret from the past to entertain the crowd she chased with? Through it all, she had refused to show Kate how it had hurt. Only her mother had known. Only her mother had seen the tears.

"If I could take it all back . . . I would. I was wrong. I know that now. I wish I'd never—" As Kate's voice broke, she hid her face in her hands.

Sandi watched her for several seconds. She knew what she should do, but she couldn't respond. Deciding it would be best to leave, she placed her half-eaten slice of pizza near the pitcher of water and reached for her coat. Slipping it on, she walked toward the door, then hesitated and looked back at Kate. The revenge Sandi had imagined for so long wasn't sweet. The bitter feeling intensified until she finally stepped back into the family room and approached her former friend. "Okay, let's talk," she said.

"I thought you left," Kate said, looking up from her hands.

Sandi shook her head and handed Kate a fresh napkin before sitting down beside her on the couch. "We need to finish this," she said, slipping out of her coat as Kate wiped at her eyes and nose.

Kate nodded. What Sandi had come back to hear, she wasn't sure, but the words finally came. Begging forgiveness, Kate poured her heart out. Tearfully, old debts were settled and discarded as the two girls began to come to terms with a painful past.

* * *

It was nearly midnight when Sandi's mother called to see if her daughter was ever coming home.

"I'll be right there," Sandi assured her, still staring at the picture of Kate's new friend, Randy. This guy was gorgeous—a clean-cut missionary who had been called to serve in Ireland. Kate had definitely improved her taste in men.

"Do you need me to pick you up?" Harriet Kearns asked, still irritated that her daughter had been singled out to fellowship Kate. Here it was nearly midnight, and she certainly didn't want her daughter walking home alone.

"I can drive you home," Kate offered.

Sandi returned the smile. "Kate can bring me home, Mom."

Harriet wasn't sure she wanted Kate driving her daughter anywhere. "I don't know," she said reluctantly, not wanting to reveal what she really thought of Kate Erickson.

Sandi eased over her mother's concerns. "I'll see you in a few minutes. Bye."

After Harriet hung up the phone, she decided she would call Lori Blanchard the next morning. As far as Harriet was concerned, Sandi had gone above and beyond the call of duty. Kate could be someone else's responsibility. Harriet was not about to let her daughter get mixed up with Kate again. And she would make that clear as soon as Sandi walked through the door.

* * *

Linda slowly staggered across the lawn. It was only a few minutes past midnight, but she didn't feel like staying until the end of the party. Getting stoned hadn't helped the depression she felt. Her head buzzed with pain. Another wave of nausea hit as she reached the driveway. She looked around for her Mustang. Cars were parked everywhere around Jace's house. His parents were gone on another business trip. Everyone was having a wonderful time in their absence. Everyone but her.

She quickly lost the contents of her stomach in some bushes near the driveway. She tried to spit out the bitter taste that lingered, then gave up and renewed the search for her car. She found it on the other side of a truck. Fortunately, she had left the keys in the ignition, something she'd learned to do after losing several sets of keys at other parties. They usually surfaced the next day when the party mess was cleaned up.

The engine started on the second try. Linda smiled. A few more minutes and she would be home, sleeping this off. She had tried something new tonight. In the past, Kate had always tried to steer her past the drugs, claiming they messed with your mind. Well, Kate had messed with her mind anyway. So, when the tiny bag of white powder was waved in Linda's face, she had readily agreed, out of spite. Anything to help her forget. Anything to make her high. And it had worked, for a while. Shifting into reverse, Linda backed the car out of the driveway.

* * *

"Remember when we smeared pine gum on the latrine?" Sandi asked as Kate turned the Sunbird down the street that would eventually lead them to the Kearns home.

Remembering their first year at girls' camp when they had been eager Beehives, Kate grinned. "Yeah. Remember the look on Sister Lyle's face?"

Sandi laughed, seeing again the look of indignation as Sister Lyle had tried to readjust the clothes that were sticking to various parts of her anatomy. "Those were good times."

"There can be others," Kate said, smiling at Sandi.

"Yeah, I—" Sandi started to reply, then her gaze shifted to the road ahead. She screamed. A car was careening toward them, swerving from one side of the street to the other. Kate gasped and offered a quick, silent prayer. She tried to turn her mother's car out of the way, but the other car moved in the same direction. A second effort to avoid the other car produced the same results. Finally, bracing herself for what appeared to be an inevitable collision, Kate made one last effort to avoid a head-on crash. Narrowly missing the other car, the Sunbird ran over the sidewalk and into a metal fire hydrant. Both girls were shaken by the impact, but the seat belts had held them securely in place. Sandi bumped her head against the window on her side of the car, and Kate's left leg throbbed horribly as a portion of the front end of the car caved in against it.

Kate leaned down to rub her leg and felt something wet and sticky. "Great," she groaned.

"Are you okay?" Sandi asked.

"Yeah," Kate lied. "Are you?"

"I smacked my head a good one," Sandi replied as she rubbed

the lump that was starting to form. Suddenly, they heard a crash and the sound of tearing metal. Kate stretched to look out the rearview mirror. The other car had plunged into a lamppost down the street. Biting her lip, Kate opened the door on her side and pulled herself out of the car. Water shot out of the hydrant, spraying her with a cold mist.

"That didn't sound good," Sandi muttered, poking her head out of the car. "Hey, your leg's bleeding."

"I know," Kate replied, hesitantly putting weight on her left leg. She winced and held her breath. "I'll go for help," she said.

A siren sounded in the distance. "I think someone beat you to it," Sandi said wryly as she tried to climb out of the car. When droplets of water pummeled her face, she pulled back inside the car.

"Are you girls all right?" a worried voice asked.

Kate turned to look at the older woman who was holding out a blanket. "I . . . guess. Sandi hit her head pretty hard . . ."

"You're both getting wet," the woman said as she led Kate away from the car toward the sidewalk. Then she went back after Sandi. Soon both girls were wrapped in blankets, and the woman examined Sandi's head, smoothing back her hair for a better look. "You've got a nasty bump forming there."

"It's okay. Check Kate's leg."

"I'll live," Kate said, flinching as the woman inspected her leg.

"We'd better get you off your feet," the woman muttered. "That's a deep gash."

"I'm all right." Kate said quickly. "What about the other car?"

"My husband went down the street to check on it," the woman said as she helped Kate to sit on the cold cement. She had a first-aid kit, from which she selected a gauze pad and gently dabbed at the cut on Kate's leg. "I'm Penny, by the way. Penny Martin. My husband, Andrew, and I were just getting ready for bed when we heard tires squealing. We saw the whole thing and called the police. It's a wonder you two weren't killed!" She readjusted the blanket around Kate and patted her awkwardly.

"Looks like they're here," Sandi said as she moved closer to Kate. Her head was starting to spin. Several spectators had gathered around, most wearing coats or robes. Ignoring them and their offers to help, Sandi closed her eyes and leaned against Kate.

Kate was staring intently at the wreck down the street. The police had stopped there first. She couldn't make out the color of the car, especially now that the street light had been knocked out of commission, but in the darkness, it looked like a Mustang.

Who is it? Kate wondered. *Who in Bozeman drives a Mustang?* There was Jack Shope, the school jock, and Peter Wilding, the president of the Elders Quorum in their branch. But it couldn't have been Brother Wilding. He didn't drink, and obviously the driver had been drunk. Or had maybe suffered a heart attack. But that ruled out both Jack and Brother Wilding, who was only in his thirties . . . and in great shape. He had run in several marathons.

Kate's eyes widened as she thought of someone else who owned a Mustang. Praying she was wrong, she tried to get another glimpse of the car, but too many people were standing in the way. A police officer approached, requesting everyone to stand back. She watched as he looked over the Sunbird, checking it for a possible fire hazard. Kate was certain the water from the hydrant had stifled that risk.

Satisfied that they were in no immediate danger, the officer focused on Kate and Sandi. "Are you the driver?"

Kate nodded. "The other car . . . who was driving?"

"Do you have your license?"

"It's in my wallet in the car," Kate responded.

"Officer, these girls are hurt—surely your questions can wait," Penny said protectively.

"Are you injured in any way?" the policeman asked, peering at Kate.

"My leg's cut. Sandi hit her head on the window," Kate said. Sandi was still leaning against her shoulder. "I don't think she's in very good shape."

"An ambulance is on its way," the officer said calmly, forcing one of Sandi's eyes open and probing it with the beam from a flashlight.

"What about the other car?" Kate asked again.

"Were you two the only occupants of this car?" he asked, looking into Sandi's other eye.

"Yes," Kate answered impatiently. "Was anyone else hurt?"

An ambulance rounded the corner and screeched to a halt. A tall, slender man and a shorter woman with blonde hair hopped out and ran toward them.

"These two are in no present danger. They're coherent and have only minor injuries," the policeman told the two paramedics. "If I were you, I'd take a look at the occupant of the other vehicle."

The tall paramedic ran toward the Mustang while the woman made her own assessment of Kate and Sandi. The officer stepped away from them to question Penny.

"Well, Sandi, was it?" the paramedic prompted, looking at Sandi closely.

Sandi slowly nodded.

"You may have a slight concussion . . . The swelling is a good sign. If you didn't have that bump, I'd be more concerned. I know it hurts like heck, but you'll be all right. As for you," the paramedic turned to Kate, "you're going to need some stitches in that leg. It doesn't appear to be broken, and the bleeding's under control for now. Let's get you onto a gurney and to the hospital." Suddenly her radio crackled.

"Sally, call for backup. We've got our hands full here. Bring that tin machine on down."

Sally unsnapped the radio from the belt around her waist. "On my way," she answered. Turning to Kate, she smiled. "We'll get you two to Deaconess as soon as possible," she promised. "Another ambulance will be here in a few minutes. The police will notify your parents, and they'll meet you at the hospital." Sally then ran to the ambulance and drove it down the street.

Kate shifted around for a better look. Who was in that other car?

CHAPTER FOUR

The drive to Bozeman Deaconess Hospital was one of the longest rides of Sue's life. Unable to sit still, she fiddled with her seat belt, then began to nervously twist her short, red hair around her fingers. The policeman who had called had tried to reassure her that Kate's injuries were minor, but in her heart, Sue feared the worst. Her husband, Greg, gripped the steering wheel and drove as fast as he dared. A few minutes later, he turned onto Highland Boulevard and then sped toward the hospital. Finally, he pulled up near the emergency entrance. Sue had her door open before he could hurry around to help her out of the car. Together, they raced inside.

Sue tried to push her way into ER but was escorted back into the hall to wait. The sound of a low groan twisted her heart, but she was told Kate hadn't arrived yet. Impatiently, she paced the floor with Greg.

A few minutes later, Fred and Harriet Kearns hurried into the building.

"Where is she? Where's Sandi?" Harriet angrily demanded.

"They're not here yet," Greg answered, glancing at the Kearns. The adage "opposites attract" always went through his mind when he saw them together. Harriet was about 5'3" with a slightly rounded figure and an often feisty disposition. Fred was tall, slim, and easygoing.

"I never should've let her out of the house tonight," Harriet continued. "Look what happened. And all because of Kate!"

Fred gripped his wife's arm. "That's enough, Harriet," he said firmly.

Harriet pulled away from her husband and marched in front of Sue. "I hold you personally responsible for this," she exclaimed. "None of this would've happened if you hadn't called Lori Blanchard!"

"Lori was trying to help—"

"And look where that got my daughter. I told Sandi this was a mistake. I never should've agreed to let Kate drive her home."

"Kate is a good driver!" Sue countered, her green eyes flashing.

"When she's sober," Harriet snapped. "The officer said drinking had been involved."

"It wasn't Kate," Sue said sharply. "Kate doesn't drink anymore!"

"That's not what I heard. You just don't want to face the truth."

"Harriet, that's enough," Fred insisted as he dragged his wife to the other end of the hall.

Greg pulled a handkerchief out of his pocket and handed it to Sue. She wiped at her eyes, then turned her back to him to blow her nose. "People say things they don't mean when they're upset," he said, readjusting his glasses.

"She meant every word," Sue sniffed.

"Let it go, Sue," Greg murmured as he pulled her close. "We have more important things to worry about."

Two gurneys were wheeled in through the emergency doors. At the sight of Kate and Sandi, both sets of parents raced to be at their daughter's side.

"Kate, are you all right," Sue asked.

"I'm in better shape than your car," she mumbled.

Sue kissed Kate's forehead. "Just so you're okay, honey," she answered. "We can replace the car. It's seen better days anyway."

"Your mother's right," Greg said.

"Excuse me, but her leg needs some attention," the paramedic insisted as he began pushing the gurney forward.

"Her leg?" Greg asked. "It's not broken again?"

"It's no big deal, Dad," Kate said as they pushed her into ER.

"I scraped it a little."

"A little?" Sue asked, following them into ER. "How little is little?"

"I'm sorry, but you'll have to wait in the hall," a nurse insisted. Sue could see that another nurse was leading a determined-looking Harriet out of ER and took a tiny bit of satisfaction from it.

Several minutes passed. Suddenly Linda's mother, Marie Sikes, burst through the emergency doors. "Where's Linda? What happened?"

Sue and Greg exchanged a look of concern. Sue stepped toward Marie, took her arm, and led her to a set of chairs. Taking a seat next to Marie, Sue said gently, "We're not sure. We were told there was a car accident . . . one that must've involved all of our daughters."

"I knew it," Harriet fumed, marching in front of Sue and Marie. "Kate and Linda were partying again, weren't they? Kate used Sandi . . . again!!! And now my daughter's lying in that room, in pain because of those two!"

"Harriet," Fred warned as he tried to steer his wife away from Sue and Marie.

"Kate and Sandi were at our house all evening," Sue said, rising to her feet. "Linda wasn't there."

"How would you know?" Harriet blazed. "You've never known what Kate's been up to. I doubt it's changed now. Why, the things Sandi used to come home from school and tell me—"

"Harriet!" This time Fred made it clear he was serious as he forced his wife back down the hall and sat her in a chair near the emergency exit.

A voice broke over the intercom, sounding a coded alarm. Several nurses and another doctor flew into the Emergency Room.

"What's going on in there?" Harriet snapped. "We have a right to know!" A few minutes later, her indignant complaints faded to a whisper when a doctor wearily stepped out into the hall.

"I'm looking for Marie Sikes," he said quietly.

Marie shakily rose to her feet, and the doctor motioned for her to follow him down the hall. When they finally stopped, he asked if anyone was with her. She shook her head. "No. It's bad, isn't it? What's wrong with my daughter?"

The doctor studied the tiled floor. "I think you'd better sit down," he said, attempting to steer her toward a group of chairs.

"No, tell me, what's going on," Marie said, stubbornly pulling away from the doctor. Reluctantly, the doctor met her heartsick gaze and confirmed her worst fears. Linda's injuries had been too severe. They hadn't been able to save her. Marie moaned, then collapsed. The doctor grabbed her before she fell to the floor, and Greg hurried forward to help. They laid her across the set of chairs, and Sue hurried to Marie's side. Kneeling beside her, she held Marie's trembling hand and silently asked the question that plagued them all. Why had this happened?

CHAPTER FIVE

During the funeral Kate sat very still as people stared and whispered. She told herself she didn't care. Caring only made you vulnerable—something Linda had told her years ago. Too late, she understood the wisdom of that philosophy. And the only person who would appreciate the irony of this moment was gone.

At the cemetery, Kate was only vaguely aware of her parents beside her, helping her to walk. It had taken fifteen stitches to close the gash in her leg, and she walked with a noticeable limp. She ignored the icy wind and tried not to look at the casket. Linda wasn't in there. Not the Linda she had known.

Someone shoved a white rose into her hand. Linda had loved white roses. Sue leaned close to whisper that Kate was supposed to lay the rose on the casket. Hobbling forward, she stared at the pink-tinted metal. She tried to speak, but the words wouldn't come. Unwanted tears descended, blurring her vision. In her mind, she could see Linda, laughing, taunting, bitter. Always bitter. Always laughing, even when life wasn't funny.

Sue managed to ease the flower from Kate's hand and placed it with the others that had been strewn along the coffin. She then guided Kate back to where the rest of the family was standing. Kate felt her Aunt Paige's arm go around her waist. Paige had flown up from Salt Lake to be here—but it hadn't helped. Nothing helped. Nothing eased what she felt inside.

As they moved away from the freshly dug grave, Kate caught a glimpse of Marie. "I need to talk to Marie," she said, her voice a strained whisper.

"What, honey?" Sue asked, leaning down.

"She wants to talk to Marie," Paige repeated softly, her concerned brown eyes meeting Sue's worried gaze. Kate wasn't handling this well at all. Not that they had expected her to. It had been a horrible, tragic experience. Something that would take time to absorb. But ever since the initial outburst of grief and rage, Kate had closed herself off from everyone.

Sue hesitated. It was the first time Kate had spoken in nearly two days. And yet, Marie was in worse shape than Kate. Sue was certain that an encounter between the two was not a good idea. Anything that would disintegrate her daughter's fragile well-being was to be avoided. There had been enough sharp words spoken, thanks to Harriet Kearns.

"Please, Mom," Kate pleaded.

Sue's heart melted. "Sweetheart, I don't think now is a good time. Maybe later . . ."

"Mom . . ." Kate's voice broke. "She has to know I never meant . . . I didn't . . ."

"I know, honey. We all know. It's going to be okay," Sue soothed, giving her daughter a supportive squeeze.

"Please . . ."

Sue gazed into the despair-filled eyes. It would mean so much if Marie could soften what had taken place, and yet, understandably, Marie, was not herself. A misplaced word or accusation would only make things worse.

"Sue," Paige said, pointing. A man and a woman were helping Marie cross the cemetery toward them.

Nodding, Sue tried to steer Kate toward the Explorer, but she refused to budge. Silently, Sue prayed for help.

Kate stubbornly held her ground, waiting until Marie was about to pass in front of them. "Marie . . . Mrs. Sikes?"

Marie slowly lifted her head, her swollen, reddened eyes focusing on Kate.

"I . . . I'm sorry. I didn't mean . . ."

Seeing Kate brought back too much. Marie closed her eyes and kept them shut until her sister and brother-in-law had maneuvered her to the waiting car.

Kate leaned against her mother and began to sob. Several minutes had passed before Sue and Paige were able to guide Kate to the Explorer where Greg was patiently waiting with Tyler. They drove home in silence.

Later that afternoon, Kate disappeared. Paige thought her niece was still in the backyard, but when they searched, she wasn't there. Tyler thought his sister was in her room, but when they looked, it was empty. Sabrina thought her big sister was in the bathroom, but when the door finally opened, it was Greg who walked out. Sue hunted every inch of the house before panicking. Even then, she didn't give her fear free reign until she discovered that the Explorer was missing, too. Greg and Paige quickly left in the rental car Paige had picked up at the airport, their faces grim.

Tyler grabbed his mountain bike out of the garage and promised to check out several popular teenage hangouts. Sue stayed home with Sabrina in case Kate returned. To keep busy, she made phone calls, including a call to Lori Blanchard, who promised to drive around to see what she could turn up. Lori, in turn, called Sandi Kearns.

"I know your mother is still upset, but we could really use your help. Do you have any idea where Kate would go?"

Sandi could hear the worry in Sister Blanchard's voice. "They're sure she took off somewhere?" she asked.

"Yes. There's no sign of her."

"Have you tried the cemetery?"

"I just came from there."

"Where are you now?"

"At the mall. There's no sign of her here either."

"Has anyone checked with Jace?"

"No," Lori said dryly. "Thanks anyway."

"Lori, I'd come help you look, but my mom won't let me out of the house. She wouldn't even let me come to the funeral."

"I know," Lori sighed. "There is something you could do, though."

"What?"

"Pray. Kate's a mess . . . we need to find her right away."

Sandi frowned, an uneasy feeling settling in the pit of her stomach.

"Well, I'm going to drive around some more. I'll talk to you later."

"Let me know if you find her."

"Will do," Lori returned before hanging up the phone.

"Find who?" Harriet asked, stepping into her daughter's room.

"Kate. She's missing."

Harriet snorted. "She's out to get more attention."

"Mom, that's not true. Kate's really upset."

"She ought to be. One girl's dead because of her. You could've been killed as well."

"It wasn't her fault! If it hadn't been for Kate, we would've died! Kate is the reason I'm still alive."

"Sandi, you're not thinking clearly." Harriet forced her daughter to lay back on the bed. "It's that head injury."

Sandi protested. "Mom, I know what happened that night. Linda was drunk and almost plowed into us. Kate swerved out of the way."

"Several people have told me Linda went to a party held in Kate's honor," Harriet told her daughter. "And yet you say Kate Erickson isn't responsible for the shape that poor Linda was in."

"Poor Linda? Is this the same Linda you couldn't say enough bad about?"

"It's not good to speak ill of the dead. Quit upsetting yourself. Kate's probably off with those wild friends of hers getting drunk. They'll find her. And even if they don't, she's no concern of yours." Harriet smoothed the blankets around her daughter. "Try to get some rest," she said before leaving the room.

Furious, Sandi sat up and threw the blankets onto the carpeted floor. "I don't care what you say," she muttered, "Kate's in trouble and I'm going to help." She quietly closed her bedroom door and changed into jeans and a sweatshirt. She then stuck pillows under the blankets on her bed to give the impression that she was still in her proper place. Grabbing a jacket, she cautiously opened the bedroom window and took out the screen. After hiding it in the closet, she climbed out into a large tree. Leaning against the trunk of the tree, she fought a sudden episode of dizziness. She took a deep breath, then reached back to shut the window until it was only open a crack. Satisfied that she could still get back in, she quickly climbed to the ground. Once there, she wheeled her ten-speed out of the garage and sped off down the street.

Kate stared at the bottle in her hands. Jace had been only too willing to give it to her. She gazed at the amber-colored liquid. It had eased the pain in the past—before her life had been turned upside down. Ever since the accident in Salt Lake, she had tried doing the right thing. She had kept the Word of Wisdom, had faithfully adhered to Church standards, and look where it had gotten her. The entire town was convinced she was still a troublemaker, she had no friends, and Linda was dead. So much for being good.

She heard the sound of laughter coming from across the park. Instinctively, she stuck the bottle of whiskey back inside the brown paper sack. Then, remembering she no longer cared what she did or who saw her, she pulled out the bottle, wadded the bag into a tight ball, and hurled it into the trees. No one cared what she did, anyway. No, that wasn't quite true. Tyler and Sabrina cared. Her mother and father cared. Lori Blanchard cared, or so she said. She had thought Randy Miles cared, but she hadn't heard from him in nearly three weeks. What would he think about what had happened? She knew what he would say about the bottle in her hands.

She pushed his face from her mind. In his place, she saw Paige. Her aunt had cared enough to fly up from Utah, but it didn't begin to touch the pained despair she felt inside. She saw again the look on Mrs. Kearn's face, blaming her for Sandi's head injury, and the way Marie Sikes had refused to look at her at the cemetery, shutting her out as completely as Linda had done. Jace had thrown it all in her face.

"*It's your fault, you know,*" Jace had taunted when she had approached him an hour ago. She didn't know why she had ended up at his house, only that she was seeking relief from the pain she was carrying inside. She didn't know where else to go. Jace was the only friend she had left, if you could call him that. He was the one who had handed her the whiskey. He always kept one or two bottles handy.

"*Linda never touched cocaine until you turned your back on her. She's dead because you walked away.*"

Jace was right; it was her fault. Even though her parents had said comforting things like *"Kate, you can't blame yourself for something Linda did. Sandi's alive because of you."* Yes, Sandi was alive, but Linda was dead, and no one understood what that loss meant. She didn't understand it herself.

Kate twisted the cap off and held the bottle to her lips. Just one swallow . . . she closed her eyes and imagined how it would feel as the whiskey burned going down. Suddenly, she saw her fourth great-grandmother's face—Colleen Mahoney, someone who had suffered more than anyone she had ever known. Colleen wouldn't be this weak, this full of self-pity. And she would never understand a broken promise, the one Kate had made in the dream. The bottle fell from her hands, spilling most of its contents onto the ground.

"I can't," Kate sobbed. Picking up the bottle, she hurled it into Glen Lake. "I can't do this . . . help me, Grandma . . . I don't know what to do," she pleaded. Falling to her knees, she buried her face in her hands.

"I'll help if you'll let me," a soft voice said.

Startled, Kate stared up at Sandi. "What are you doing here?"

"I was worried," Sandi explained. "We all are . . . everyone's out looking for you. Lori called me when she couldn't find you. I prayed about it and had a feeling you'd be here."

Kate stared at Sandi, then turned to gaze out at the lake.

"I'm sorry I haven't been by to see you . . ." Sandi stammered.

Kate remained silent, wiping at her eyes.

"My mother hasn't let me out of the house. She's treating me like an invalid because of this stupid concussion. I keep reminding her it's mild, but she won't listen to me."

"You don't need to cover for her. She's made it perfectly clear how she feels about me," Kate said glumly.

"She's wrong about what happened . . . and about you."

"Maybe."

"Maybe, nothing. Kate, we're both alive because of you. I've never seen anyone drive like you did that night."

"It didn't save Linda, did it?!"

Unsure of what to say, Sandi silently prayed for inspiration as she sat beside Kate on the dry grass.

"Linda's dead," Kate said hoarsely.

"I know and I know it hurts, but it wasn't your fault."

Refusing to answer, Kate drew her knees up and hugged them. Her left leg began to throb, but she ignored it.

"Linda made her own choices that night. You had no way of knowing she was going to get stoned."

"I should've guessed. I knew she was upset. She always gets that way when—"

"What were you going to do, hold her hand every minute of every day? She was hooked on that stuff."

"She'd never tried cocaine before."

"And who's to say you could've stopped her? Linda was one messed-up girl."

"We had a fight the afternoon before she died. You should've seen the way she looked at me. She said—"

"She probably said a lot of things she didn't mean, Kate."

"But I—"

"Quit beating yourself over the head with this," Sandi said firmly. "I'm sorry Linda died. We all are. I wish I could change what happened. But none of us could do anything to stop it. You had no idea she was driving in that kind of shape. The only ones who did were at the party. Why didn't they stop her?"

Unfolding her legs, Kate stretched out, wincing as her injured leg continued to throb. Why hadn't anyone stopped Linda from driving? Surely they had seen the condition she was in. Maybe. Maybe they were all so strung out, Linda had appeared normal. That was the way it usually was at those parties. Only before, everyone had always made it home in one piece. Jace had dented his dad's fender once, pulling into some trash cans, but that was it, until now.

Kate nodded slowly. "Jace should've stopped her. But he was probably too busy entertaining one of his female guests."

"The party was at his house?"

"He said it was my fault Linda died," Kate said in a whisper.

Sandi reached into her pocket and handed a wad of tissue to Kate. "And you believed him? C'mon, Kate, think about it! Jace has never owned up to anything in his life. It's too convenient to blame everyone else."

Kate wiped at her eyes and nose.

Sandi continued. "Jace never has been good for you. He's only out to use you. You do know that, don't you?"

"Yeah . . . I guess."

"He's the one who gave you the bottle you threw into the lake, right?"

Kate stared at Sandi.

"I saw the whole thing. I started to panic when it looked like you were going to chug that stuff. I almost yelled for you to stop, but something held me back. I knew I could stop you this time, but what about the next?"

Kate gazed at the lake, realizing how close she had come to giving in.

"Linda made her own choices, too. Nobody forced her to take cocaine—just like nobody forced you to throw that bottle away."

"I came here to get drunk . . . but I couldn't. I kept seeing Mom's face, and Dad's . . . Aunt Paige's, then Randy's . . . and my great-grandmother, the one I told you about."

Sandi nodded, sensing it was her turn to listen.

"It's been so hard since Saturday night. At first, I couldn't believe it when Mom told me about Linda. It didn't seem real. But now . . . I keep wondering if I'd handled things differently . . . if I'd been more patient with her . . . ."

"Kate, you told me yourself the reason she was so angry was because you refused to go to that party."

"But if—"

"Let go of it. No one's blaming you, except for that clueless nimrod who's still trying to drag you down to his level. Everyone else is worried sick about you. You can't believe how many people are out looking for you right now."

"Why?" Kate asked tonelessly.

"Because we care."

Kate looked up at Sandi. "Do you care? After everything that's happened between us, do you honestly care?"

"I'm here, that should tell you something. I'll admit, I thought it was all an act when you first came home, but I was wrong. I know that now, and I'm sorry I made things so hard for you the past few weeks."

Unable to speak, Kate dabbed at her eyes with the tissue.

"Friends?" Sandi asked, reaching for a hug. Kate clung to her and cried. Sandi cried with her, the events of the past few days overwhelming both girls. That was how Lori Blanchard found them, several minutes later. Relieved, but not wishing to intrude, Lori quietly left, anxious to let everyone know Kate was all right and in very good hands.

CHAPTER SIX

Later, Kate and Sandi hooked the ten-speed to the Explorer, and Kate drove Sandi home. Kate parked in the driveway and as she helped unfasten Sandi's bike, she offered to come in to help explain. Sadly smiling, Sandi shook her head.

"No. I'd better handle this one alone. Thanks anyway. I'll call you tomorrow after school. I'm going, despite what Mom thinks."

Kate nodded. Her parents had said she could wait until next week to return to school. She was glad—she needed a few more days before attempting to go on with life. "See you later . . . and thanks."

Sandi gave Kate a quick hug before wheeling her bike toward the house. As Kate drove down the street, Sandi sighed and put her bike in the garage. Enough time had passed, she was certain her mother had figured out what she had done.

Reluctantly, she opened the front door and stepped into the house. When no one confronted her, Sandi peered into the living room. Her mother was sitting on the sofa. One look revealed she had been crying. Sandi pulled a face and forced herself to approach her mother. "Mom . . . I'm sorry. But Kate—"

"Here I am, worried sick, wondering if you're all right, and you pull up with that . . . that girl!"

"Kate needed me this afternoon. She's having a rough time."

"And I suppose it's your own personal duty to help her. Well, I've got news for you, young lady. I told Lori Blanchard just what

I thought about the entire situation."

"What?"

"She came by a while ago to let me know you were at East Gallatin State Park with Kate—to tell me how much she appreciated what you were doing."

Sandi almost smiled. How had Sister Blanchard known? The woman was a marvel.

"You needn't look so smug," Harriet snapped. "You openly defied me. I still can't believe you climbed out that bedroom window. Something that had better never happen again if you know what's good for you!"

"Mom, I—"

"I don't want to hear any more excuses! You're grounded for the next two weeks!"

"Okay," Sandi said meekly. Turning, she headed out of the room.

"I'm not finished."

Sandi sighed as she turned to face her mother. She should have known it wouldn't be this easy.

"I want to make it perfectly clear you are to have nothing more to do with Kate Erickson."

"Mom!"

"Don't argue with me! I won't have her running your life into the ground like she did with Linda Sikes."

"Kate didn't . . . Linda was the one who—"

"I don't want to hear another word about it! You stay away from that girl, she's nothing but trouble. I told Lori Blanchard the same thing, and I let her know that if you two are going to persist in this nonsense, I want you released as class president!"

Sandi stared at her mother.

"Now, march yourself upstairs and get back to bed. A person with a concussion has no business running around town on a bicycle!"

Too stunned to argue, Sandi obediently headed upstairs. When she reached her room, she stepped inside and closed the door. "Why is she acting this way?" she whispered. "Why?"

On the way home, Kate purposely avoided the street where the accident had taken place. When she finally pulled up in front of her house, the front door opened and several people came running out to greet her. Her mother was the first to reach the Explorer.

"Kate, are you all right?"

Nodding, Kate leaned into her mother's hug, then endured more of the same from her dad, Paige, Lori Blanchard, and even Tyler and Sabrina. Tim Randolph, the branch president and his wife, Shelley, came forward, each enfolding her in an embrace. Together, they led Kate to the house, surrounding her with concerned love.

Several minutes later, President Randolph approached Sue. "What do you think about giving her a blessing?" he asked, his gaze shifting to Kate who was sitting on the couch in the living room between Lori and Paige.

Sue glanced at Greg. They had talked about it, but when they had approached Kate the night of the accident, their daughter had refused. "I don't know. I think we're treading water with her right now. Her head's above the surface, but that's about the extent of it."

The telephone rang. Tyler answered. He set the phone on the counter and approached his parents. "It's for Kate."

"Who is it?" Greg asked, afraid it was another reporter.

"Some lady. She wants to speak to Kate."

Sue frowned and headed for the phone. She didn't want anyone talking to her daughter unless she knew who it was and what they wanted. "Hello?"

"Hello, Kate?"

"No, this is her mother, Sue."

"Oh, Sue. How are you holding up?"

"Fair, all things considered."

"I'm sorry, you probably have no idea who this is."

"Well, as a matter of fact—"

"Jan Miles, Randy's mother."

"Oh, Jan," Sue said, relaxing immediately. "I'm sorry. We've had a lot of unwanted phone calls the past few days. Reporters, thrill seekers, that kind of thing. We've been screening calls. Especially the ones for Kate."

"I don't blame you. How is she doing?"

Sue played with the phone cord. "It hasn't been easy for her. Linda was a close friend for a long time."

"I know. We all felt terrible when Paige called the other day. Randy's worried sick about Kate."

"He knows?"

"Yes. I committed a tiny sin and called him. I would've written, but I figured a letter would take too long to reach him. Randy's sending a letter to Kate. He would've called, but you know how missionary rules are. I was barely allowed to speak to him. Anyway, he wanted me to call and check on Kate. I've got a message from him if she's up to talking to me."

"I'll get her," Sue said, hoping this was the boost Kate needed. She set the phone down on the counter and moved into the living room. "Kate, you're wanted on the phone."

Kate looked up. "I don't want to talk to anyone right now."

"It's Jan Miles."

"Jan . . . I mean, Mrs. Miles . . . Randy's mother?"

Sue nodded, relieved to see the tiny spark of excitement in her daughter's eyes. "She talked to Randy. She has a message for you."

"A message?"

Paige smiled at her niece. "Go on, Kate. Talk to her."

Kate crossed the room and picked up the phone. "Hello," she said hesitantly.

"Hello, Kate," Jan said warmly. "I know this is a difficult time for you, but I wanted to let you know how concerned we all are."

Kate closed her eyes.

"I can't tell you how sorry we are about Linda. I wish I could've come up with your aunt. We sent flowers for the funeral. Randy's name is on the card." Jan paused, concerned by Kate's silence. "Kate, I know it's rough right now, but it will get easier. Each day, it'll hurt a little less."

"Promise?" Kate stammered, wiping at her eyes.

"Yes. I learned that lesson years ago when I lost a good friend in Vietnam."

"Vietnam?"

"During the war. Shawn and I had dated in high school. Then he was drafted. A year later we received word he had been killed in the line of duty."

Kate caught her breath. "That must've been horrible."

"It was. The first week is just a blur. I don't even remember the funeral. It seemed so unreal."

"I know. Today was awful."

"Facing the loss of a loved one is hard, harder than most ever realize until they're in the same situation. But tomorrow will be easier, and each day that follows. Gradually, the pain you're carrying inside will fade."

"I thought I understood that after losing Shannon," Kate sniffed. "But this is so much harder."

"Shannon?"

"In the dream I had . . . during the coma."

"Randy said something about that."

"This time it's for real. I mean, Shannon really did die, but I wasn't actually there."

"Any kind of loss hurts, and the heartache won't go away overnight. It's hard to let people go . . . even when we know their time on earth is over."

"But if Linda hadn't been so stoned—"

"Kate, even if she'd been sober, if it was her time to go, she would've been taken anyway."

"Are you sure?"

"Yes. Just like you, I had a lot of questions when Shawn died. He was a wonderful person. We'd planned on getting married after his mission. Then, suddenly, he was gone. I kept asking, 'Why? Why Shawn? Why now?'"

"And?"

"Sometimes there are reasons we can't begin to understand in this life. Someone told me they thought Shawn had been called to serve a mission in the spirit world. It helped, thinking of him in that way."

"I doubt that's what Linda's doing."

"Don't judge her, Kate. It might be she'll accept the gospel in the spirit world, something she might not have done here on earth."

"Do you really think so?"

"I think it's possible. From what Randy's told me, Linda led a pretty hard life."

"Her father walked out years ago. She hasn't seen him since. I'll bet he didn't even come to the funeral."

"Did her mother have much to do with the Church after the divorce?"

"No." Kate chewed her bottom lip. "I think I see what you're saying. Linda was on a bad road . . . like me, only, she didn't have anyone to turn her around."

"You never know. That's why we should never judge. We all progress on different levels at different times. Some embrace the gospel and live it their entire lives. Others struggle with it for years."

"It seems so unfair!" Kate burst out. "If Linda had been in a different family, she might have been okay."

"Now, you're getting into some deep water. I know of several good families who have ended up with kids just like Linda. Kids who have been taught the gospel and still turn away from the happiness it offers."

"It happens," Kate murmured, thinking of herself.

"Anyway, before I forget, I called Randy after your Aunt Paige called me."

Kate turned to look at Paige. Someday she would have to tell her aunt how wonderful she was.

"If there was any way he could call you himself, he would. But until the letter he's promised to write reaches you, he gave me strict instructions on what to tell you. He even made me write it all down."

"Really?"

"Yes, really. First thing on the list, he wants you to wrap your arms around yourself and give a big squeeze because that's what he'd do if he was there right now."

Kate's eyes began to mist.

"He wants me to tell you that he's very glad you were watched over the night of the accident. He'll be praying for you. And he wants you to look up a scripture."

"A scripture?"

"Yes. Do you have a pen or pencil handy and a piece of paper?"

"Just a minute," Kate said, turning around to the notepad posted near the phone. A pencil hung from a string near the pad. "Okay."

"Doctrine and Covenants, section thirty-eight, verse nine."

"Got it."

"Third Nephi, chapter twelve, verse four."

"There's more than one?"

"Actually, about five."

"That sounds like Randy," Kate said, her lips almost curving into a smile. "Give me the rest of them."

"Okay, but remember, you asked for it. Doctrine and Covenants, section one hundred and twenty-two, verse five, the first line. Then he wants you to skip down to verse six and read the first two lines, skip down to verse seven and start with the middle of the fourth line and read to the end of the section."

"Hold on, I'm running out of room on this page," Kate said, tearing off the top sheet of paper and stuffing it into the pocket of her jeans. "Okay."

"Only two more. Doctrine and Covenants again, section one hundred and five, verse 41."

"Got it."

"And Alma five, verse twenty-six. He said to tell you that he often feels to sing the song of redeeming love, whatever that means." Jan smiled. She knew perfectly well what her son had meant. Not that she blamed him. There was something pretty special about Kate Erickson. She would gladly welcome her into the family if things worked out between the young couple.

"Anything else?"

"I'm sure it will all be in his next letter."

Kate smiled for the first time in several days.

Sue breathed a prayer of gratitude for Randy and his mother. Maybe they would survive this after all. She'd had her doubts, especially today, but now a glimmer of hope was radiating from her daughter's face. Stepping into the kitchen, she checked on the casserole in the oven, and continued to watch Kate out of the corner of one eye.

CHAPTER SEVEN

It was nearly nine-thirty when Fred Kearns walked up the sidewalk that led to his house. He had spent the day in Butte, attending a dental seminar. It was a challenge, keeping up with the latest techniques and equipment on the market. But he prided himself on running a top-notch dental practice and knew that continuing education was the key.

As he moved to the porch, a car pulled into the driveway. Turning, he watched as Lori Blanchard got out of her small Celica. "Hello," he called. "I suppose you're here to see Sandi."

"Let's just say I didn't like how I left things earlier with your wife."

"Oh," Fred sighed. He'd been alarmed by his wife's behavior lately. "I hope she didn't upset you."

"It's okay," Lori said, attempting a smile. "She had a point. It *was* my fault Sandi was with Kate that night."

"Sister Blanchard, you can't blame yourself. What happened was an accident."

"I think I'm finally starting to realize that. Still, if anything had happened to either of those girls . . ." She shuddered. "Anyway, I understand that Harriet is worried about Sandi, but I wish she'd listen to us concerning Kate."

"That's what set her off today?"

Lori grimaced. "You might say. Kate has had a horrible time since the accident. The one involving Linda Sikes . . . and the one she had in Salt Lake. She's trying so hard to put the past behind her—we need to be supportive. That's why I asked for Sandi's help. They used to be friends . . . I thought this would be the right time to mend a few fences."

"Harriet doesn't agree."

"I know. Believe me, I know." Lori explained about Kate's disappearance earlier that afternoon and how Sandi had eventually found her. "I don't normally encourage my Laurels to sneak out their bedroom windows, but, under the circumstances, I'm grateful Sandi did. Your daughter did a wonderful thing. She pushed aside the grudges she might still be carrying to reach out to a young lady who really needed her. I'm very proud of her."

"Well, thank you. She's always been a good girl."

"And she's just the kind of influence Kate needs," Lori continued. "It's essential for Kate to have the love and support of good friends, especially now, with Linda's death. From what I understand, I'm not the only one shouldering blame for what happened that night. Kate thinks she's responsible for Linda's death."

"Why?" Fred asked, surprised. "It wasn't her fault."

"I wish your wife shared that opinion. She still thinks Kate's to blame."

Fred looked puzzled. "At first, I thought it was because she was in shock over the accident, but it isn't getting better. I don't know what's wrong with Harriet. She's never been this unreasonable before."

"Hopefully, it'll blow over, but in the meantime, I don't want to lose Sandi as the class president."

"What?"

"This afternoon, Harriet said if I persist with helping Kate, she wants Sandi released from the presidency."

Fred adjusted his glasses thoughtfully, then said, "You have my assurance that our daughter will continue in her calling. I don't know what Harriet is thinking these days, but I have no problem with what you're doing."

"Thank you," Lori said gratefully. "Would it help if I came in to talk the situation over with your wife and daughter?"

Fred smiled slightly. "No, I'd better handle it myself. Thank you for stopping by, though. And don't worry, I'll straighten this out." He waited near the porch while Lori climbed into her car and pulled out of the driveway. Then, with a look of determination, he opened the front door.

When he stepped inside, he felt prompted to check on Sandi. Deciding that would be a good place to start, he set his briefcase in the hall and walked upstairs. He knocked softly. When there was no reply, he turned the knob and stepped inside the darkened room. "Sandi?"

"Yeah?" came the muffled reply.

Fred crossed the room and looked down at his daughter. Even in the darkness, he could tell she had been crying. "What's wrong?" he asked, knowing what the answer would be.

"Mom," Sandi said, sitting up. "Why can't she understand what I'm trying to do?"

"I'm not sure," Fred replied. "Sister Blanchard caught me before I came in and filled me in on what happened today." He loosened his tie. "I'm proud of you, honey. But don't make a habit of sneaking out that window," he teased.

"Dad," Sandi complained. "You know me better than that."

"True," he admitted, gazing at his daughter.

"I wish Mom would give me a little credit."

"She will . . . she does. I'm not sure what's going on with her right now, but I'll talk to her. As for Kate, I don't mind if you spend some time with her. You could be a good influence. Just don't let her drag you down while you're trying to lift her up."

"You know that'll never happen," Sandi said mournfully. "I wish I knew why Mom's so worried. Doesn't she trust me?"

"Yes, we both do." He leaned forward and kissed her gently on the forehead. "Don't lose hope. Things'll get better. In the meantime, get some rest. I'll go see what's eating your mother." He moved to the door, then turned to look at Sandi. "Do you want the light on?" he asked.

"No, it's okay. Thanks, Dad."

After leaving his daughter, Fred went in search of his wife. It didn't take long to find her in the utility room folding towels. Studying her face, he wondered what would be the best approach.

"You're late getting home tonight," Harriet observed as she

folded a fluffy blue towel.

"I've been home for a while."

"I know. I heard you pull up in the driveway. Have you eaten anything yet?"

"Have you?" he countered.

"No," Harried sighed. "Sandi said she wasn't hungry and I can't say that I have much of an appetite. I figured you'd probably pick up something to eat on the way home."

"Actually, I did grab a sandwich on my way through Butte," he impatiently admitted. Food wasn't the issue at stake. "I'd like to talk to you about Sandi."

Harriet avoided his probing gaze and continued folding towels. "I'm busy right now. Maybe later."

"The towels can wait, Harriet, but our daughter can't. She's been through a lot the past few days—"

"Thanks to Kate Erickson!"

"Kate isn't the problem. You are."

Harriet raised an eyebrow, but didn't speak. Nor would she meet her husband's questioning gaze.

Fred spoke first. "I don't understand. You're usually the first one to reach out to help someone else. Why are you denying our daughter that same opportunity?"

"I don't want her hanging around with Kate!" Harriet said stubbornly.

"If it hadn't been for Kate, we might've buried our daughter today."

"If Sandi had stayed home where she belonged, none of this would've happened."

"Maybe Sandi and Kate wouldn't have been involved, but from what I was told, Linda still would've died and might have taken someone else with her in the process. She was in no condition to drive—she'd had a bad reaction to the cocaine. Her injuries were severe, but she died from cardiac arrest triggered by the cocaine."

Harriet was quick to add, "And from what I heard, Linda had attended a party held in Kate's honor. A party where they were drinking, doing drugs, and heaven knows what else."

Fred shook his head. "Sandi said Kate had nothing to do with that party. In fact, Kate and Linda had fought over it the night before. Kate had no intention of going."

"Maybe not to that one. There are others I've heard about," Harriet sniffed.

"Is that it? You're afraid Kate will drag Sandi to one of those parties?"

"All right, you asked, I'll tell you." Harriet glared at her husband. "Yes, I'm afraid that's exactly what'll happen. But I won't let it. I won't let Sandi end up like . . ." She turned away, clenching at a towel.

Fred moved in front of his wife. "You don't want Sandi to end up like what? What is it you're not saying?"

"Fred, how many children do we have?"

"Six, last time I counted." His eyes widened. "Are we about to increase that number?"

Harriet violently shook her head, and Fred breathed a sigh of relief. Still, it would've explained the mood swings.

"How many have served missions?" Harriet persisted.

"Three," Fred said, puzzled. "Both of our sons and one of our daughters."

"How many have been married in the temple?"

"Four. Heidi's still in college, but I have no doubt that one of these days, she'll pop up with Mr. Right and a dazzling diamond on her finger."

"That leaves Sandi."

"Yes," Fred answered, still confused.

Harriet gazed intently at her husband. "I've spent my entire married life teaching those children the gospel. I want every one of them to be there when we're reunited in heaven. We're a forever family, right?"

Fred wondered at her intensity. "Yes, at least I'd like to think so. But what does this have to do with—"

Harriet didn't let him finish. "Stephanie and Lacey tell me I'm too protective of their youngest sister. Maybe they're right. But Sandi's my baby and always will be."

"Harriet, your baby is seventeen years old—"

Harriet interrupted him. "Let me finish. Have I ever mentioned the resemblance between Sandi and Laurie?"

Fred shook his head. Actually, he didn't know much about his wife's youngest sister. Just that she had died in a tragic accident when she was sixteen.

"They look alike, talk alike. And like Sandi, Laurie was always eager to please. Anxious to help. A friend to everyone. Then she started chasing with a neighbor girl down the street. Brenda Burch. Brenda wasn't active in the Church, and Laurie thought she could reactivate her. Only the more time they spent together, the more enthralled Laurie became with Brenda's lifestyle. Laurie ended up turning away from the Church and away from us, in spite of what we tried to do or say. About the time my parents finally decided to send her to live with an aunt to get her away from Brenda, there was a terrible boating accident. Brenda and Laurie had gone out onto the lake with two or three boys. They'd all been drinking. One of the boys started showing off. He revved up the engine, turned a corner, and steered into a large rock. Laurie and Brenda were both thrown from the boat. They saved Brenda. Laurie drowned."

"Honey, I'm sorry. I had no idea . . . Your family's never really talked about it."

"It's too hard. We loved Laurie so much." Harriet fumbled for the piece of tissue stuffed in the front pocket of her jeans.

"It won't happen like that with Sandi," Fred comforted his wife, brushing the hair from her face. "She has a very strong sense of who she is."

"Laurie did, too."

"Harriet, be honest. Was Laurie as strong in the Church as you thought?"

"What a thing to say!"

"I don't want to upset you, but I want you to realize something. What happened to Laurie was tragic, but it doesn't mean Sandi is destined for the same fate."

"But . . . look at Kate. She was a good girl until she started running around with that wild crowd of delinquents. And then—"

"And then, she made poor choices. Harriet, we're here to gain experience, to learn to tell the good from the bad. Kate has had enough experience with the bad to realize how precious the good is. If Sandi can help her finish making that transition, then I say, let her try."

"Fred!" Harriet exclaimed, repulsed by his suggestion.

"I mean it. Who are we to judge our Father's children? Does He love some more than others? Does He want us to turn our backs on those who make mistakes? Didn't the Savior reach out to everyone around Him, regardless of their race or creed? He loved the righteous man and the sinner and invited both to partake of the blessings of the gospel."

Harriet stared at her husband.

"Can we in all good conscience turn away from a troubled young lady, a daughter of our Heavenly Father, someone He loves as much as Sandi or you?"

"This isn't fair," Harriet complained. "I know you're right—but my children will always come first!"

"And if it was your child who was in trouble? Would you want everyone to walk away?" Fred waited a few moments while Harriet focused on her hands, then said, "Here's something else for you to consider. Right now, Sandi's convinced you don't trust her—which isn't good. She rebelled enough today to climb out her bedroom window."

"I about died when I walked into her room and—"

Fred held up his hand as if to stop the flow of speech. "She wouldn't have done it if you had listened to her earlier. Sandi has never given us cause to doubt her. She's one of those rare kids who seem to come with a built-in compass. Let's give her the freedom to use it. With teenagers, resentment triggers more rebellion than anything else I know. On the other hand, teens aren't so apt to turn away if they know we're there for them. If they know we love and support them."

"What makes you such an expert?" Harriet said dryly.

"How many kids did you say we've raised so far?" Fred asked.

"But—"

"Not to mention the years I've served in the scouting program. I've seen more than my share of parent-teen contention. It's something I'd like to avoid with our youngest. She's trying to do a good thing, and right now, she needs to know we're with her on this. Okay?" Fred asked, his eyes pleading with her.

"Oh, all right," Harriet sighed. "I'll try. But if I ever find that Kate is leading Sandi astray, that's the end of it. I won't sacrifice my daughter to save someone else."

"Fair enough," Fred said, leaning for a kiss. He felt drained, but happy. Harriet was a compassionate woman. It was one reason he had married her. Another reason was apparent when they kissed.

Later that night, Harriet began trying to make amends. She started with Sandi. Swallowing a vast portion of pride, she climbed the stairs to Sandi's room, and even though her daughter was asleep, decided to settle things between them. She flipped on the hall light, walked into the room, and gently shook Sandi awake.

At first, Sandi thought she was dreaming. But, as her mother haltingly explained why she had been so upset, Sandi realized this was no dream. As she listened, she tried to understand the ordeal her mother had lived through years ago—one Harriet had feared was repeating itself with Kate's help.

"I was wrong to think you were following in Laurie's footsteps, and I'll try to be supportive if you want to remain friends with Kate." Harriet nervously picked at Sandi's quilt, avoiding her daughter's inquisitive gaze.

Quickly forgiving her mother, Sandi reached for a hug. Afterwards, Harriet tucked her back under the covers, kissed her goodnight, and retreated from the room. An inner glow assured her she was on the right track.

* * *

The next morning, Harriet succeeded in talking Sandi out of going to school. Together, they made a couple of pies to take on the visits that needed to be made. Their first stop was to see Lori Blanchard.

Surprised by who was standing on her front porch, Lori hoped this wouldn't be a repeat of yesterday's confrontation. She didn't know what to say when Sandi carefully handed her a warm pie. Hoping it was a good sign, Lori set it on the dining room table to finish cooling. She then led Sandi and her mother into the living room as Harriet made nervous small talk about the weather. Somewhat embarrassed, Lori hastily tried to clear the room that had been cluttered by her preschoolers.

"Don't worry about the toys," Harriet tried to say kindly. "You should've seen my house when my kids were small. It always looked like a cyclone had hit it." Sandi gave her mother an incredulous look, but Harriet ignored it.

"I don't normally let them drag this much in here, but I was busy hemming a new pair of Wade's jeans. Either he shrunk or the size changed," Lori said, in an attempt to keep things light.

Sandi smiled politely at the intended joke as her mother fidgeted with a small stuffed lion that had been left on the couch. "Sister Blanchard," Harriet began.

"Lori," Lori insisted with a smile.

"Lori," Harriet repeated. "This isn't easy, so I'm going to come right out with it." She gazed steadily at Lori. "I was out of line yesterday, and I want you to know I regret what took place."

Lori glanced from Sandi to Harriet. In her opinion, Fred Kearns had worked a miracle. "Sister Kearns," she started to say.

"Harriet," Harriet replied.

"Harriet," Lori said obediently. "I don't want hard feelings to exist between us."

"Neither do I. Especially since my daughter will be working closely with you in Mutual, or whatever it's called these days."

Lori smiled at Sandi, relieved that she would not be losing her class president.

Harriet continued. "I'm not offering excuses—this has been an emotional time for me. But it doesn't give me the right to—"

"It's okay," Lori assured her.

"No, it's not. You were only trying to be a good leader, and I haven't exactly made things easy for you."

"Harriet, I've felt horrible since the accident," Lori blurted out. It was something she had longed to say to this woman for days. "It *was* my idea to have Sandi spend time with Kate that night. If I hadn't called . . . if I hadn't asked Sandi to—"

"I said some terrible things to you yesterday, that's why I'm here. I was wrong. You were trying to reach out to Kate in the only way you could think of. I came today to say I'm sorry, and to let you know that I'll support whatever you and Sandi think is best for the girls in our branch."

Lori was visibly touched by Harriet's apology. "You can't

possibly know what this means to me," she replied. "Thank you."

Harriet nodded, acutely aware of how she had contributed to Lori's feelings of guilt. "I lost a younger sister in a similar situation, years ago," she said slowly. "Her death doesn't make what I said or did right, but I hope you'll try to understand. I couldn't stand the thought of losing Sandi the same way."

Sensing the tremendous effort Harriet was making, Lori offered a sympathetic smile. "I'm sorry for the loss of your sister. It must've been difficult."

"Yes, it was," Harriet murmured.

"Thank you for helping me understand what you've been feeling."

"Can you forgive me for yesterday, for what I said?"

Lori nodded. "Don't give it a second thought," she said, offering another smile.

Relieved, Harriet returned the smile. Then, glancing at her watch, she rose from the couch. "Well, I hate to rush off, but we really should be going. Thank you for letting us drop in on you."

"I'm glad you did. It means a lot. And thanks for the delicious-smelling pie. Would you and Sandi stay long enough to have a piece with me?"

"No. We really have to be going. I'd like to see Sue and Kate this morning, too."

Lori's eyes widened. As she led Harriet and Sandi to the front door, she marveled at the change that had taken place. Yesterday she would have said it was next to impossible. But now she believed anything could happen, even a truce between Harriet and Sue. She knew only too well how upset Sue had been, but if Harriet could somehow smooth things over, it would definitely pave the way for Sandi and Kate to pick up the threads of friendship.

After Harriet and Sandi left, Lori retreated to the master bedroom and knelt beside her bed to plead for another miracle.

* * *

Carefully holding onto the fresh cherry pie, Harriet rang the doorbell. When an unsmiling Sue answered, Harriet nearly lost her nerve. Sandi, uncomfortably aware of the tension, broke the silence.

"Hi, Sister Erickson. How's Kate today?"

"A little better," Sue responded, glancing from Harriet's worried expression to the imploring look on Sandi's face. Struggling with resentment, she stepped aside and motioned for them to come in. Harriet handed her the pie, which Sue carried into the kitchen as her guests took a seat on the couch in the living room. Giving herself a few minutes to calm down, Sue took a deep breath, then walked into the living room and sat on a chair across from the couch.

Harriet forced a nervous smile. "Sue, I realize I'm probably the last person you want to see right now, and I can't say that I blame you. What I said to you that night at the hospital was unforgivable. I shouldn't have said those things about Kate and Linda. I was wrong to judge either girl."

Sue didn't trust herself to speak. Instead, she stared out a window, willing herself to remain calm.

"It's difficult for me to explain why I—"

"There's no excuse for how you behaved that night or for the things you've said since the accident," Sue said in a strained voice. "Kate has been through more than anyone will ever know! She didn't need anything else. You have no idea how difficult you've made things for her!"

"I didn't realize . . ." Harriet stammered.

An inner voice warned, but Sue ignored it, allowing harsh emotions to control her words. "You didn't realize that my daughter's heart had been shattered? That this has been a living nightmare, made worse by people like you?!" Rising, she glared at the trembling woman on her couch.

Harriet stood, blinking rapidly. "Sue, I . . . I came to say I'm sorry."

"I'm sorry, too," Sue snapped, remembering too clearly the unkind words that had been spoken. Words that had sliced through Kate's heart. "I'm sorry a grown woman thinks she can say what she wants no matter who it hurts, and then smooth it over by baking a pie!"

Flinching under Sue's harsh stare, Harriet bolted from the

room and out the front door. Fumbling with the car door, she slid behind the wheel and bowed her head. Sue watched her through the living room window, forgetting that Sandi still stood beside her.

"Sister Erickson, my mother made a mistake, but she came here to apologize."

Startled, Sue turned to face Sandi.

"You didn't even give her a chance to explain."

"I'm sorry I lost my temper, but Sandi, you of all people should know how she's hurt Kate. I'm Kate's mother. How am I supposed to feel?"

"Maybe I'm wrong here, but I think you reacted like my mother did in the hospital. You're both so anxious to protect us, neither of you can see the harm you're really doing."

"Sandi," Sue began.

"My mother—"

"Your mother has no idea how hard it's been."

"And you don't know why she acted like she did," Sandi countered. Before Sue could reply, Sandi quickly explained about her mother's sister, ending with Laurie's death.

Sue gazed at Sandi. "I had no idea—how could we know?"

"You couldn't. I didn't know either until last night. Dad finally dragged it out of her." Sandi gazed out the front window at her mother. Harriet was sobbing into the steering wheel. "Sister Erickson, I'm sorry my mom upset you, but she did try to make things right this morning. I wish you'd given her that chance." Turning, Sandi walked out of the room. She was startled when Sue beat her to the front door.

"Sandi, could you do me a favor and go upstairs to check on Kate?" Sue asked. "I'd like a few minutes alone with your mother."

"You're sure?"

Sue nodded, then disappeared through the front door. Sighing, Sandi walked upstairs. A few minutes later, she entered Kate's room. Fully dressed, Kate lay on top of her bed. Her eyes were closed, but tears were sliding down each cheek. "Kate," she said quietly.

Kate opened her eyes and stared up at Sandi. "I thought you

and your mom would already be on your way home," she said.

Shaking her head, Sandi sat down on the bed. "I guess you heard what took place downstairs," she asked.

"Most of it," Kate answered, wiping at her face.

"Mom wanted to straighten things out," Sandi said, glancing out Kate's bedroom window. She watched as her mother climbed out of the car to talk to Sue. "And your mom, well, she's worried about you. This didn't turn out like we'd planned, but they are talking. It's a start."

Kate sat up, gazing in the same direction as Sandi. They watched for several minutes, each praying for an end to this feud. Tears and laughter blended when their mothers finally embraced. Following their example, Kate and Sandi hugged each other tight.

CHAPTER EIGHT

For Marie, the holidays came with a cruel intensity. Between Halloween and Thanksgiving, she put her life on automatic pilot; one day blended into another as she stumbled through the routine. Thanks to the sleeping pills her doctor had prescribed, she had been able to sleep at nights, usually from about three a.m. till the alarm buzzed at six-thirty. Numb with exhaustion, she would shut off the alarm, and head for the shower. After the semi-warm water finished waking her up, it was back to the bedroom to pick out something to wear. Her job as a bank teller dictated the selection— sedate hues that washed out what was left of the color in her face.

She wore her blonde hair tightly smoothed back in a chignon. At one time she had frequently worn it down to her shoulders, curling the front, then brushing it back for a soft, feminine look. She had caught the eye of several male customers in the past, not that she had ever encouraged their advances. Memories of Dwight had kept her polite, but aloof, and there had always been Linda to consider. She had gone on an occasional date, but had never allowed a serious relationship to develop.

Marie didn't like looking in the mirror anymore; she didn't recognize the woman who stared back. The dark circles under her eyes, the hollow cheeks that deepened as she continued to lose weight, the lifeless look usually seen on the faces of prisoners of war. Imprisoned by guilt, memories, and grief, Marie went through the motions of living while her spirit withered with pain.

Keeping busy helped her make it through each day. She invented things to do to keep occupied, at work and at home. Her small booth at the bank had been reorganized a thousand times. The house had never been cleaner. Eventually she would have to sell it and take an apartment closer to work. It was too hard living in a place where every room reminded her of Linda. She was constantly haunted by thoughts of what might have been. Memories tormented her, making it difficult to relax, to fall asleep at night. Even though fatigue overwhelmed her, peace eluded her and the combination took its toll.

Her sister called frequently. The soothing words she spoke helped, for a time. Samantha was the only link to a family who disapproved of her. Their father, a widower for twenty years, hadn't had much to do with her since her marriage to Dwight. Not that she blamed him; she had disappointed herself more than anyone else. This was not the life she had planned, but like her daughter, Marie had made decisions that refused to relinquish their hold on her.

Marie stumbled across a temporary solution in the basement one afternoon. As she moved and sorted boxes, she came upon Linda's private stash of vodka. Stunned, Marie stared at the bottle in her hands. After a while she took it upstairs to the kitchen, where she opened a cupboard and took down a glass. Filling it with vodka, she took a tiny sip and shuddered before setting the glass on the counter. It had been years since she had allowed herself to get drunk. She had lived that way for a time, after Dwight left. Linda was the reason she had finally pushed it away.

"Not that it did you any good," Marie mumbled angrily to her absent daughter. "You still drank . . . you tried pot and any other drug you could get your hands on," she accused, slapping her hands on the counter. "Why? Was it to punish me? Well, it worked! See what you've done?! See what I am?" Marie knocked the glass to the floor, watching as it shattered, spilling its contents over the broken pieces of glass. Picking up the bottle, she hurled it at the wall. The bottle didn't break, but the vodka spilled out onto the floor.

"What did you want from me?" Marie moaned. "I tried! I loved you . . . wasn't it enough? Wasn't it ever enough?" Sinking to her knees, she buried her face in her hands and began to sob.

CHAPTER NINE

"If thou art called to pass through tribulations . . ." Kate softly read aloud one of the scriptures Randy had told her to study from the Doctrine and Covenants. She had read the other passages, but this was the one she kept coming back to, especially after a hard day. Skimming through the verses, she skipped ahead to reread, "Therefore, hold on thy way . . . fear not what man can do, for God shall be with you forever and ever." Closing the book, she held it against her chest and quietly cried.

At supper Kate picked at the food on her plate, then retreated to her room. Sensing Kate's wish to be alone, Sue and Greg kept their distance until it was nearly ten o'clock. Then Greg went upstairs to talk to Kate while Sue slipped across the hall into Sabrina's room to check on their first-grader.

"Hi, Mommy" came a little voice.

Sue was startled. "Sabrina, I thought you were asleep."

"I woke up," Sabrina answered. "Kate was yellin' at Tyler. Why was she mad?"

"I'm not sure," Sue sighed. She hadn't had time to talk to Kate yet. After supper, she had gone with Greg to help him finish his home teaching. They hadn't been able to get away from the elderly widower until almost nine-thirty.

"Is Kate still sad 'cuz her friend died?"

"Something like that," Sue replied. Leaning down, she kissed Sabrina's soft cheek. "Kate will be fine," she soothed. "And you need to go back to sleep or you'll be tired at school tomorrow."

"'Kay," Sabrina said, nestling under the covers. "'Night, Mommy."

"Goodnight, honey." Sue slipped out of the room and walked down to Tyler's room. "Ty?" she said, peering into the darkness.

"Yeah," a cracked voice replied.

Sue smiled. Tyler hated what puberty was doing to his vocal range. "Mind if I flip on the light for a minute?"

"No."

Sue walked in and turned on the light. "I understand you talked to Kate while we were gone," she probed.

"Uh, yeah," he answered, sitting up in bed.

"Sabrina said she heard you two fighting."

Tyler scowled. "How did she hear that?"

"Think about it, Tyler. Her bedroom is right below Kate's. It must've come through the heat vent."

"Oh," Tyler said, suddenly alarmed. How much had Sabrina heard?

"What's up with your older sister?"

Tyler frowned. "She won't talk about it. That's probably what woke Sabrina—Kate telling me to mind my own business and leave her alone. She wasn't exactly quiet."

"Okay. Thanks anyway." Turning around, she flipped off the light. "See you in the morning," she said.

"Yeah," Tyler answered. He lay on his back for a while, staring into the darkness. Had Kate let Jace kiss her today at school? He had overheard some of the high school students talking about it as he had walked home this afternoon. Hoping it was only another rumor, he had waited until their parents had left before trying to talk to his older sister. But Kate had refused to answer his questions. "Man, Kate," he mumbled. "Not Jace. Mom and Dad'll have a stroke." Shaking his head, he rolled onto his side and tried to go to sleep.

* * *

"Kate?" Greg said softly, knocking at her bedroom door. When there was no response, he turned the knob and entered the room.

Kate had fallen asleep reading the scriptures. Greg pulled the triple combination away and set it on the nightstand. Kate moaned but didn't wake. Picking up the folded quilt on the end of the bed, Greg covered her with it, shut off the light beside her bed, and quietly left the room.

"How is she?" Sue asked, coming up the stairs.

"Asleep," Greg answered, pulling Kate's door partially shut. "What do you think set her off this time," he asked, following his wife to their bedroom.

"I'm not sure. She was awfully quiet when she came home from school this afternoon. Somebody must've said something, or . . . who knows. Maybe she went by the cemetery after school. She was late coming home."

"You don't suppose she tried to see Marie again?" Greg asked.

"I hope not—it just makes it that much worse. Marie can't deal with Kate right now. She can barely deal with herself."

"I know," Greg murmured, slipping off his shirt. "I saw Marie a couple of days ago at the bank. She looks terrible." Troubled, he glanced up at Sue. "I remember how it was, waiting for Kate to snap out of the coma. I can't imagine how it would've been if we'd lost her."

"Don't think the same thought hasn't crossed my mind a few hundred times," Sue replied as she sat on the bed. "My heart goes out to Marie," she sighed. "I wish there was something we could do."

Greg nodded and sat beside his wife. Then, reaching for her hand, he helped her to kneel beside him as he offered a worried prayer.

* * *

"NO!" Kate shrieked, waking with a start. Sitting up, she grabbed for a pillow and held it against her. The nightmare had been so real. First Marie, staring at her, those grief-stricken eyes expressing what she couldn't say. Then Jace, taunting, laughing, telling her she couldn't run from herself. Finally Linda, angry, accusing, following her everywhere she turned.

"Why?" Kate sobbed into the pillow. "Why won't it end?"

"Kate, what is it?" Sue asked, stepping into the room. She turned on a lamp, then reached for her daughter. Several minutes passed before Kate could talk about the nightmare, and the day she'd had at school.

Sandi had stayed home with the flu that day, leaving Kate without a friendly anchor. Jace had taken full advantage, following her around, finally cornering her in the gym. Grinning at the gathering crowd, he had triumphantly proclaimed Kate would never be free of him. He reminded her that he was the one she had turned to after Linda's funeral.

"You came to me, begging for a bottle of whiskey. Go on, deny it," he had challenged.

"I didn't beg—you gave it to me, you jerk! Leave me alone."

"I just want to help," Jace had said innocently.

"You can't help," she had replied, giving him an dirty look. "You don't even understand—"

"You've got that right—I don't understand! I don't understand you at all. We had a good thing goin', Kate, remember," he said as he had locked his hands behind her neck.

"Let go of me!"

Instead of releasing her, his grip had tightened. "Oh, no, sweet cheeks, we ain't through talkin'. We got a problem. You think you've changed, but you haven't! That bump on your head knocked the sense right out of you," he had said, his fingers straying to Kate's face. Kate had flinched at his touch, but he had held her firmly in place. "Maybe this will jar your memory." Leaning close, he had forced a kiss on her, bruising her lips with a cruel intensity. Then, he had pulled away, laughing as she had angrily wiped at her mouth. "Just like old times, babe," he had crowed as she ran out of the gym. "Just like old times!"

Even now, as Kate spoke, she shuddered at the memory.

"That's it! This time he's gone too far," Sue said angrily.

"That's not the worst part, Mom."

"Oh," Sue said, already plotting what she would like to do to Jace.

"Everyone thinks I'm dragging Sandi down. She's the only friend I have . . . the only one I can even talk to. She tries to stand up for me, but I hate what it's doing to her. I hate how Jace and his gang treat her. Last week when Jace started mouthing off again about the whiskey, Sandi stepped between us, telling him what I'd done with it."

"And?"

"He laughed and told everyone she had probably helped me drink it. It's not fair, Mom. It's not fair to Sandi—"

"And it's not fair to you," Sue murmured. "Look, I've been thinking about the offer Paige made a couple of weeks ago. Maybe it's time to take it seriously."

Kate stared at her mother.

"I know it's not a perfect solution, but if we don't do something soon, I won't be held accountable for what your father or I will do to Jace. It's obvious he's not going anywhere, and I won't have you this miserable the rest of your senior year."

"Maybe you're right," Kate said. "But I hate to let him win."

"He lost a long time ago," Sue replied. "He just doesn't realize it yet. As for Sandi, surely the other girls in the branch—"

"They're furious with me. They blame me for how Sandi's being treated at school. Like it's my fault. Maybe it is . . ."

"You know that's not true." Sue brushed the hair out of Kate's eyes. "Under normal circumstances, I'd advise you to be patient, but this is getting out of hand. At least in Salt Lake . . ."

"Sandi's life could get back to normal and maybe I could go on with mine," Kate said, finishing her mother's thought. "Aunt Paige said the same thing to me the last time she called."

"Well, it's something to think about," Sue replied. "We don't need to make a decision tonight. We'll talk it over later." She patted Kate's hand. "Think you can sleep now?"

Kate nodded.

"Let's start by getting you into a nightgown. When you fell asleep earlier, your dad didn't have the heart to wake you." Sue pulled a nightshirt out of the dresser as Kate slipped out of her t-shirt and jeans.

* * *

"Is everything all right," Greg sleepily asked when Sue returned to the master bedroom.

"No," Sue answered. Sitting on the edge of the bed, she revealed the cause of Kate's current nightmare—the one they were all living. Greg reacted as she had anticipated and it was all she could do to keep him from going after Jace. "Greg, you're not going to accomplish anything this time of night. Besides, Kate doesn't need any more stress right now," Sue pleaded. "She's been through enough. We don't need to make it worse for her."

"I'd like to make it worse for him," Greg growled as he reluctantly stepped out of his pants and reached for his pajama bottoms. "I still think I could knock some sense into that degenerate," he said, scowling. "If he so much as breathes on her again . . ."

"I feel the same way. But none of that will help Kate. I think our only option is getting her out of Bozeman."

Greg sat down on his side of the bed and picked up the family portrait sitting on the nightstand. He touched Kate's smiling face.

"I don't want to let her go either, honey," Sue said softly, sliding an arm around his shoulders. "I've been trying to convince myself I can handle it next fall when she heads to college. Sending her away now tears at my heart." She sat down beside him. "But I can't watch her suffer anymore. It's not getting better—if it was, I'd want her to keep trying. I don't see the light at the end of the tunnel this time."

Slowly nodding, Greg set the picture back on the night stand. Gripping his wife's hand, he silently pleaded for the strength they would need in the days ahead.

CHAPTER TEN

Y ou're not serious." Sandi stared at Kate, hoping she hadn't heard right.

Looking up from the piece of pecan pie in front of her, Kate nodded.

"Why?"

"You know how it's been lately. I can't deal with it anymore." Avoiding the look on Sandi's face, Kate concentrated on the antique decorations lining the walls of Frontier Pies. She had invited Sandi here to tell her about the decision to move to Salt Lake. If things worked out, she would leave after Christmas.

Sandi continued to stare at Kate. "I never thought I'd see the day when Kate Erickson ran away from a challenge," she said at last.

"I'm not running away—"

"Then what do you call it?"

"Sandi, it'll be easier for both of us if I leave."

"I don't think so. I finally get you back as a friend, and you're willing to walk away again." Sandi angrily sliced at the piece of cherry pie she had ordered.

"I'm not walking away," Kate protested. "We'll still see each other at the Y . . . if I get accepted. In the meantime—"

"In the meantime, you'll desert me—leave me here to face everyone alone."

"You're not making this easy," Kate mumbled, stabbing at her pie.

"Good! Turning your back on a friend shouldn't be easy."

"I'm not turning my back—"

"You're giving up, without a fight. You might as well walk up to Jace and congratulate him on his victory."

"Sandi—"

"Let him take the credit for ruining your life. Another notch in his belt."

"You don't understand—"

"I understand more than you think," Sandi said, sadly.

"I can't expect you to keep facing this, day after day."

"It'll let up eventually."

"Right," Kate replied. "People have been telling me that for weeks. I don't buy it any more."

"Kate, there are more people on your side than you know." She ignored the look on Kate's face and continued. "Okay, it's been rough, but the only voices you seem to be listening to are the ones you need to ignore."

"What?"

"Let me finish. There are several kids at school who admire you for the way you've stood up to Jace."

"I really believe that one!"

"I'm serious. Yesterday, Patty Reynolds said—"

"Patty . . . the one who's been making your life miserable since you started hanging around with me?"

"She's a good person and friend . . . which is partly why I picked her as my first counselor."

"I don't believe this," Kate sighed before cramming a piece of pie into her mouth.

"I know she's been critical of you. It's taken a while for her to see how things really are."

Kate rolled her eyes and continued to chew.

"She found out this week her dad's being transferred to Boise. They're moving during Christmas vacation."

"So?"

"So, she started to rethink a few things, like how much she's going to miss me. She came over to tell me last night. We had a long talk and I straightened her out on a couple of items. Your name came up."

"That must've been interesting," Kate murmured.

"It was. She told me a lot of kids were upset after Jace manhandled you Thursday. Some of them don't think he's funny anymore. And they're starting to believe you really have changed. If you walk away, you'll give Jace more ammo to use against you."

Kate pushed the half-eaten piece of pie away and slumped in her chair.

"Kate, we can do this. We can show people how wrong Jace and his crowd are. In fact, we might even be able to make this into something positive."

"How?"

"Well . . . I got the idea from Sister Blanchard. Mom thinks it's worth a try." Kate gave Sandi a skeptical look. Ignoring the look, Sandi smiled brightly. "What would you think about starting up a chapter of the SADD organization in our school. You know, Students Against Drunk Drivers?"

"Sandi, I don't—"

"We could make a difference. Linda's death has had an impact on several people. Patty told me Bob Quentin quit drinking because of it."

"Bob? I don't believe it."

"Believe it, Kate, it's true. I asked around. I think there are others we could influence too."

"What's this "we" stuff?"

"C'mon, Kate, don't give up now. We're on the verge of turning things around. Are you with me, or are you going to bail? Either way, I'm going through with this. I think it's important."

"Can I think about it for a while?" Kate replied, reaching for her coat.

"Sure," Sandi said, picking up her own coat.

"Where are you going? You haven't finished your pie yet."

"Neither have you," Sandi pointed out.

"I'm not hungry," Kate said, slipping her coat on. "Nothing personal . . . but I need some space for a while."

"Okay. Don't skip town without letting me know," Sandi responded.

Nodding, Kate picked up the check, moved to the cashier to pay, then walked out of the restaurant.

CHAPTER ELEVEN

C an you believe it, Linda? Me, in charge of a SADD bunch?"
Kate complained, grimacing at the unintended pun. "That was bad,
sorry." She brushed the snow away to lean against her friend's
headstone. "It'd never work, right? I mean, no one would listen to
me—especially now." Moving away from the headstone, she angrily
wiped at her eyes. "I thought I had all the answers when I came back
to Bozeman. I figured, I'd throw out a few apologies, make things
right with everyone, and life would be great. I even thought I'd be
able to turn you around. Instead, I'm the one who's being turned
around, and you're dead, thanks to me. I'd give anything if I could
change that night . . . if I could change what I said the day before!

"But I can't. You're gone, and I'm supposed to go on with my
life like nothing's happened. No one understands what I'm
feeling—and I'm surrounded by people who either ignore me or
won't let me forget, and I can't deal with it anymore!" She turned
and began to walk away, then broke into a run.

Stunned by what she had overheard, Marie stepped out from
behind the tree she had slipped behind at the first sight of Kate.
She watched in silence as Kate climbed inside the Explorer and
roared away from the cemetery. Sighing, Marie moved to Linda's
grave and brushed the remaining snow from the headstone. She
picked up the white silk roses Kate had dropped and added them to
the fresh arrangement she had brought, setting the vase in the
rounded opening in the cement near the headstone.

* * *

"Kate, I know you're in there," Sue insisted, knocking again on her daughter's bedroom door. "Are you all right?"

"I'm fine," Kate yelled.

"Uh huh," Sue said dryly. "Do you want to talk about it?" She waited, but there was no response. "Okay, I give up. When you're ready to unload, you know where to find me." Sighing, she walked downstairs as Tyler burst in from outside.

"Dad says the Explorer isn't hurt too bad—just a couple of dents from where she plowed into the garage," Tyler said, pulling off his gloves.

"Good," Sue replied.

"He thinks she must've hit an icy spot on the driveway. You should see the garage door."

"I saw it," Sue informed him. When she had heard the initial crash, she had raced out the front door. Kate had come flying past her, sobbing as though her heart would break.

"First the Sunbird, now this. Maybe we'd better get her a chauffeur, it'd be cheaper," Tyler quipped.

Sue frowned at her son. "Tyler, I'm really not in the mood for this right now, okay?"

"Okay," Tyler said sullenly. Opening the front door, he hurried outside.

Sue closed it behind him, grateful that Sabrina was down the street playing at a friend's house. The last thing they needed was her endless questions.

Moving into the living room, Sue absently picked up a pair of Tyler's dirty socks. She took them to the utility room and threw them into the hamper. As she stepped back into the kitchen, she wondered if she should start dinner, or approach Kate again.

What had upset her? She knew Kate had planned to break the news to Sandi today about leaving for Salt Lake. Deciding that must be the answer, Sue headed for the stairs. The doorbell rang out sharply. "Now what?" she muttered. Turning around, she moved to the door. Her eyes widened when she saw Marie Sikes standing on the porch.

"Marie . . . come in," Sue stammered.

"Are you sure?" Marie asked hesitantly. "It looks like I've come at a bad time."

"Oh . . . the garage . . . well, it's been one of those days." She motioned for Marie to step inside. "Kate came flying in and—"

"She's here, then?" Marie asked as she followed Sue into the living room.

"Yes," Sue answered, wondering at the thoughtful look on Marie's face.

"Is she all right?"

"I think so."

Marie glanced around, wondering if she had done the right thing by coming here. She glanced nervously at the colorful cardboard pilgrims taped on the front window in celebration of Thanksgiving.

"Marie, is something wrong?" Sue asked, instantly regretting it. *Idiot,* she thought to herself. *Of course something's wrong—she buried her daughter five weeks ago.*

Marie was too preoccupied to take offense. "I'm . . . concerned about Kate," she said softly.

"Oh?" Sue replied.

"Could I talk to her?"

Sue hesitated. She doubted Kate would talk to anyone, let alone Linda's mother. Praying for inspiration, she finally settled on the truth. "Kate came home very upset this afternoon. She plowed into the garage, ran in the house, and headed up to her room. I tried to talk to her, but she wasn't very receptive. I'm not sure I can get her to come out."

Marie glanced toward the stairs, then back at Sue. "Earlier, I took some flowers up to the cemetery. Kate was there, talking to Linda. She said some things . . . I had no idea she was blaming herself for what happened."

"Still? But, I thought we'd convinced her—"

"Sue, I feel terrible. I turned her away a couple of times—not because I thought she was responsible. Seeing her hurt too much. I can't explain it—"

"You don't need to," Sue interrupted. "I have no way of knowing what you're going through right now, but I know how I felt when Kate was in that coma. It was awful."

Marie nodded, her gaze shifting back to the stairs. "Would you mind if I tried to explain things to her? Maybe it would help."

"Under the circumstances, I think it's worth a try," Sue responded, touched by Marie's willingness to help.

"Where's her room?"

"Upstairs, the first door on the left. Do you want me to come up with you?"

"No, if it's all right, I'd like to try it alone first." Marie looked to Sue for permission, then began climbing the stairs. She hesitated in front of the closed door as the painful memory of another closed door surfaced. Trying her best to block it out, she knocked. When there was no answer, she tried the knob. It turned easily in her hand. Taking a deep breath, she pushed the door open and entered the room.

"Mom, I don't want to talk right now," Kate sobbed into her pillow.

"I know how you feel," Marie said softly.

Startled, Kate rolled over to stare up at Marie.

"But it's what I need to do," Marie continued, stepping close to the bed. "There are some things I should've said before now. Kate, I never meant to hurt you. The reason I've been avoiding you . . . it wasn't because . . .what happened the night Linda . . . the night of the accident . . ." Marie paused. "It wasn't your fault. I've never blamed you for any of it."

Fresh tears slid down Kate's face as she sat up. "But the day of the funeral, at the cemetery . . . and those times I stopped by . . ."

Marie closed her eyes. "I see you and I see Linda—you two spent so much time together. I'm sorry for turning away . . . for making it harder for you. Will you let me help now?" She looked at Kate and held out her hand. As Kate slowly reached to take it, Marie pulled her up into an embrace. "We have to help each other, Kate," she murmured. "It's the only way we're going to get through this."

Nodding in silent agreement, Kate clung to Marie as a torrent of emotion bonded them in a way few people would understand.

CHAPTER TWELVE

. . . Which is why we decided to pull this together. We can help our friends avoid and overcome the dangers associated with drugs and alcohol."

"Like you helped Linda?" Jace yelled from the back of the auditorium.

Kate blinked. What was Jace doing here? He had already discouraged several students from coming tonight. He probably thought it was his duty to ruin the meeting for everyone else.

"What happened to Linda wasn't Kate's fault," Sandi replied, standing next to Kate in front of the podium. "We all know that," she added.

"Do we?" Jace taunted, strutting down the aisle. "Whose fault was it then?"

"We're not here to point fingers at anyone," Sandi said angrily. "We're here to stop idiots like you from ending up like Linda."

"Did I hear right?" Jace asked. "Idiots like us?" His friends laughed and cheered him on. "Okay, tell us, we're all *dying* to know . . ." Jace paused to grin at the small crowd that had gathered in the auditorium. "How can idiots like us stay alive?"

Kate gripped the microphone. "By using a little common sense," she said, glowering at Jace. "Something you wouldn't know anything about."

"I'm wounded and she twisted the knife," Jace said, pulling out an imaginary blade. When that brought laughs, he began acting out a dramatic death scene.

Sandi frowned. This was too important—she couldn't let Jace destroy it before it had even had a chance. She wished she had agreed to let parents come to this first meeting. She had thought it would go over better if they asked for students only. Students helping students. That was the goal of SADD. She glanced up, two junior boys were starting to walk out.

"Wait, don't leave, please," Sandi pleaded.

"If you insist," Jace quipped, picking himself up off the floor. He turned to his captive audience. "You heard the woman, she begged me to stay."

"You heard wrong," a voice challenged from the middle of the auditorium.

"Who said that?" Jace asked, glancing around.

"It sounded like Bob Quentin," Jace's closest friend, Gary Leavitt answered.

Jace glared back at the large senior and mumbled several obscenities.

"You can stay if you'll sit down and listen," Kate said firmly, hoping to avoid a fight. She knew how hot-headed Jace could be.

"I wouldn't have it any other way, Katie—dear," Jace said, giving Bob another dirty look before motioning for his friends to fill in the seats on the front row.

Convinced the damage was done, Kate tried to continue. "We want to organize a hot-line—"

"A hot-line run by a hot-mama," Jace hollered. "I love it."

"It would be run by students from our school. Volunteers, people like you . . ." Kate stammered, trying to ignore the look on Jace's face.

"People like us?" Gary feigned shocked surprise.

"People like us," Jace sarcastically assured his best friend.

"We would try to discourage students from getting drunk in the first place and arrange rides for those who insist on drinking," Kate continued. "Our goal is to keep people from drinking and driving."

"I'm sure we can think of better ways to use that hot-line," Jace sneered. "I know an expert who can tell you everything you want to know about 900 numbers. Kurt, take the floor."

"Remain seated, Kurt," Sandi said sharply, moving closer to the microphone. "Why don't you guys leave? We're here to help people—something you wouldn't be interested in."

"Oh, yeah? I'd love to help Kate with a few things. Would you like to see my list?" Jace asked, reaching into his pocket.

Sandi glanced at Kate. This wasn't turning out like she had hoped.

"Shut up or leave," Bob Quentin demanded.

"What?" Jace stood up, glaring at his opponent. "I don't think I heard right."

"You heard me all right," Bob said, rising to his feet. The six-foot four-inch senior stared menacingly at Jace.

"Would you look at that? Little Bobby Quentin can stand up all by himself these days." Jace turned to grin at Kate. "What a good influence you've been having. You must be proud."

"Kate had nothin' to do with it," Bob said. "Linda's death is what did it for me. I don't want to end up like that."

"Bobby, my man, you've got it all wrong. Kate had everything to do with it. That's why she's up there trying to make herself feel better about it." He turned to face Kate. "Isn't that right, Kate? This is your way of glossing over what happened. Linda's dead because of you!" he accused.

"You're wrong," an angry voice replied. Everyone turned around as Marie Sikes made her way down the aisle. "You couldn't be more wrong," she added as she continued to the front of the auditorium and climbed the stairs that led to the stage. Crossing the stage, she smiled at Sandi, then seeing the shape Kate was in, drew her into a hug.

"I'm sorry I told you I wouldn't come. I didn't think I'd be able to handle it," she whispered to Kate. "But I'm here, and there's something I'd like to say to these kids."

Kate nodded.

Keeping an arm around Kate's waist, Marie moved back with her to the podium. She motioned for Sandi to join them and slid her other arm around Sandi's tiny waist. "These two are still alive, thanks to Kate's quick thinking. Kate is guilty only of trying to be a good friend to my daughter. She tried to talk Linda out of throwing the party that was held the night . . ." Marie couldn't finish the sentence. "My daughter had a drinking problem . . . and she messed around with drugs, despite what I said or anyone else for that matter. I can see now that I should've gotten her some help. Instead, I told myself she'd be fine, that eventually, she'd realize the danger of what she was doing. She was just having a good time, right? Wrong!" She looked down into the audience at Jace. "When having a so-called 'good time' ends a life, it's time to make some changes."

Tightening her grip around Sandi and Kate, Marie gave each girl a quick squeeze before she continued, "I'm proud of these two girls. What they're trying to do is wonderful. And if any of you want to do something to help, join them. Support them. Stop other young people from meeting a tragic death."

The auditorium was silent. Then Bob Quentin stood up and shouted, "Tell me what to do!"

"You can count on us," two sophomores cried out. Soon everyone, with the exception of Jace and company, stood to pledge their support. Applause began and continued as Kate, Sandi, and Marie tearfully gazed down at them. Disgusted, Jace and his friends slunk out quietly. Triumphant, Marie reached for Kate and Sandi and held their hands up into the air. Another door had opened, one that would lead to healing and peace.

CHAPTER THIRTEEN

Dec. 27

*D*ear Elder Randy M.,

Thanks for the cute leprechaun doll. I love it. Now, whenever I miss you, I'll give him a squeeze—not that you look anything alike.

Kate smiled as she gazed at the mischievous-looking doll sitting on her bed. Picking up her pen, she continued writing.

I'm sorry things are so slow in your district. Don't lose hope. There are people waiting to hear the gospel. Keep trying—don't ever give up.

You probably can't believe I said that after everything that's happened the past few months. It's true though. Sandi was right—things are starting to get better. Moving to Salt Lake wouldn't have solved anything. Bozeman seems like home again, and I've had the chance to get closer to some people who are pretty great. People like Mom, Dad, Sandi, Marie, Sister Blanchard, Aunt Paige, your mother, and you. I never would've made it through any of this alone. I'm so grateful for all of you and for everything you've done.

The support we've had for SADD has been overwhelming. Students, teachers, and parents have been wonderful to help. Especially Marie. I never really knew her before. The sad thing is, I don't think Linda did either.

She is such a neat lady. She helped us establish our hot-line, and has spent hours answering phones. Sometimes we run short of student help, but Dad, Mom, Sister Blanchard, even Sandi's mom and dad have been really good to fill in. We've been told that our efforts have already saved lives. It won't bring Linda back, but it does seem to ease what we've all been feeling.

We invited Marie over for Christmas. She refused at first, then showed up on our doorstep Christmas Eve. She couldn't handle it alone. Mom made her stay the night in the guest room. It was kind of awkward for all of us Christmas morning. We didn't want to say or do anything to make Marie uncomfortable. I thought I'd blown it when I handed my gift to her. It was a picture I'd had blown up and framed—one of Linda I had taken during our junior year. One where she's actually smiling. Marie cried for a while, but assured me she loved it. It's the way we both want to remember her.

The Sunday after Christmas, Marie went to church with us—it was the first time in years. A musical number got to her during sacrament meeting. Some Primary kids sang, "I'm a Child of God." I'll admit, it hit me pretty hard, too. It was one of the songs performed at Linda's funeral. I guess there will always be moments like that.

A man named Stephen Ross came to our SADD meeting last night. He came to the one we held the week before Christmas, too. His wife and daughter were killed in an accident involving a teenage drunk driver nearly three years ago. I noticed he spent a lot of time talking to Marie. I'll keep you posted on that one.

We're trying to pull together an alcohol-free party for New Year's Eve. We're thinking of having a dance. The superintendent told us we could use the school gym. Sandi's still trying to line up a band. Mom said she'd help me with refreshments. I hope it turns out. I keep having nightmares about Jace showing up to ruin it. Don't worry though. Sandi and I are getting pretty good at dealing with him. Besides, Bob Quentin will be there and he can handle just about anybody. That guy's huge!

Well, take care, have a super day, and always remember how much you mean to me.

Love,
Kate

P.S. Sandi picked me as first counselor to replace Patty Reynolds in our Young Women class presidency. It's great, and it's giving me the chance to get closer to the girls in our branch. Things are definitely looking up.

Jan. 20

Dear Sister Erickson,

Congrats on your new calling, and thanks for the Christmas care package! The cookies arrived mostly in one piece. The hat, gloves, and scarf will come in handy.

Sorry I haven't written until now, but things have finally picked up in our district. We're teaching an entire family—I know they have to be golden! I won't make any predictions concerning baptism dates, but I know it'll happen this time.

How did the New Year's Eve dance turn out? You're having quite an impact on Bozeman. Have I mentioned how proud I am of you? (Don't let it go to your head!) Seriously, it's a good thing you're doing. And I'm glad you have people like ME in your life. We all need love and support, including yours truly. Last week, I had a horrible day. My pants caught in my bicycle chain, and I tore a good-sized chunk out of my leg when I fell. Then, as I hobbled uphill pushing my bike, some jerk threw a rock at me. He nailed me in the forehead. My companion said I was a bloody mess. (I'm not so sure he didn't mean it the way people use that phrase over here. Don't worry, I've already called him to repentance.) I was about as discouraged as I've ever been. To top it off, it started raining and our roof leaks. But . . . waiting for me in the mailbox was a letter from Mom. It made all the difference in the world. When you know someone is on your side, there isn't much you can't do.

Love,
Elder Randy Miles

P.S. If you get bored in the near future, another batch of homemade cookies would be greatly appreciated!!

Feb. 10

Dear Elder M.,

I hope you enjoy this batch of cookies. (I loved the subtle hint in your last letter!!) I tried a new recipe in your honor. Let me know if it's edible.

How's it going with your golden family? I hope it works out. You're getting a few battle scars over there. For your sake as well as mine, please be careful. As for life in Bozeman, the battle continues here as well. The New Year's Eve dance was, for the most part, a success. We counted heads and nearly half of the student body was there.

    Unfortunately, just as I'd feared, Jace arrived to make a fool and a nuisance of himself. When we started the countdown at midnight, I thought we were in the clear. Wouldn't you know, that's when Jace and his friends decided to show up—drunk. They sauntered in like they owned the place, grabbed me, and tried to force me to drink out of a bottle of gin they'd brought with them. Mom and Dad were chaperoning, as well as Marie Sikes and Stephen Ross. I thought Dad was going to kill Jace for a minute. It took Mom, Marie, and Stephen to pull them apart. By then, the police arrived to escort Jace and his friends downtown to cool their heels for a while. I've heard Jace has threatened to make me pay for getting him in trouble. Sandi's worried, but I don't think anything will come of it. Besides, Mom won't let me go anywhere alone. Now I know what it must be like to have a companion. You have my sympathy. (Kidding.)

Eternally yours,
Kate

Feb. 14

Dear Elder Randy Miles,

    I know I just sent off a letter, but I had to thank you for the gorgeous flowers that arrived today. Your mom called this afternoon to make sure they got here okay. She's sure a sweetheart—like her son. Thanks again. Have a super day.

Love ya,
Kate

P.S. I hope you receive the box of chocolates on time and in good shape.

Feb. 24

Dear Kate,

    You're welcome for the flowers. The box of chocolates showed up in good shape and were wonderful—ask my companion. He ate most of them, the rat.

Speaking of rats, Jace had better steer clear of you if he knows what's good for him! Listen to your parents and play it safe. Have you considered taking a self-defense class? In the meantime, maybe your guardian angel would be willing to work a little overtime?! When I think about everything's that's happened to you this year, he or she is probably ready for a vacation.

That family I mentioned may not be as golden as I thought. The head of the house is starting to drag his feet. He loves a good pipe in the evening and the occasional beer, and is struggling with the Word of Wisdom. But we're not giving up. I can see a desire for the gospel burning in his wife's eyes.

Mom sent me a picture of my newest nephew this week. He looks like me—the lucky kid!

Well, try to behave and know that someone in Ireland loves you. (It's my new companion. I caught him lusting after your picture!)

Love,
Elder M.

P.S. A couple of days ago I was able to take some wonderful shots of the coast. I'll send you some of them.

March 12

Dear Elder Randy,

You'll be happy to know that Jace's parents sent him to live with an uncle somewhere in Wyoming. I guess they decided he was getting into too much trouble around here. I can't say that I've missed him. Since he left, his friends have been keeping a low profile. They give me a bad time at school once in a while, but most of the time they leave me alone.

The SADD bunch is doing great. Sandi came up with an idea to hold a fund-raiser—a talent show. She wants me to sing. I told her I'd think about it. We want to raise money for SADD and for some kind of a memorial for Linda. I don't know what that will be yet, but we'd like it to be a surprise for Marie.

Speaking of Marie, she brought Stephen to church last Sunday. I didn't mean to eavesdrop, but I overheard Marie talking to my mom the other night. Marie's afraid Stephen is getting too serious. In a way, I hope it will work out between them. Stephen is a great guy. He's not a member of the Church, which has Marie concerned. Now that she's active again, she doesn't want to give it up. I think Stephen realizes how much it means to her. And he did seem impressed Sunday. He asked Dad all kinds of questions. I hope it works out. I'd like to see Marie and Stephen rebuild their lives . . . maybe even together.

Your eternal romantic,
Kate

P.S. Tyler wants to know if you've spotted a pot of gold yet. (He has a thing for rainbows!)

March 29

Dear Kate,

    Thanks for the letter. I'm glad Marie is staying active in the church. If it works out with Stephen, that would be great, but don't be disappointed if it doesn't happen. Sometimes things don't turn out the way we want them to—like the family we were teaching, the Dalys. Their two-year-old boy, Billy, has developed a serious case of viral pneumonia. It doesn't look good. The mother, Maureen, wants us to administer to him, but her husband, Jim, won't let us near their son. At the moment, Jim doesn't want anything to do with us or the Church. It didn't help when his neighbors told him this happened because he was thinking of becoming a Mormon. I keep praying for a miracle, but I'm not sure what to do any more. I've had more doors slammed in my face this week than in my entire life. It gets old in a hurry.

    Sorry if I sound a little down. Things'll get better, and I know the Lord's work will go forward.

Yours in the gospel,
Elder Miles

P.S. Tell Tyler real gold is found in the hearts of good men and women. It's a saying Mom sent me last week.

Sandi looked up from the letter and gazed at Kate.

"Well?" Kate said glumly.

"I don't see the problem."

"'Yours in the gospel'? That's like saying, 'Have a good day.'"

"What's wrong with that?" Sandi asked as she sat down on Kate's bed.

"Compare it with how he's ended the last five letters." Kate picked them up from her desk and brought them across the room to Sandi.

Sandi obediently read the lines pointed out by Kate. "Kate, just because he—"

"He doesn't love me anymore," Kate sighed, moving to the window.

"I think you're being silly. It's obvious this guy adores you. He has other things on his mind right now. Not that you're not important to him," she hastily added, avoiding Kate's glare. "He's on a mission, Kate. He's supposed to focus on teaching the gospel, not on writing mushy love letters."

"I suppose you're right," Kate said, moving back to the bed. She sat down and stared at the letters Sandi had scattered across the quilt. "But if he didn't care . . ."

"You'd go on with your life and someday meet someone else."

"You're full of sympathetic comfort," Kate grumbled.

"Sorry, but I just went through this with Bill, remember."

Kate frowned. "I know. I shouldn't have dumped this on you."

"No problem," Sandi said, offering a smile. "I never thought Bill and I would last forever. We've been drifting apart for quite a while. He's either working or studying—"

"That reminds me, is he going to make valedictorian?" Kate asked.

"I hope so. It's probably the only way he'll make it to college."

"And you two broke up because he's been so busy?" Kate prompted. She hadn't asked earlier, figuring Sandi would tell her when she was ready.

"No. There were other reasons," Sandi replied. "We've both changed so much this year, and he's right. I have spent more time with SADD than with him lately. It's probably for the best," she sighed.

"You're taking it better than I would," Kate commented.

"Tell me about it! You're having a fit over how Randy signed his name. I'd hate to see how you'd react if he ever quit writing."

"Don't say it," Kate pleaded. "It can't happen."

* * *

"It might," Sue murmured later, glancing at her daughter. Sandi's visit had done nothing to boost Kate's spirits. "Kate, people grow and change. It might not work out between you two."

"Mom!" Kate complained.

"I'm not saying I don't want it to. I'd be tickled to have Randy as a son-in-law *someday*—emphasis on someday. Right now, he needs to concentrate on his mission, and you need to concentrate on graduating from high school and getting into college."

"You're not cheering me up, Mom."

Sue pushed the letters to the side and sat down on Kate's bed. "Sweetheart, you know I only want you to be happy."

"Randy makes me happy," Kate said quietly.

Sue prayed for the right words that would help her daughter. She had been afraid that Kate had become too dependant on Randy. He had helped Kate through so much, she knew it would crush Kate if their relationship ended. But Randy couldn't be an effective missionary if his only thoughts were of Kate. "Right now, Randy is trying to do the Lord's work—" she began.

"I know that, Mom," Kate interrupted. "I'm not trying to stand in his way. But it would be nice to know he still cares."

"You know he does," Sue soothed. "When he gets back, you two will have plenty of time to work things out. Until then, allow him the freedom he needs to be a successful missionary. Spend this time furthering your education. I'm sure I've mentioned before that I wish I'd gone after that business degree I was working on when I met your dad. Fortunately, I've never had to work outside our home. Your father's job has always been stable—he was wise to go into computer technology. And his salary has provided us with a good living. But if anything ever happened to him, I don't know what I'd do to support the family. And in today's world . . ."

Kate rolled her eyes. "A woman needs an education. I know, Mom. I'm planning on going to college."

"Good girl," Sue said, patting Kate's leg. "There's something else I wish you'd consider."

"What?"

"It wouldn't hurt you to date other people once in a while." There, she had finally said it. She braced herself for the explosion that would follow. Kate didn't let her down.

"Mom! I'm not gonna date anyone while Randy is—"

"Mike Jeffries wants to ask you to the senior prom."

"I can't believe you would even suggest . . . Mike Jeffries?"

Sue nodded.

As Kate pictured the handsome senior in her mind, she blushed. Mike's large brown eyes framed by long lashes and his thick head of dark hair had often captured her attention in the past.

"Mike wants to go out with me? Not that I'd even consider it."

It was all Sue could do to keep a straight face. "His mother mentioned it to me the other day at the grocery store. We were talking about getting our visiting teaching done."

"You went from visiting teaching to Mike asking me to the prom?"

"One thing led to another. I've always thought that he was a nice young man, even your father's impressed with him. Wasn't Mike the youngest scout to earn his Eagle in our branch?"

Kate shrugged. "I've never been into scouting much," she said, still trying to absorb this new information.

"Betty, Mike's mother, mentioned that he's wanted to ask you out for quite a while, but has been too timid."

"Mike—timid? That's a new one!"

"He knows you're writing to a missionary," Sue added. "For some guys, that's a bit intimidating." She paused for several seconds, but Kate remained silent. "Randy doesn't expect you to put yourself into cold storage for two years. He'd want you to enjoy things like the senior prom. I think he'd like Mike."

"Yeah, right," Kate said as she rolled her eyes. "Look, Mom, Mike's okay, I've always liked him, but I couldn't—"

"Kate, you're only a high school senior once. I hate to see you miss this chance."

"I know. I'd love to go to the prom, but I'm afraid Randy wouldn't understand."

"Sure he would. I'll bet he went to his senior prom."

"I know he did. I've seen the pictures," Kate replied, seeing Randy's arm around another girl's waist. "I guess it wouldn't be like a real date," she added contemplatively. "And Randy's so busy right now . . . he probably wouldn't want me to bother him with little details like this."

"Even if you did, I doubt he'd mind too much," Sue said, hoping Kate was taking this suggestion seriously.

"I'll think about it," Kate responded, imagining how wonderful Mike would look in a tux. "You're sure Mike's going to ask me?"

Sue nodded. "I told his mother you'd love to go to the prom."

"Mom!"

"It's true, isn't it?"

"Well, yeah, I guess." A smile appeared, then faded.

"Now what's wrong?" Sue probed.

"Sandi. How can I go to the prom when she has to stay home?"

"Who says she's staying home?" Sue asked, a mischievous twinkle in her eye. "I saw how Keith Taylor was looking at her Sunday at church."

Kate stared at her mother. Keith was Mike's best friend. It seemed like Mike and Keith were always together. Both participated in school sports and had made the varsity football squad since they were sophomores. Mike was one of the fastest wide receivers Bozeman had seen in several years. As for Keith, his defensive record had netted him a place on the state's all-star team. Tall and broad-shouldered, Keith was a natural choice to play defensive end.

"In a way, I'm kind of glad Sandi and Bill split up. I've never been in favor of steady dating in high school," Sue said, interrupting Kate's train of thought.

"Why?"

"Because it can lead to trouble."

"Aunt Paige dated Uncle Stan in high school," Kate said impishly.

"That's different," Sue quickly replied. "They didn't . . . that is to say, they never—and anyway, times have changed."

"I see," Kate replied, enjoying her mother's embarrassment.

"Is it five o'clock already?" Sue said, glancing at the clock on Kate's nightstand. "I'd better get supper going."

"I'll help," Kate volunteered, following her mother out of the room. "And Mom . . ." she added.

Sue paused at the staircase.

"Thanks for listening. It helped."

Smiling, Sue waited until Kate moved forward, then slid an arm around her daughter's waist. Together they walked downstairs, conspiring about the future purchase of a prom dress.

CHAPTER FOURTEEN

W hat do you think?" Kate nervously asked, gazing at her reflection in the bathroom mirror.

Sue smiled as she finished fastening a strand of pearls around her daughter's neck. She was loaning them to Kate for the evening, along with the matching teardrop earrings. "I think we'll have to glue Mike's eyes back in place when he sees you. They're going to pop right out of his head."

"Mom!"

"I'm serious, Kate. You're beautiful." Ignoring the lump forming in her throat, Sue forced another smile. "I want you to promise me that you'll relax and have a wonderful time tonight."

"I'll try," Kate said, glancing in the mirror again. She had spent nearly two hours at Ruth's Beauty Shoppe. If the reaction she was getting from everyone was any indication, the results had definitely been worth it. Her father had already threatened to lock her in a closet to preserve what he called his "fatherly sanity." Her mother claimed she was stunning with her hair softly piled on top of her head, small feathered curls framing her face. The forest-green formal they had doctored to be comfortably modest, complimented her coloring, drawing out the emerald green in her eyes.

"Mikey's here," Tyler sang out, hollering up the stairs.

"Am I doing the right thing?" Kate gave her mother a worried look.

"Yes," Sue answered, blending in the blush on Kate's cheek

with her hand. "Now hurry downstairs before your father has a chance to chat with Mike."

"He wouldn't."

"He might. He said it isn't safe to let anyone of the male gender see you in this condition."

"What condition?"

"Drop-dead gorgeous," Sue replied, forcing her daughter out of the bathroom. "Let's go. You've primped enough."

"I'll say." As Tyler came up the stairs, he stared at his sister, then gave a low whistle. "Wow," he mumbled. "I'd better warn Mike."

Tyler!" Sue threatened as Tyler began bounding down the stairs.

"It's okay, Mom. Mike can handle Ty—and Dad."

"Just so you don't let Mike handle *you,*" Sue said, ignoring the indignant expression on Kate's face.

"Mom!"

"I'm a parent—I'm supposed to say things like that. Now, let's get you two on your way," Sue said. "Only let me go down first. I want to see the expression on Mike's face when you make your entrance."

"Okay," Kate said with a smile. She waited a minute, then took a deep breath and began to make her way down the stairs.

Sue wasn't disappointed. The look of adoration on Mike's face said it all. He smiled nervously at Greg and Tyler, then moved to gallantly offer his arm to Kate as she approached the bottom of the stairs.

"I want a dress like that," Sabrina said, staring up at her big sister.

Kate knelt down to give Sabrina a hug. "If you still want it in a few years, you can have it, Breeny, I promise," she whispered.

"'Kay," Sabrina agreed, then added with a lisp, "Don't get it dirty."

Laughing, Kate nodded as she took Mike's extended hand.

"Hold it," Greg said sternly. "Before you leave, there's something I want to—"

"Greg," Sue warned, giving him a stern look.

"Something I want to do," Greg said, enjoying the moment.

Smiling brightly, he pulled out his camera. "I'd like to get a few snapshots. Would you two mind posing in front of the fireplace?" he said with a grin.

"Sure, Brother Erickson," Mike nervously agreed.

Sue smiled, convinced she had never seen a sharper-looking couple. Mike looked great in a grey tuxedo with a forest green bow tie and cummerbund. The colors complimented Kate's dress perfectly. Pleased with her success at remodeling the originally low-cut dress, Sue watched as Mike picked up the clear plastic box from the coffee table and pinned a white rose corsage on Kate. At the sight of the white roses, Kate's eyes clouded briefly with pain. Then, quickly regaining her composure, she smiled and reached for the white carnation boutonniere she had picked out for him. They obediently stood together in front of the fireplace as Greg took several pictures. Finally, Sue took the camera away and sent the young couple out the front door. She refrained from crying until they pulled out in the car Mike had borrowed from his father.

"Need this?" Greg asked, offering a handful of tissue.

"What?" Sue asked.

"I've lived with you long enough to recognize the signs," he said, gently leading her into the kitchen.

"She looked so happy tonight and so grown-up," she tried to explain. "I'm proud of her. Especially the way she handled it when Mike pinned on that white rose corsage."

"He had no idea it would hit her like that," Greg said gently, pulling Sue close. "Besides, I think it hit you harder than Kate."

"I want tonight to be wonderful for her. She needs something like this to make up for everything else that's happened."

"Well, if Mike keeps his promise, I don't think we have anything to worry about."

"Greg, you didn't," Sue accused, pulling back to give her husband a quizzical look.

"Let's just say Mike and I reached an understanding while you two were up there stalling in the bathroom. Kate will definitely be in the hands of a gentleman tonight."

"Oh, no," Sue groaned.

"Relax. It was the same speech your father gave me the first time I met him."

"Now I'm worried," Sue replied, laughing. "You owe Mike an apology."

"Your dad never apologized," Greg said. "And if you've got the waterworks under control, I have plans for my lady tonight too."

"Greg," Sue protested as he dragged her through the side door into the garage.

"Tyler said he'd watch Sabrina. We're going out to dinner."

"What? I'm not dressed up for anything."

"You're fine—this is a casual date. I figured it'd be a good idea to give you something else to chew on besides your fingernails. Now, let's go." Ignoring her protests, he escorted her to the car.

* * *

Kate and Sandi walked into the decorated gym, followed by their beaming escorts. Keith immediately led Sandi onto the dance floor while Mike found Kate a chair and offered to get her a glass of punch. A few minutes later, as they both sipped at the fruit-flavored beverage, Mike took a deep breath and approached a subject that had come between them at dinner. At the Avellino, the restaurant where he and Keith had made reservations, Mike had pulled out a chair for Kate to sit on and in the process of helping her slide closer to the table, touched her shoulder. Kate had sharply pulled away, knocking over the glass of ice water that had been placed in front of her. Both were embarrassed and were now feeling extremely uncomfortable with the semi-romantic setting.

"Kate, I'm sorry about what happened at the restaurant," Mike said awkwardly.

"No problem," Kate assured him. "You didn't do anything wrong. It's me. I know it sounds crazy, but I feel like Randy's watching me." She blushed.

"He must be quite a guy."

"He is," Kate said. She started to describe Randy, then turned red again. "I'm sorry, Mike. You don't want to hear this."

"Sure I do," Mike lied. "And when you finish, I'll tell you all about Emily, Angela, and Amber," he grinned as Kate laughed. "Should I go on with my list?" he asked, counting on his fingers. "There was also Melissa, Julie, Tricia, Dusty . . . let's see,

Rachelle . . . Ronette, Maria, Becky, Janene . . . uh . . . Ginger, Michelle, Adri, Kandy, Jessica, Amy . . ."

"That's okay, Mike. I get the hint," Kate laughed.

"Not to mention, Idella, Anna, Deidra, Camie . . ."

"Mike," Kate warned, although her eyes twinkled with amusement. She glanced up and saw that Keith and Sandi were dancing to a song with an upbeat tempo. "We came here to dance, right?" she said suddenly standing. "Let's dance."

"You're sure?" Mike asked, standing beside her. "I didn't get to finish my list."

"Trust me, we're through with the list. Let's go," she replied, pulling him out onto the dance floor. Forcing herself to relax, she began to enjoy herself as they moved in time to the music. The fast number was followed by another buoyant song, then the pace of the evening changed with a slow dance. As Mike's arms went around her, she stiffened.

"Want to sit this one out," Mike murmured in her ear.

"No," Kate stammered. "I'm okay." As they began to gently sway in time to the music, she realized that having Mike's arms around her was actually rather pleasant. She didn't even mind when he tightened his grip during the next song, which was also a slow number. After it ended, she smiled up at him. "Thanks for being patient with me."

"Same here," Mike joked. "I'm not exactly light on my feet, or yours," he said with a grin. "Hope I didn't step on you too many times."

"Only a couple," she teased as he led her from the dance floor.

"I don't know about you, but I could sure use another glass of punch," he said breathlessly.

"Sounds good." Kate took a chair beside Sandi.

"We'll go get our picture taken after the punch," Mike promised as he pointed to the corner where couples had begun lining up.

Kate nodded, then turned to Sandi as Mike walked toward the refreshment table.

"Looks like you two are finally starting to hit it off," Sandi said.

"Yeah. Mike's a neat guy."

"Your mother and I have only been trying to tell you that for weeks. He really likes you, Kate."

"I know," Kate sighed.

"Is that a problem?"

"Maybe. Where's Keith?"

"I think he went to find the little boy's room."

"He went to fluff up his hair again?" Kate chuckled.

"Probably. He's as nervous as you've been all night."

"He's just excited to be out with the sexiest lookin' babe in town!"

"Right," Sandi countered, secretly pleased with the compliment. "You're the one everyone keeps staring at."

"Here you go," Mike said, handing a glass of punch to Kate. He handed another to Sandi, then went back after two more glasses for himself and Keith.

"It's hot in here," Sandi said before taking a sip. "I needed this."

Kate nodded in agreement and began to drink out of her own cup. Frowning, she peered at the contents.

"What's the matter?"

"I'm not sure." Kate tasted the punch a second time. "Oh-no," she moaned.

"What?" Sandi probed, lifting her glass up to her lips for another taste.

"Don't drink any more," Kate said sharply.

"What's wrong?"

"Somebody spiked it."

"You're kidding?"

"I wish," Kate said, quickly standing as Mike approached with two more cups of punch. "Don't drink it, Mike. It's spiked," she said, glancing around the room.

"What?" Mike asked, staring at Sandi for confirmation. "Are you sure?" he asked, sniffing one of the cups in his hand.

"Oh, yeah. This punch has more than the normal kick to it. Trust me."

"I guess you'd know . . . I mean . . ." Mike stammered, realizing his mistake immediately.

"You're right, I would know," Kate said quietly. "And if you'll excuse me, I'm going to bring it to someone's attention." Taking Sandi's cup, she began walking across the gym floor.

"I didn't mean that the way it sounded," Mike groaned, sliding down into the chair Kate had vacated. "Now what do I do?"

"Pull your foot out of your mouth and go after her," Sandi said.

Leaning down, he covered his face with his hands.

"Don't give up on her, Mike, please," Sandi pleaded. "She's touchy on some subjects. Like, white roses, for instance."

"What?" Mike asked, sitting up.

"They were Linda's favorite flower."

"Strike two," Mike grimaced.

"You couldn't possibly have known. She understands that. We talked about the corsage earlier at the restaurant when she and I went into the rest room."

"Oh, great!"

"It's okay, Mike. While we were alone, I asked her about it. As for the comment you just made to Kate . . . it's going to take some effort to dig yourself out. But you can do it, big guy," Sandi said brightly, patting him on the back. "If you like her as much as you say you do, go after her."

"Maybe you ought to talk to her first," he said hopefully.

"Nope. You're on your own. It's the only way you'll get through to her. Good luck." As he walked away, Sandi shook her head. "You're going to need it."

"Need what?" Keith asked, suddenly appearing at her side.

"A miracle," she replied. Sandi waited for him to sit beside her before explaining what had happened.

*　*　*

After bringing the punch to the attention of the proper adult authorities—namely the three high school teachers who were experiencing the great joy of being chaperones—Kate wandered outside for some fresh air. Even though she knew Mike hadn't meant anything by it, his comment had still stung. "Why can't people let go of the past?" she murmured, staring off into the darkness.

"Because it keeps turning up to haunt you!" a familiar voice said, laughing.

Whirling around, Kate found herself staring at Jace. Panicking, she tried to move past him, but he held her firmly in place.

"Don't you look nice?" he murmured, drawing her close. Kate shuddered, smelling the liquor on his breath.

"You're the imbecile who spiked the punch, aren't you?" she demanded.

"No need to thank me, at least, not here where everyone can see." Jace grabbed her by the wrist and pulled her down the sidewalk. "Let's go somewhere private. Then you can thank me all you want."

"Let go of me," Kate hollered. "I mean it, Jace!"

Jace paused long enough to force a kiss on Kate's protesting lips, then continued dragging her toward the parking lot. Kate struggled to free herself, but Jace's grip intensified. She tried to scream, but he clamped a hand on her mouth.

"Jace, what are you doin'?"

Jace froze, then laughed at his friend. "Gary, what are you doin' out here? I thought you'd be in there partyin' it up with the rest of the crowd. You dumped the stuff in the punch bowl, right?"

"Yeah. But someone caught on pretty quick. They're tryin' to figure out who did it. We need to get out of here, now," Gary said, nervously glancing over his shoulder.

"That's what I had in mind, only I'm taking some entertainment with us," Jace said, continuing to keep a hand over Kate's mouth. "I think this little lady will show us a real good time tonight, isn't that right, Katie?" Grinning at his friend, Jace wasn't prepared for the kick when it came. As he doubled over, he released Kate and cursed with pain.

"You touch me again and I'll—" Kate sputtered.

"You'll what?" Jace said, still trying to catch his breath. She had managed to connect with where it hurt the most. "You're gonna pay for that mistake," he growled, grabbing her arm. He reached back to slap her, but someone intercepted his hand. Turning to take a swing at his new assailant, Jace missed and received a sharp upper cut to the jaw. Kate pulled away as Jace wiped at the blood that was now seeping from one corner of his mouth. Scowling, he glared at Mike Jeffries.

"Don't you ever touch her again," Mike threatened, pushing Kate behind him protectively. Jace started to take another swing at him, but Mike skillfully ducked and plowed a fist into Jace's abdomen. "I mean it, Sloan," Mike said.

Wheezing, Jace glared at Mike. "I'm gonna tear you apart, you dirty—"

Anger overcoming fear, Kate stepped out and slapped Jace hard across the face. "Get out of here, you jerk," she exclaimed. "I never want to see you again! Do you understand?!"

"If it's still foggy, I can make it perfectly clear for you," Mike volunteered, quickly stepping between Kate and Jace.

"Let's go, Jace," Gary said, his eyes widening at the size of the crowd that was heading their direction. "I'm leavin'," he said, bolting to the parking lot.

"This isn't over," Jace said, pointing first at Mike, then at Kate.

"Yes, it is." Sandi's date, Keith, suddenly appeared beside Mike. Sandi stepped forward and pulled Kate out of the way as Jace was surrounded by a crowd of young men, including Bob Quentin.

"You don't know when to quit, do you?" Bob said.

"You ever touch Kate again, and you'll be walking funny for the rest of your life," another voice growled as several senior boys from the football team gathered around Jace.

"Got it yet, Mr. Sloan?"

Still breathing hard, Jace glowered at those surrounding him. "All this because of her?" he asked, pointing at Kate. "She must really be showin' you boys a good time."

At this insult, Mike knocked Jace to the ground. Keith grabbed Mike to hold him back.

"We'll take it from here," Coach Waters said, leading a police officer through the crowd. "I think this young man needs a lift downtown," he said, handing an empty bottle of whiskey to the officer as he reached down to pull Jace to his feet. "Let's go, Sloan. The party's over, at least for you. As for the rest of you, that gym floor is looking a bit empty. Get inside and see what you can do about that."

Slowly, the crowd dispersed as another police officer took statements from Mike and Kate. His partner managed to catch

Gary Leavitt, who was only too willing to confess to what had taken place. Soon the patrol car pulled away from the school on its way to the police station.

"Are you sure you're all right?" Sandi asked Kate.

"I'm a little shaky," Kate admitted, allowing Sandi to lead her back inside the gym.

"Let's go freshen up," Sandi suggested, noticing that Kate's mascara had run a bit.

Kate looked at Mike, then said, "Give me a minute, okay?"

Sandi nodded and moved away to stand discreetly next to Keith while Kate talked briefly to Mike.

Kate took Mike's still-clenched first in her hand. "How is your hand?" she asked softly.

"It's okay."

"Let me see that," she insisted, pulling him closer to a light for a better look. "It's already starting to swell. We'd better get some ice on it."

"It'll be all right. I'm glad I came out when I did, though."

"Me too. It means a lot. Thanks for . . ." Kate struggled for the right words.

"Can you forgive me for being such an idiot earlier?" Mike interrupted. "I didn't mean what I said . . . It came out all wrong."

"Don't worry about it." Reaching up, she softly kissed his cheek. "I'll be right back," she promised. Grinning, Mike rubbed thoughtfully at his cheek.

"Here, Mike," Keith said, handing Mike a cold pack from Coach Waters' office. "Hope it cools you down." Holding the bag against his knuckles, Mike ignored his best friend's teasing as he watched as Kate walked away.

"She's quite a lady," Keith observed, his attention riveted on Sandi. The pink formal seemed to float as she walked by Kate's side.

"Yes, she is," Mike agreed. "A real lady."

* * *

The rest of the night was a blur for Kate. What had started out to be one of the worst nights of her life quickly became one of the best. She hoped the picture she and Mike posed for would capture some of the excitement she felt.

Dancing with Mike seemed natural after the traumatic adventure they had shared. She didn't even mind when he held her tight during a series of slow dances. Finally the music stopped—it was time to crown the king and queen of the festivities.

It was a tradition for the senior class to pick two seniors who had contributed the most to making it a great year. Most years, the honor went to athletic stars, cheerleaders, or student council members. Kate knew how many hours Sandi had put into creating their chapter of SADD and hoped her friend would be selected. She was stunned when her own name was announced.

They called Kate up three times, but she was in such a state of shock, Mike and Sandi finally had to push her to the front of the room to accept the crown. Mike placed it gently on her head, then leaned down to kiss her cheek. Sandi gave her a hug, then stepped out of the way as the king's identity was revealed—Keith Taylor. Sandi squealed, leading Keith up to stand beside Kate. Concerned, Kate studied her friend's face, convinced Sandi should have been sharing this moment with Keith. There were tears in Sandi's eyes, but the expression on her face was one of pure joy. Kate relaxed as Keith put a protective arm around Sandi's slender shoulders and gave her an intense squeeze. Then, reaching for Kate's hand, Keith led her onto the deserted gym floor for the traditional dance.

"Congratulations, Kate," Keith whispered in her ear as they whirled around the applauding room.

"You too, Keith," Kate managed to say, tears streaming down her face. "I can't believe this."

"I can. You deserve it."

"But, there are so many others who—"

"Enjoy it Kate. This is your moment," Keith gently chided, expertly waltzing her around the room.

Deciding to do just that, Kate tried to relax until the song was finally over. Grinning, Keith led Kate back to Mike. He turned at the sound of Sandi's voice.

"You two looked pretty good out there," Sandi said, smiling brightly.

"A little too good," Mike complained, slugging his friend in the arm.

"You taught me everything I know," Keith quipped, going along with Mike's good-natured teasing. "How about a glass of punch?" he added, reaching for Sandi's hand. "I understand they mixed up a fresh batch." Sandi nodded, allowing Keith to lead her across the crowded room.

Sensing this was a good time to let Sandi and Keith have a moment alone, Mike escorted Kate to the gym doors. A few minutes earlier, he had spotted a set of parents who were impatiently waiting to congratulate their daughter.

"Oh, Kate," Sue said, hugging her daughter, "I'm so happy for you."

"We *both* are," Greg said, reminding his wife of his presence. Sue reluctantly pulled away from Kate to let him take over.

"I can't believe it, Dad," Kate said, trying to keep her crown in place.

"No one deserves it more," he whispered before releasing her to Mike's custody. He reached to shake Mike's hand, wondering at the way Mike suddenly winced. Convinced it was his own masculine strength, Greg grinned.

"How long have you guys been here?" Kate asked, wondering if the police had called her parents.

"We arrived in time to see you receive your crown," Sue answered. "We wanted to catch the senior parade. We haven't missed it, have we?"

"No," Kate assured her mother. "It's next, though. Stick around."

"We will," Greg promised. "Come along dear," he added, "I think I can find us a place to sit with some of the other parents." Holding Sue's hand tightly in his own, he helped her across the gym floor.

"Why didn't you tell them about what happened earlier?" Mike asked as they walked to where the seniors were lining up.

"I will, later. I want to enjoy this moment for as long as I can."

Silently agreeing, Mike reached to hold her hand. As far as he was concerned, this moment could last forever.

CHAPTER FIFTEEN

M om, I know it's not a good idea to kiss on the first date, but tonight . . ."

Sue smiled. Last year, this conversation would have never taken place. There were times when she was still overwhelmed by the changes in her daughter. "Under the circumstances, I'd say Mike deserved a kiss. In fact, he may get one from me next time I see him."

Kate was aghast. "You're not serious?"

"Just a peck on the cheek—something to show him how much I appreciate what he did."

"He was pretty great," Kate agreed. "I don't think anyone's ever dared to knock Jace around like that."

"Jace had it coming," Sue said firmly. "Why didn't you say anything about this earlier when we were at the gym?"

"Think about it, Mom. In my place, would you have said anything?"

"Probably not," Sue sighed. "Your father wouldn't have made a very pleasant scene. It was still a bit ugly here at home when you finally told us." Sue sipped at the cocoa she had heated up for this private conversation.

"Think Dad'll eventually calm down?" Kate asked before trying her own mug of cocoa.

"Talking to the police helped. Especially when they said Jace is headed for a juvenile detention center for a while." Sue frowned.

"Are you sure about testifying? I'm still not sure I want you involved in this."

"Mom, Jace had no business spiking that punch. And from the way he was talking, he would've really hurt me. I tried to get away, but if Mike hadn't come out when he did . . ."

"I know." Sue closed her eyes, trying to block out what Jace had had in mind. "Unfortunately, spiking the punch and being drunk and disorderly won't be enough to put him away for very long." She opened her eyes to gaze at Kate. "You've been through enough, Kate. Things need to settle down."

"It'll happen—eventually, I hope." Frowning, Kate took another sip from her mug. "Dad said Jace's parents are all for sending him to a rehab center when this is over. It's probably a good idea, if it works. It's time Jace started facing up to a few things—like tonight. I'll never forgive him for what he tried to do."

"Never's a long time," Sue said sadly.

"Maybe I'll be over it by then."

Sue smiled. It was good to see Kate was getting some of her spunk back.

"Mom, there's something else I want to ask you."

"Okay."

"Tonight . . . when Mike kissed me, I felt something. Like with Randy, only different." Kate frowned. "I'm not making any sense, am I?"

"You're making perfect sense," Sue soothed. "Give it time. A lot of things happened tonight. Some wonderful," she said, picking up the crown Kate had set on the table. "Some not so wonderful," she added, thinking of Jace. "Through all of it, Mike was there. You might be confusing several emotions. Next time you're together, it'll be more apparent how you really feel."

"If there is a next time," Kate sighed, taking the combs out of her hair and shaking it down.

"I don't think you need to worry about that. I saw how he was looking at you tonight." Sue lifted an eyebrow, then said thoughtfully, "In my own humble opinion, Randy's much safer."

"Why?"

"Because he's halfway around the world."

"Another typical parental viewpoint?"

"You've got it," Sue laughed. Glancing at the clock, she groaned. "Here's another parental viewpoint. If anyone makes a peep before ten o'clock tomorrow morning, I won't be held accountable for my actions!"

"Same here." Kate slowing rose from the table. "But it's Sunday tomorrow," she reminded her mother.

"Oh, no," Sue groaned. "I have to fill in for Sister White during Primary."

"You'll make a great chorister," Kate said, grinning as her mother handed her the crown.

"Goodnight, princess."

"Goodnight, Mom," Kate said as she brushed her mother's cheek with her lips. "Thanks for everything."

As Sue drank the last of her cocoa, she relived the moment Kate had been crowned queen of the senior prom. A memory she would treasure almost as much as her daughter.

* * *

The next morning, as a yawning Sandi and Kate made their way to the room used by the Young Women, they were unaware of the admiring glances being cast in their direction. Following tradition, they had each worn their new formals, complete with the corsages.

"You two look beautiful this morning," Lori Blanchard said as she walked into the Young Women's room. "And I'm proud of both of you for wearing gowns that are not only stunning, but also very modest."

"It wasn't easy finding one," Sandi commented.

"Yeah. Mom had to remodel this one," Kate added.

"It was well worth the effort," Lori said, smiling warmly at both girls. "You're to be commended for setting a good example for the other girls." Sandi returned her smile, then moved across the room to round up some help for opening exercises. Lori slid an arm around Kate's waist and led her into a vacant corner of the room. "And congratulations to you on earning a well-deserved crown last night."

"I don't know if I'd say well deserved," Kate began to protest.

"I would. I'm impressed with you, young lady. And I'm not the only one. President Randolph mentioned the other day that he'd like to ask you to speak in church in the near future."

"You're kidding?"

"No. He'd like you to share some of your experiences, as well as your testimony. He wanted me to see if you'd be willing to do it."

"Maybe."

"Don't sound so thrilled. You'll do a great job."

"I'll try," Kate finally replied.

"Good," Lori said. Then as other girls clamored for her attention, she hurried across the room. Kate smiled, grateful for a leader who always went the extra mile.

CHAPTER SIXTEEN

April 22

*D*ear Elder Miles,

I'm sorry I haven't written for a while. Things have been crazy here. The homework continues to pile up, but it's easier to concentrate now that Jace is no longer part of the picture. He was taken to a juvenile detention center last week. After serving his time there, his parents are going to sign him into a rehab center. I'm just glad it's finally over. Testifying against him was one of the hardest things I've ever had to do.

On a brighter note, we pulled off the talent show last night—the fund raiser for SADD. Sandi talked me into singing—I did a rendition of "The Greatest Love of All." Sandi danced, Bob Quentin juggled, and I could probably fill this page listing the people who agreed to perform. Marie Sikes was our MC. She did a great job.

We had a good turnout. Marie doesn't know it yet, but we've decided to spend part of the money on a special plaque in memory of Linda. We'll present it to the school at graduation, and it will be hung in the hall near the trophy case. We want everyone to remember the price paid for drinking and driving. It's also kind of a parting tribute to Linda. No one will ever forget her.

Kate paused, nibbling on the end of her pen. She had put off writing to Randy for weeks. In the meantime, there had been no word from him. Figuring he was too busy to write, she decided to quit pouting and send off a letter. The trouble was, she wasn't sure what to write. She was dating Mike on a regular basis; they doubled most of the time with Keith and Sandi. Kate loved being with Mike, but doubted Randy would understand. She was more at ease with Mike than with any guy she had ever known—with the exception of Randy. Sighing, Kate tried to finish the letter.

I finally received a reply from BYU. They thanked me for my interest in their school, then said I don't have the grade point average they're looking for. I've pulled straight A's all year, but it doesn't make up for the grades I earned before—back when I didn't care.

I guess I'll take Uncle Stan up on his offer and go to work for him this summer. I'll make more than I would at Burger King. Uncle Stan says his construction company needs another secretary now that the Olympics are coming, and he's willing to train me. I'll head down in June. Mom talked me into sending an application to the LDS Business College in Salt Lake. If I get accepted, I think I'll go after a degree in computer technology. Aunt Paige said I could stay with them, and I could work part-time for Uncle Stan while I go to school. I'll be busy, but maybe it'll keep me out of trouble.

Sandi was accepted at the Y. We're both upset I was rejected. We had planned on being roommates. Oh, well. Maybe there's a reason for the way things turned out.

Mike Jeffries, the guy who took me to the prom, was accepted at Ricks. I won't be seeing much of him after May. He's planning on sending in his mission papers next February. He'll be nineteen then.

Kate smiled, wondering if Randy would object to her seeing Mike until June. Maybe he wouldn't catch that part.

"And maybe he won't care," she said, suddenly feeling depressed.

Closing the letter, she sealed the envelope and stuck it inside of her purse. She'd mail it later when she met Sandi at the library to cram for a major history test that was coming up. Regret tugged at her heart as she thought about Sandi going to BYU without her. Maybe, if she kept her grades up at the business college, she would have a shot at being accepted by BYU in another year. By then, Randy would be home. Frowning, she wondered how he would react if she still couldn't get into BYU.

"Guess I'll cross that bridge when I come to it," she murmured. Gathering her purse and books, she flipped off the light and walked out of her room.

CHAPTER SEVENTEEN

May arrived with unseasonable warmth, promoting rampant episodes of spring fever. As the second weekend approached, Sandi and Kate planned a picnic in the hills with Keith and Mike. However, their plans changed when Sandi's sister, Stephanie, had her baby—another black-haired boy. So Sandi and her parents headed to Billings to take a peek at the new arrival, and Kate, Mike, and Keith were left on their own to decide how to spend Saturday. Keith's decision was made for him when he was called to work. After considering several options, Kate and Mike concluded it was too nice to spend the day moping around Bozeman. They decided to stick with their original plans, minus Keith and Sandi.

With her mother's help, Kate packed a basket full of food, then impatiently waited for Mike to arrive. When he finally pulled up in his father's newly washed truck, Kate rushed out the door to greet him. He jumped out of the cab and teasingly whirled her around in the air. Setting her down, he planted a firm kiss on her lips. Realizing that Sue was standing on the porch, holding a forgotten picnic basket, Mike flushed a deep red. With an embarrassed smile, he walked over to retrieve the basket.

Kate moved closer to the truck, careful not to meet her mother's eyes. Her mother's warning to be cautious nagged at her.

"Are you sure this is a good idea?" Sue had asked earlier as they had prepared the food for the picnic. "You could rent a movie, stay here, eat in the family room—"

"Where you can keep an eye on us," Kate had replied, finishing the sentence. "That sounds romantic."

"Works for me," Sue had countered. "It's the romantic setting that has me worried."

"You trust me, don't you?" Kate asked.

"You know I do, but I'd feel better about this if—"

"If Sandi and Keith were going. I know. You've repeated that about a hundred times this morning. Mike is a total gentleman," Kate had responded.

"True, but good kids can make mistakes. You and Mike are very close—I'm not saying that's a bad thing, but you need to be careful."

Kate had met her mother's pleading gaze with a look of determination. "I appreciate your concern, but we'll be fine."

"Just . . . be careful today," Sue had said, as she began turning the chicken.

"We will," Kate had answered stiffly. An uncomfortable silence grew between them until Sue steered the conversation to safer topics. By the time Mike had arrived, the tension between mother and daughter had disappeared.

Now, as Kate helped Mike load the bulging picnic basket in the truck, she sensed the worry that had returned to her mother's expression. She forced herself to face her mother and wave. Sue returned the wave, then slowly stepped into the house as Mike helped Kate climb inside the four-wheel-drive truck.

It didn't take long to find a perfect spot up a nearby campground in Gallatin Valley. New green grass was making an appearance now that most of the snow had melted. A tiny brook bubbled nearby, finally free of the ice that had hampered its flow during the winter. Spreading a blanket on top of the grass, Kate laid out the fried chicken, salad, and dinner rolls she had made with her mother's help.

They ate until they were stuffed, then each forced down a slice of apple pie. Moaning pitifully and holding his stomach, Mike stretched out on the blanket and dozed as Kate put things away. After carrying the basket back to the truck, Kate sat on a rock not far from the brook and watched the water as it gurgled by. She was so caught up in her thoughts, she didn't hear Mike when he walked up behind her. Startled, she nearly fell in. Mike laughed and grabbed her, pulling her close for a lengthy kiss. Enjoying the electric current that it generated, they kissed again. Then, taking her hand, Mike led her back to the blanket where the kissing continued, intensifying feelings that both had been harboring. Caught up in a sudden burst of desire, Mike's lips slipped down to Kate's neck, his hand straying along her body. Alarmed by what she was feeling, Kate pulled away.

"No, Mike. We can't let this happen," she said softly.

"What?" Mike asked, taking a deep breath.

"You know as well as I do where this is heading," she said, sitting a safe distance away on a fallen log.

Angered, but knowing Kate was right, Mike walked down to the brook, gathered up a handful of rocks, and threw them one at a time into the water.

"Mike?" Kate finally said, remaining on the log.

"Yeah?"

"I think we'd better go home."

Mike turned around and walked back to where she was sitting. "I never meant for this to happen."

"I know," she replied, her eyes filling with tears. "We've never talked about it before, but I think you should know I never . . . Jace might've said some things, but they weren't true. I've never been with a guy . . . not like—"

"It doesn't matter. Even if you had . . . it doesn't give me the right to . . . I wasn't trying to take advantage of you." He paused. "Kate, I'm sorry. It's my fault. I got carried away."

"We both did. We never should've come here." Kate stared at her hands, tears splashing down. "Mom tried to tell me that all morning, but I didn't want to hear it. I ignored the uneasiness I felt. I figured it was my imagination working overtime."

"I never meant to hurt you," Mike mumbled.

"I know. But do you realize what we were doing?" she asked, staring at the ground. "It was leading to something neither one of us want . . . at least, not now, not like this."

Mike sat down in front of her and began to pick at a pile of dried pine needles.

"In less than a year, you'll send in your mission papers."

"Yeah, I guess."

"I know how much that means to you. We can't let anything jeopardize that dream for you. I have dreams too, Mike. We can't let what we're feeling destroy what we really want."

"But I've never felt this way about any girl I've ever met. I don't want to lose you," he said, reaching to wipe the tears from her face.

Kate leaned into his touch, then pulled back, wary of emotions that threatened to overpower her. Rising, she moved to a tree and leaned against it. "We can't be alone like this. It's all I can do to pull away from you. Next time, it won't be as easy."

Mike slowly nodded. "Let's head back," he said, moving to pick up the blanket. They walked side by side to the truck, fearing what the other was thinking, neither knowing how to repair the rift that now existed. They drove in silence back to Bozeman until they finally pulled up in front of Kate's house. Shutting off the engine, Mike turned to look at Kate. "I think we need to talk this over. Nothing turned out like it was supposed to this afternoon."

"You can say that again," she replied, forcing a tiny smile before she opened the door on her side of the truck.

"Wait, I can get that for you." Mike hurriedly opened the door on his side. He wanted another chance to explain, to somehow make things right between them. Kate wasn't making it easy.

"Under the circumstances, I think it's best if you leave now and we'll talk later," she said, reaching for the picnic basket.

"Let me," he replied, slipping out of the truck before she could argue. He insisted on carrying it to the house and set it on the porch for her. "I guess I'll see you in the morning . . . at church?" he said hopefully. "Maybe tomorrow it won't seem so bad."

"Maybe," Kate muttered, focusing on one of her mother's flower beds.

"Kate, look at me," he said, sharper than he'd intended. He waited until Kate finally glanced at him. "We made a mistake today, I admit it, but it wasn't anything either of us expected. It just happened and we need to deal with it, together."

"Being together is what got us into trouble in the first place!" she retorted, angry with him, but more so with herself.

"I don't think you mean that the way it sounded," Mike said, trying to keep his own temper from flaring. "I said I was sorry. What more do you want?"

"I don't know!" she said, running a hand through the front of her hair. She closed her eyes in an attempt to block out the embarrassment she still felt.

"Kate," he said, trying to put a hand on her shoulder.

"No, Mike," she said, pulling away.

"Kate?"

Shaking her head, she fled into the house.

Cursing under his breath, Mike walked back to the truck and roared off down the street.

CHAPTER EIGHTEEN

Kate spent nearly an hour alone in her room. Then, deciding she needed a shoulder to cry on, she went outside to the backyard where her mother was working in the garden. Sue looked up from where she had been raking rocks. She saw Kate's troubled expression immediately. She had heard Mike drive off, then a few minutes later, pounding music had radiated from Kate's room—something that hadn't happened in nearly a year. Sensing a confrontation wasn't a good idea, she had spent the past hour offering a silent prayer. Now she waited for what Kate had to tell her.

"You were right, Mom. We never should've gone on that rotten picnic," Kate said tearfully.

"I didn't want to be right," Sue murmured as she dropped the rake to lead Kate to the large, wooden swing Greg had recently built for their backyard. Heartsick, she sat down and motioned for Kate to join her.

Kate sat beside her mother, then before she lost her courage, told her everything that had happened.

Relieved, Sue breathed out slowly. Taking off her gardening gloves, she searched for words that would console, and yet let her daughter know she had come dangerously close to falling through the ice.

"Now I know why you said what you did about steady dating," Kate whispered.

"It can lead to problems," Sue answered. "That's why I wanted you to wait until Sandi and Keith could go with you. There's safety in numbers."

"I know. I thought I could handle it. But when Mike kissed me like that, I couldn't even think straight. And the longer it went on, the more I wanted him to touch me and then when he tried . . . if it hadn't felt so wrong . . . I might've let him."

"Part of why we're down here is to learn how to control this body we've been given. Those passions we feel only overpower us when we let them. We're in the driver's seat. We have to let our spirit control our body, not the other way around. And sometimes, even when we think we're strong," Sue said, lifting her daughter's chin until their eyes met, "we have to avoid situations that add fuel to the fire we sometimes feel."

"I'm so glad it didn't go any further than it did."

"You're not the only one," Sue said softly. "But I am proud of you. It took a lot of strength to stop before things totally got out of hand."

Kate stared down at the ground, realizing how easy it would have been to give in.

"And I want you to know how much I appreciate your honesty," Sue continued. She brushed Kate's long hair away from her face.

"I have a question."

"Just one?" Sue asked.

"Probably not," Kate admitted. "What do Mike and I do? How serious is this? Do we need to go see the branch president?"

"I think it would be a good idea to talk this over with President Randolph. If I understood what you were saying, you were necking and it was leading to petting."

Kate blushed and slowly nodded.

"Do you have any other questions?"

"Should Mike and I stop seeing each other?"

Sue fought back an instinctive reply, relying on the Spirit to guide her answer. "It's up to you and Mike. It won't be easy, either way."

"Tell me about it. The ride home today was awful. And when we finally pulled up out front . . . we were both so angry and embarrassed. I was afraid to let him touch me, and yet, a part of me wanted him to hold me. It doesn't make sense, right?"

"It does." She slid an arm around her daughter's shoulders. "You'll both be heading in different directions after graduation. Maybe it would be a good idea to cool things down between you. To just be friends for a while."

"If he's still speaking to me. He was pretty upset when he left."

"I heard," Sue said, trying not to smile. "We probably have some interesting tire tracks in front of our house."

Nodding, Kate leaned close to her mother. Sue squeezed Kate's shoulder and for several minutes, they did nothing but rock together in the swing. The peaceful moment was soon interrupted.

"Mommy!"

Sue looked up to see Sabrina come racing across the lawn.

"Can I swing too?" the six-year-old excitedly asked.

Sue glanced at Kate who smiled in agreement. They both slid over to let Sabrina sit on the other side of Sue. Draping an arm around both of her daughters, Sue started the swing in motion again, aided by Kate and Sabrina.

Sabrina giggled. "Faster," she encouraged. "Higher."

Sue and Kate tried to oblige, but the wooden swing wasn't designed for this kind of abuse and before they knew what had happened, all three ended up on the grass, laughing.

In the garage, Tyler looked up from the lawn mower engine he was trying to help his father fix to stare out a small window. "What's with them?"

Greg wiped a greasy hand on his shirt before glancing out the window.

"Dunno," he said, shrugging. "Looks like one of those female bonding moments we have to endure on occasion."

Tyler shook his head, then picked up the screwdriver he had been using and went back to work on the engine.

Greg watched his wife and daughters for a few more minutes before lending his son a hand. He grinned as Kate threw a handful of grass down her mother's neck, successfully drawing Sue's attention away from tickling Sabrina. Sue then chased Kate around the yard, threatening bodily harm. Apparently giving up, Sue quietly went after the garden hose. Catching Kate off guard, she hit her with a cool blast of water. Kate ran toward her mother and a struggle ensued over the garden hose. As the two of them tumbled to the ground, Sabrina shut off the faucet.

Greg watched in amusement as his six-year-old daughter walked over to her mother and older sister and gave both of them what appeared to be a stern lecture. Sue and Kate tried to look contrite, but were having a difficult time controlling their giggles. Finally, Sue allowed Sabrina to pull her to her feet, and Sue in turn reached back for Kate. Arms around each other, they headed for the house. Still smiling, Greg adjusted his glasses, then searched for the wrench he had been using.

"Think we'll ever understand that species?" Tyler asked, gesturing toward his mother and sisters.

"Probably not, but that's what makes it fun," his father answered. He smiled when Tyler pulled a face.

CHAPTER NINETEEN

President Randolph glanced around for several minutes before spotting Kate. He had been trying to track her down for nearly two hours. He would have tried to telephone, but he liked to make this type of visit in person; it was easier to read expressions and gauge reactions.

As the branch president walked across the park, he reflected on how far Kate had come in recent months. He didn't want to do anything to jeopardize her progress, but he could not ignore the prompting that had come since Sunday. Kate's name had haunted him for nearly two days. It was time to do something about it.

"Hello, young lady," he said warmly. Startled, Kate jumped. "No need to get up," he said quickly, sitting on the grass beside her. "I swung by your house. Your mother gave me a couple of places to check out."

"You want to talk to me?" Kate stammered. She had almost gotten up enough nerve to talk to him on Sunday. But after what had taken place during Young Women, Kate had spent the remainder of the day avoiding him. She pushed the unpleasant memory away.

"Yes. Your name has been on my mind for a couple of days. I decided it was time we had a chat." He stared out at Glen Lake, wondering at Kate's nervousness. They'd had several long talks the past few months, but she had never acted like this. "Sister Blanchard—" he started to say.

"She told you, didn't she?" Kate accused, mentally kicking herself for talking to Lori. At the time, it had seemed like a good idea. Lori had tried to help, had tried to smooth things over. It hadn't changed anything, but it had eased what she was feeling, knowing someone was on her side.

"Well, no, she didn't," he answered, puzzled. "She mentioned quite a while ago that you would be willing to speak in church. I was wondering about this coming Sunday." He was careful not to probe. If there was something Kate needed to tell him, it would eventually surface. Unlike some of the other youth in the branch, he didn't have to fish it out of her. When Kate Erickson was ready to talk, it all came spilling out.

"That's why you came out here? You want me to speak in church Sunday?"

"Yes," President Randolph responded.

Kate shook her head. "I can't. Not this week. Not after what . . ." She cringed. Why couldn't she learn to keep her big mouth shut?

"Would the next week be better?"

Kate took a deep breath before meeting the branch president's quizzical gaze. "There's something you should know—and after I tell you, I doubt you'll want me to speak in church."

"You let me decide that one," he said kindly, his twinkling blue eyes encouraging her to tell him what was wrong.

"This past year, I've come to you with a lot of things that I've done, things that I needed to clear up."

President Randolph nodded.

"It hasn't been easy, but I've really tried to make things right— to keep the commandments and do everything 'by the book,'" she said, referring to the advice he always gave to live as Christ taught in the Book of Mormon.

"That's why I would like you to speak in church. I think the people in our branch, the youth especially, could gain from your insights and testimony."

"President, they would do nothing but laugh in my face and call me a hypocrite, especially now."

"Why would they do that?"

"I've been debating whether I should tell you. Mom and Lori . . . Sister Blanchard, both suggested that I talk to you. But I'm not sure that what I did is serious enough to bother you with."

"If it's bothering you, I want to hear about it."

"Okay. You're here, so I guess I might as well." Drawing up her knees, she hugged them. "Mike and I have been dating kind of steady since the senior prom."

"I've noticed," he said, instantly concerned. He always worried about the teens in his branch, especially when they started dating.

"Yeah, well, Saturday, we went on a picnic. Keith and Sandi were supposed to go with us, but, it didn't work out that way." Hesitantly, Kate revealed everything that had taken place. When she finished, she stared out across the lake, avoiding the disappointment she knew she would see in his face. "So, you see, I can't get up and speak to anyone—"

"Why not?" he softly challenged.

"I just told you . . . Mike and I, we—and anyway, everyone knows. Somehow, Mike's little sister found out. I don't think she's ever liked me. She told the other Beehives about it and made it sound like it was my fault. Sandi heard those girls talking—I hadn't told her yet, but I was planning to—only the story that's spreading isn't what happened." She blushed. "Anyway, I was so upset after Sandi hit me in the face with what Mike and I had supposedly done, Lori—I mean, Sister Blanchard—had to spend nearly an hour talking to me during Sunday School to calm me down."

President Randolph offered Kate a handkerchief as he considered everything she had told him. Sighing, he decided to start at the top. "Kate, I'll admit, you and Mike were playing with fire. I hope you understand the serious nature of sexual sin. It's second only to murder in the eyes of our Heavenly Father. In today's world, we're told we're old-fashioned if we uphold moral standards. But our Father in Heaven knows that the only way we can truly be happy is through living the commandments. Remaining chaste before marriage is one of them.

"The special feelings and desires planted within each of us serve a sacred purpose. If we tamper with them, we desecrate the holy temple—our body—that houses our spirit and we invite Satan into our lives. Satan would have us believe we're nothing more than animals who must satisfy every urge, every base instinct. If he had his way, there would be nothing left of beauty in this world. And in my opinion, there is nothing lovelier than a young lady who has kept herself pure, or more handsome than a young man who has maintained his physical integrity. I can't stress enough the importance of heeding the standards taught by our church." He paused, sensing Kate's misery. "But I think you already know that."

Kate nodded, tears spilling down her cheeks.

"I also know that this past year, you've learned that our Heavenly Father has provided a way for us to come back into his presence if we make mistakes. It is possible to be forgiven for our sins if we'll humble ourselves and truly repent."

Gripping a handful of grass, Kate tore it loose.

"Now, in this instance, it's clear you recognized you were heading for trouble. Hopefully you understand why we caution you young people to steer clear of necking and petting. You've seen that it can lead to a desire that is overpowering. What you haven't seen is the heartache that engaging in sex before marriage can trigger. The guilt and shame alone can be staggering, not to mention the risk of disease and pregnancy. I've been in a position to see lives nearly ruined because of uncontrolled passion. It's not something I would ever want for you, nor would your Father in Heaven." He paused, very much aware of Kate's soft sobs.

"Young lady, I want you to know how proud I am of you. In many instances, it is the girl who controls the situation. You're to be commended for having the courage and strength to pull away. The greatest mistake you made Saturday was to ignore your mother's advice and the prompting you had about the picnic. That soft inner voice can keep you on the right path, if you'll let it. Listen more closely next time. Heed those promptings. You're a precious daughter of our Heavenly Father—always remember that, Kate. Know that you are his child, and as such, entitled to his help and loving guidance."

Kate wiped at her eyes and nose with the branch president's handkerchief. Turning her head, she glanced at the middle-aged man sitting beside her. "So, what do I do now—to make this right?"

"You've told me everything?"

"Yes," Kate answered, her cheeks flushing.

"Well, in my opinion, you've already taken the biggest step by talking to me. And I think I can safely say this is something you'll avoid in the future."

Kate nodded.

"All right, then, forgive yourself, and forgive Mike, knowing your Father in Heaven will forgive you."

"It's that simple?"

"This time. Let's not make a habit out of this, however."

"I won't," Kate replied fervently.

"I know you well enough to know that when you make a promise to stay away from something, you will. I appreciate that with you, Kate." He glanced down at his hands, making a mental note to arrange a visit with Mike in the near future. "There is something else I should add. I think it would be in your best interest to keep things light between you and Mike the next few weeks. Double or group date—it's safer, and it really is a lot more fun that way."

"My mom said the same thing."

"She's right. You two need to avoid any kind of situation where your standards could be compromised."

Kate nodded.

"As for the rumors that are going around, I think it would be a good idea for this branch to hear what's in your heart. To realize what a special young lady you are."

"There's nothing special about me," Kate sighed. She stood up and ran a hand through the front of her hair. "And I'm so tired of having to prove myself over and over! It's like my entire life is a test right now. Every time I turn around, there's something else I have to deal with!"

"Everybody's life is a test. That's why we're here," the branch president gently reminded her. "Satan sees the potential you have, and he's not about to make it easy for you. He knows the choices you're making now will determine who you're going to be."

Frowning, Kate moved closer to Glen Lake. She reached down, picked up a handful of stray pebbles, and tried to skip them across the water. President Randolph followed, watching as she unsuccessfully threw stones into the lake. Reaching down, he scooped up three rocks, picking those that were smooth and flat. Then, aiming carefully, he skimmed the first stone across the top of the water. It skipped in three places before sinking.

"How did you do that?" Kate asked.

"My father taught me years ago. Want me to show you how?"

"Yeah, I guess," she replied half-heartedly.

"First, you need to choose the right kind of rock. You have to be selective with this kind of thing, or you'll sink to the bottom every time." He opened his hand to reveal the stones he had chosen.

Kate compared them to the misshapen rocks in her own hand. Dropping them to the ground, she began looking around for a round, flat stone. Finally discovering one under a dried piece of moss, she cleaned it carefully, then held it out for inspection.

"That'll do. Now hold it in your palm like this," President Randolph demonstrated. Kate obediently followed his example. "Slip it between your fingers," he continued. "Draw it back and aim for the top of the water." He threw out the second stone, skipping it perfectly across the lake.

Kate threw her stone out, heeding his instructions. This time, her rock skipped once before disappearing.

"That's better," he said enthusiastically. "Let's try it again," he said, pointing out a perfectly shaped rock. Kate picked it up and after watching President Randolph skip his third stone across the water, she tried again, this time meeting with greater success.

"It takes practice. Before long, you'll have this down pat. Then you'll see something my father used to call the ripple effect. Every time that stone lands like it's supposed to, it sends out ripples in every direction." He turned and smiled at Kate. "Just like you and me."

"Right," Kate said sarcastically, suddenly catching on that this conversation had greater depth than had been implied.

"I'm serious, Kate. That's part of why we're here—to help each other. With what you've learned, there's so much good you can do in the world."

"Do you really believe that?" Kate looked up at the branch president. "After the mistakes I've made, do you honestly think I could ever help anyone?"

"Yes," he answered. "Don't give up on yourself. We all make mistakes."

"Even you?"

"Especially me. There was only one perfect being who ever walked the face of this earth and that was the Savior."

"I guess you're right," Kate murmured as she selected another stone. This time she managed to skip it four times across the water.

"See what you can do when you start giving yourself a little credit?" President Randolph quietly asked.

Picking up another smooth rock, Kate tried again, this time sending it as far as the branch president had ever managed to reach with the stones in his hand.

"Like I said . . ." he commented with a grin.

Returning the grin, Kate took a deep breath. The depression she had felt since Saturday was finally starting to slip away. Life was good, especially when you had friends like President Randolph to share it with.

CHAPTER TWENTY

Later that night, a very penitent Sandi came by for a visit.

"Let me guess, Lori or President Randolph sent you?" Kate stiffly asked as Sandi followed her into the deserted family room.

"No," Sandi replied, her eyes soft with regret. "Keith told me what really happened. Mike talked to him Sunday—Mike's as upset as you are about the rumors going around." She met Kate's wounded look and frowned. "Kate, I know I hurt you Sunday, and I'm sorry. I was so worried about you two anyway—then when I heard those girls talking . . . it's no excuse, I should've known better. Can you ever forgive me?"

Kate slowly nodded, reminding herself that Sandi had once reached out to her through forgiving love. Her eyes misting at the memory, she embraced Sandi.

"You're the best friend I've ever had," Kate said in a choked voice. "What hurt the most was thinking I'd lost you."

Sandi began to cry.

"What is it?" Kate asked.

"I was about to say the same thing," Sandi answered softly.

* * *

The next day, after school, Mike hurried down the hall after Kate.

"Kate, wait up," he panted, racing to catch her.

Kate stopped, turning to look at Mike.

"We need to talk," he said breathlessly.

"Bad idea," she said, glancing around. The rumor that had started at church had spread to school. Lewd comments had followed both of them all week.

"Hey, hey, Mike, picking up where Jace left off?" one of Jace's former buddies hollered.

"Go for it, dude," another hooted.

"See what I mean," Kate hissed angrily. She began walking away.

"Why are you letting them get to you?" Mike asked, trying to keep up. "Where's your spunk?"

"I don't know," she snapped, her eyes blazing. "Maybe I lost it on our picnic!" she retorted. "Ask around, it's not the only thing I supposedly lost up there!"

"Kate—" he began.

"It's different for you, Mike. Everyone cheers you on as the conquering hero. 'Look at the stud-man,'" she said, enraged. "With me, it's, 'Hey, look at the sleaze!' This double standard makes me sick!"

"Not everyone thinks—"

"No, you're right," she said, whirling around to face him. "You, me, Sandi, Keith . . . that pretty well sums up who really knows what happened."

"Would you calm down and listen to me?" Mike said sharply. "I've set several people straight—you're not in this alone. Do you think I like people thinking you and I—" he blushed. "I'm just as upset as you are, okay. I can't believe how it's spread—and what really gets me is it started with my sister!"

"Yeah, that was a nice touch. How did she find out?" Kate asked, pushing her way out of the school. Mike followed her down the cement steps.

"She must've heard me talking to my dad about it."

"You told your dad?" Kate asked.

"Didn't you?"

"For your information, I told my mom, she told my dad, my dad gave me the third degree, then I told Lori after she heard what your sister was spreading, and finally, I told President Randolph."

"You talked to President Randolph?" Mike asked.

"Yes, yesterday, after school. And until I came back to school today, I was feeling better about this entire disaster."

"I talked to him, too, last night. It was really bothering me."

"What, the fact that we made out, or that everyone knows about it?"

"Boy, you're on one today. What happened? I thought things were dying down. It's not like we're the only ones . . . not that we did . . . I mean—"

"Why don't you quit while you're ahead," Kate said brusquely.

"Would you answer one question, please?"

"What?"

"What set you off today? Sandi said— Never mind."

"Sandi said what?" Kate demanded.

Mike stared at the books in his hand. "She's worried about you. She said something happened today in biology, but she's not sure what."

"Then why isn't she out here dragging it out of me?"

Mike shook his head. He had never seen Kate this angry before. Taking a deep breath, he prayed he was up to the challenge. "Because she thought it was time you and I settled things between us. And I think she's right. This is something only you and I can fix."

"Can we fix it, Mike?" Kate asked, her voice softening. It suddenly became apparent that her anger had been a front to disguise how close she was to tears. "I can't take much more." As the tears came, Mike set his books down and held her. "We shouldn't be . . . this isn't a good idea," Kate murmured, her protests muffled against his chest.

"You need to get this out of your system," he replied, aching with her. "I promise, all I want to do is hold you." He felt her relax a little and tightened his grip. Kate was right. It had been a rough week, and he would do anything to take away the pain he had caused her. Last night he had promised President Randolph that he would straighten things out with everyone, including Kate. He began by telling anyone who would listen that Kate's virtue was still intact. Some had believed, others had scoffed. But it was a start. What mattered most was Kate's opinion of him.

"Tell me what happened today," he encouraged when he could see that Kate's tears were subsiding. Taking her hand, he led her to a tree and they sat side by side, leaning against it for support.

"Sandi's right. It started in biology. She has an English class that period, so she has no idea what took place." Kate rested her chin on her hands, staring across the sidewalk. "Toward the end of class, Coach Reynolds had a phone call. He told us to study for the final that's coming up in a week. I started thumbing through my notes—I guess they didn't think I could hear them . . . or maybe they didn't care."

"*They* who?" Mike prompted.

"Tracy and Annette."

"Tracy?"

"Warnick," Kate sniffed.

"And Annette Powell," Mike finished, picturing the two Mia Maids from their branch. "What did they say?"

"It's a long story . . . President Randolph wants me to speak in church this Sunday." Mike looked alarmed. "It has nothing to do with what took place Saturday. He's been after me to do this for a while. Anyway, somehow those two found out about it."

"And?" Mike asked softly, already guessing the answer.

"And they made several entertaining comments about what I could talk on." She buried her face against Mike's shoulder. "Oh, Mike, it was awful. Especially when some of the others in the class—nonmembers, no less—added their suggestions. They thought it was a riot that someone like me would be speaking in church."

Mike let her cry for several minutes, then slowly eased himself a short, safe distance away. He hadn't forgotten the stern warning he had received from the branch president, nor could he ignore the way he felt about Kate.

"Kate, we can't stop people from talking, but we can control how it makes us feel."

"How?" she sniffed.

"By knowing we didn't do what they're saying and that we've both done what we could to make things right." He knelt down in front of Kate and wiped the tears from her face. "And by you getting up Sunday to give a talk they won't forget."

"You really think I should go through with this?"

Mike nodded. "I think it's the only way, Kate. Maybe then everyone will realize how special you really are."

Kate scowled.

"What's wrong?"

"That's the same thing President Randolph said."

"Well, it's true, and it's time everyone knew it." As he looked at her, the desire to kiss her so strong it made him weak. Nervously swallowing, he leaned forward and kissed her cheek. Then, standing, he reached down to help Kate to her feet. "C'mon," he said with a grin.

"C'mon where?" she asked, thoughtfully holding the cheek he had kissed.

"I think we could both use a hot fudge sundae."

"Mike, I really don't feel up to going anywhere right now. Besides, if anyone sees us together . . ."

Mike brought a finger up to his lips. "Hush, Katie my dear, we're going to a place that will guarantee us a private table."

"Where?"

"Your house. Your mom told me Sunday that any time I wanted to come over, I was welcome."

"Mom said that?"

Mike nodded. "She's a pretty neat lady."

"I know." Kate liked the idea of going home. Lately, it was the one place she felt comfortable and loved.

"Your chariot awaits," Mike offered, gesturing to his car.

"I don't know about this," Kate murmured as Mike led her to his car.

Pausing by the passenger side, Mike quickly unlocked the door, then pushed a lever and folded the front bucket seat out of the way. Still grinning, he pointed to the back seat. "I'll play chauffeur today," he said gallantly. Kate decided to go along with his suggestion, impressed by his willingness to give her what she needed most, time and space.

CHAPTER TWENTY-ONE

In the minutes before Kate was to speak, Sue was nearly as nervous as her daughter. All through the earlier portion of the meeting, Sue had twisted the tissue in her hands until it was in tatters, her heart filled with silent pleas for help from above. She needn't have worried—this was to be one of Kate's finest hours. Her daughter stood, looking around at those who had refused to believe in her, as well as those who had been at her side. She spoke softly at first, the Spirit prompting her when she faltered, giving her the strength she needed.

Her voice grew steadier as she spoke of the accident that had taken place in Salt Lake City, of the dream she had had while in the coma, and of the changes it had brought into her life. Tearfully, she touched on the death of her friend, Linda, and how her testimony had pulled her through that horrible time. She bore witness of never being alone, quoting scriptures she had memorized, those comforting words that had served as a balm to her soul. She spoke of the importance of avoiding the very appearance of evil, testifying that Satan will try everything in his power to make people fall, but that it is possible to overcome every test, every trial, by clinging to high standards and maintaining a testimony of the gospel.

Glancing at Mike, Kate smiled warmly, then added that the challenges and temptations that had come into her life had been a source of pain and growth. But she had withstood this trial by fire and was eager now to go out into the world to do all that she could to help others find their way. Closing with her testimony, she shared her love of the Savior, of the Book of Mormon, and of a gospel that provides a way to achieve eternal happiness. When she sat down, there was hardly a dry eye in the house, and later, after the closing prayer, Sue Erickson wasn't the only one hurrying across the room to gather Kate up in a hug.

CHAPTER TWENTY-TWO

Randy picked up his pen and tried again to answer Kate's most recent letter. Bozeman, Montana, seemed light years away from Ireland. Things were happening so fast in his district, he was always on the run. He and his current companion had baptized two families during the past three months, including the Dalys. He smiled as he remembered how it had felt when the Dalys finally entered the waters of baptism. Their son had recovered fully after Randy and his companion had given him a priesthood blessing. Not long after that, the Dalys started taking the discussions again.

Distracted by the memory, he stared out of the small apartment window for several minutes before picking up the letter he had read a half dozen times.

June 8

Dear Elder Miles,

Can you believe it, I'm finally a high school graduate! This year has flown by so fast, it all kind of runs together. I look back, amazed that it happened and that I survived.

I still can't believe they asked me to sing a solo at graduation. I wasn't sure I could do it. We were supposed to present Marie with the plaque in Linda's honor before I was scheduled to sing. I said a quick prayer and somehow made it through.

It was tough saying good-bye to Sandi yesterday. She left to work in Billings for the summer and will stay with her sister, Stephanie. We'll try to get together before she heads down to the Y. I'm sure going to miss her!

Scanning the letter, Randy saw that for the first time in weeks, there was no mention of Mike Jeffries. Wondering if that was a good sign, he continued reading.

Next week, I'll be heading down to Salt Lake to stay with Aunt Paige and Uncle Stan. I'm excited, but it kills me every time I see the tears in Mom's eyes. I'm going to miss her so much, and Dad, Sabrina, even Tyler. I wish I'd caught on sooner to how wonderful they are.

Sorry if I sound sentimental. Now I know how you must have felt when you left on your mission. Speaking of which, I hope things are going well for you in Ireland. I'm enclosing my aunt's address. If you get a spare minute, drop me a line. Take care, and have a wonderful day.

Sincerely,
Kate

Sighing, Randy reached for a fresh sheet of paper and began to answer her letter.

CHAPTER TWENTY-THREE

Kate gazed dismally at the short note Randy had finally sent her. Pushing it away, she walked out of the bedroom that was hers, at least for the summer.

She could hear Paige talking to someone upstairs. Wanting to be alone, Kate walked quietly past the kitchen where Paige was having a heated discussion with one of her twelve-year-old identical twin daughters. Kate couldn't tell if it was Rachel or Renae that was being chewed out for sloppy bedroom mainte-nance, and she tried to keep a low profile, slipping outside into the backyard. Too late, she remembered that her cousin, Tami, had come over to weed the garden.

There was no place to plant a garden in the apartment complex where Tami lived with her husband and two small boys. When Tami had mentioned to her mother that she wished it were possible to grow a few fresh vegetables, Paige had readily agreed to share the family garden plot.

"Hi, Kate," Tami said brightly, pulling at a handful of stubborn weeds. "I don't suppose you'd care to join me?" she added, smiling at her younger cousin.

"Might as well. I don't have anything else to do tonight," Kate grumbled.

"Good. I could use some help. These rotten weeds are practi-cally choking out the beans."

Kate knelt beside the row in front of her cousin and began

pulling out weeds. After several minutes, Tami looked up from her row and studied the look on Kate's face.

"Want to talk about it?" she invited.

Shaking her head, Kate continued to work. How could she explain what she was feeling when she didn't understand it herself?

Later, after taking a refreshing shower, Kate sat on her bed and tried to focus on the scriptures she had set in front of her. When she found herself reading the same verse six times, she gave up and shut the triple combination. She set it on the nightstand, then jumped when someone knocked at the door.

"Come in," she called out.

"Hi. Thought I'd slip down to say goodnight," Paige said, entering the room. Touched by the troubled expression on her niece's face, Paige moved to the bed and sat down. "You've been awfully quiet this evening. Is everything all right?"

"Yeah. It's nothing."

"Are you sure," Paige pressed.

"I'm a little homesick."

"A little?" Paige asked.

"A lot," Kate admitted. "I'll get over it."

"It takes time," Paige said softly. "It'll get better." She smiled mischievously at her niece. "I noticed a letter from a certain young missionary in that pile of mail upstairs," she said, trying to change to a happier subject.

Kate glanced up at her aunt. "I wouldn't exactly call it a letter," she countered, pointing to the nightstand. Paige looked at Kate, then at the letter. "Go ahead. Take a look," Kate invited.

Leaning forward, Paige picked up the offending piece of paper. "You're sure you don't mind?"

Kate nodded, tracing the quilt pattern with her finger as her aunt began to read.

June 20

Dear Kate,

By now, you'll be in Salt Lake. I hope you enjoy your stay in Utah, better known as Zion!

Things are hectic here. We're teaching two new families!

I can't tell you how great it is seeing the changes that come into the lives of others as they accept the gospel of our Savior. What a humbling experience to be part of that process. I think I mentioned last time that the Dalys were taking the discussions again. They finally set a baptismal date! My companion and I got to do the honors. What a wonderful day it was!

I hope we have the same success with the families we're teaching now.

Well, I guess I'd better close. I still need to write a couple more letters. Take care, and have a great summer.

Sincerely,
Elder Randy Miles

"The Dalys were baptized? That's terrific!" Paige said enthusiastically. Then, noticing the look on Kate's face, she set the letter back on the nightstand. "All right, what is it?"

Fighting tears, Kate stared at her hands.

"It's me, remember?" Paige gently reminded her niece.

"I don't know . . . I'm confused," Kate finally said.

"Confused?"

"About everything. I can't go the 'Y' with Sandi. Mike and I are . . . actually, I don't know what we are anymore, just that I miss him so much it hurts, and Randy writes to me like I was his sister."

Paige tried not to smile at this last observation.

"And I miss my family so much . . ." Kate couldn't finish the sentence.

Paige spoke gently. "Kate, it's normal to feel that way, especially when you're facing decisions that will affect the rest of your life."

"I'll bet you were never confused about anything," Kate replied.

"You'd be surprised," Paige answered. "I remember when your uncle left on his mission. I didn't know what I was going to do with myself."

"Serious?"

Paige nodded. "I think my mother nearly went out of her mind trying to convince me that my life wasn't over."

"You must've really loved him," Kate said wistfully.

"Yes—I still do, actually," Paige said with a smile.

"Did he write letters like Randy's?"

"No."

"See, you don't know—"

"He didn't write at all," Paige said, gazing steadily at her niece.

"What?"

"His mission president didn't believe in elders corresponding with girlfriends. He said it caused too much distraction."

"Really?"

"Really. It was the longest two years of my life."

"How did you do it?"

"I cried a lot. Then, when I could see that wasn't going to do any good, I got a job."

"I have one of those," Kate replied. "And, as long as I stay busy, none of this bothers me, at least, not as much."

"So, it's the free time that's getting you down?" Paige asked.

Kate nodded. "All I do is worry about the future. I mean, I know I'll go to LDS Business College for at least a year, but after that, I'm not sure. I'll be working toward a degree in computer processing, but lately I've been thinking that I might like to be a teacher."

Paige smiled. "You'd make a wonderful teacher, Kate."

"Maybe. If I get the chance. Somehow I'd have to get into a university. I kind of blew things big time during high school."

"It can still happen, Kate."

"I guess. The thing is, by then, Randy will be coming home. I'm sure he'll be going back to BYU."

"Is that a problem?"

"I don't know. Even if I get accepted next year, what if things don't work out between us? And then there's Mike. We're still writing to each other. How do I choose between them?"

"Maybe you'll meet someone else," Paige offered, a twinkle in her eye.

"You're not helping," Kate accused.

"I know. Sorry." Paige reached over to pat her niece's leg. "When was the last time you read through your patriarchal blessing?"

"Last night," Kate said. "In places, it's so vague, it really doesn't help. Don't get me wrong, there are a lot of neat things in it. But right now I'm not getting any answers. Just more questions."

"Let's take inventory. You have a good job for the summer. One that will become part-time when school starts. You've been accepted at the business college of your choice, and you will be receiving training in a field you seem to enjoy." Paige gazed at Kate. "And, as long as you want it, you'll have room and board here among people who love you."

"I know," Kate sighed. "I shouldn't complain—but I hate having the future so unsettled."

"Don't we all?" Paige's voice was sympathetic. "None of us know what lies ahead, no matter how well we plan."

"I guess you're right."

"I think the problem is, someone has too much free time on her hands. And that's something we can fix in a hurry."

"What did you have in mind? Weeding the garden didn't seem to make a dent in it tonight." Kate made a face at her aunt.

"How about something you might enjoy, like detective work?"

Kate stared at her aunt. "Detective work?"

"Family history. I don't have time to keep up with it right now. Since they gave me this wonderful new calling in the Relief Society, I feel like all I do is chase around town."

Kate knew her aunt wasn't serious. Paige made a *wonderful* Relief Society president. But there was an element of truth to what she said. She was extremely busy with her new calling. "What do you want me to do?"

"Tomorrow when you get off work, I'll take you over to the Family History Library and show you around. There's a line on your mother's side of the family that I've been trying to work on for months. With your computer skills, maybe you could turn up a few pieces of data so we can submit their names to the temple."

"To the temple?"

"To have their ordinance work done."

"Oh, you mean like baptisms for the dead."

Paige smiled. "And endowments and sealings—everything needed for a family to be linked eternally."

"Sometimes I think about how Aunt Molly must've felt, finally having her sons sealed to her," Kate said, reflecting on the journal she had discovered last year.

"Can you imagine how wonderful you'd feel, knowing you were able to help someone else receive the necessary ordinance work for eternal salvation?"

Kate nodded.

"Some of the most spiritual temple sessions I've attended are the ones where I've had the opportunity to go through for an ancestor. There's such a feeling of love . . . you can almost feel their joy when they accept the work that's done."

Kate studied the distant look on her aunt's face. As she thought about helping with this search into the past, she experienced a shivering sensation along her spine. Startled, she glanced around the room, accidentally brushing Paige's arm.

"Sorry, I didn't mean to tune you out," Paige apologized. "I can't explain it, but, I feel like family history is something you need be involved in right now."

Kate nodded—she was getting that impression herself. "How soon can I get started?"

"How about tomorrow, after work?"

"Great," Kate said, finally certain that she was on the right path.

CHAPTER TWENTY-FOUR

The next day seemed to drag on forever. At last, it was five o'clock. As Kate made her way out of her uncle's office, Paige met her at the door.

"Ready to do some snooping at the Family History Library?"

Kate grinned. "You bet," she replied. She waited until her aunt finished talking to Stan, then walked with her to the minivan and climbed up front into the passenger side. Paige walked around and slid behind the wheel.

Kate looked around the empty van. She saw no sign of her cousins. "Where is everyone?" she asked.

"Tami came over again to work in the garden this afternoon, so I put Rachel and Renae to work helping her."

"What about Johnny?" Kate asked, referring to Paige and Stan's youngest child, a boisterous seven-year-old.

"He's busy entertaining his nephews. Before I left, I mentioned that if they tore the house apart, Tami and her sisters would get to put it back together. I think they'll keep an eye on things for me."

"I'm sure they will," Kate said.

"Oh, I almost forgot," Paige said as she stopped the van before turning into the busy street. Reaching for her purse, she pulled out a letter and handed it to Kate. "This came for you today."

Curious, Kate flipped it over to look at the address on the front. "It's from Marie," she said.

"How has she been doing?" Paige asked, guiding the van

through the rush hour traffic.

"Pretty good. I think getting back into the Church has helped a lot."

"Didn't your mother mention a while ago that there was someone who was interested in her?"

"Yeah, a guy named Stephen Ross. I thought maybe he'd ask her to marry him. Mom said he would've, but Marie wasn't ready. Marie told Mom she's not about to marry outside the Church again."

"I can't blame her there." Paige smiled at her niece, then focused on the road ahead.

Kate opened the envelope and began reading. "Yes!" she exclaimed.

"What's up?"

"Stephen's getting baptized. In two weeks! I can't believe it."

"Let me guess, she wants you there?"

Kate nodded. "Maybe I could take a bus or something."

"We'd be happy to take you up. It'll give Stan an excuse to take some time off."

"Really?"

"Plan on it. We'll be there."

It didn't take long for Paige to maneuver into the parking lot intended for visitors to the Family History Library. Locking the minivan, they crossed the street and hurried up the sidewalk toward Temple Square. As Paige continued to talk about the upcoming trip to Bozeman, she neglected to notice the gate she had led them to. Walking a couple of steps ahead, she chattered brightly, not realizing she had left Kate behind. When she caught on that her niece was no longer by her side, Paige stopped and turned around. Puzzled, she retraced her steps. As she approached Kate, it suddenly dawned on her why her niece looked so strange.

"Kate, I'm sorry. I wasn't thinking. We should've gone the other way."

"It's not your fault—it caught me off guard," Kate said, still staring at the street where the accident had taken place. "The last time I was here—"

"I know. It wasn't exactly pleasant for any of us." Paige shuddered.

"It feels so weird. I can see the whole thing in my mind."

"Let's go inside," Paige suggested, pointing to the temple grounds. I think you'll feel better if—"

"This is going to sound crazy, but could I have a few minutes alone?"

Surprised by the request, Paige nodded and stepped inside the gate, moving to wait by a beautiful flower garden. Her eyes soft with concern, she watched as Kate remained where she was, staring into space. Several minutes later, Kate walked inside the gate, glancing around as if seeing the temple grounds for the first time. Heading for the visitors' center, she was only vaguely aware of her aunt's presence. Something seemed to lead her on as Kate entered the building. She paused, reliving the argument she'd had with her mother. Wincing as she recalled the sharp words that had been exchanged, she mingled in with a crowd of tourists as they moved along a winding path that led upward.

As Kate moved up into the large dome-shaped room, she stared at the statue of the Savior. His hands seemed to reach out to her. Seeing the nail prints, she flinched, covering her mouth with a trembling hand. Just as she thought her heart would break, a comforting peace settled within. Lifting her head, she gazed up at the image of her older brother.

She felt her aunt's arm around her shoulders and for several minutes, leaned against Paige. Finally, she spoke. "I know this must seem strange—"

"You don't need to explain, Kate," Paige assured her. "Under the circumstances . . ."

"I was reliving that day. Only this time, I could see how wrong I was. Then, coming up here, it was almost like I could sense what Jesus did for me—how He suffered for my mistakes," Kate said, fresh tears making an appearance. Unable to speak, she didn't protest when her aunt drew her close.

CHAPTER TWENTY-FIVE

Kate's first day at college proved to be disastrous. She had come early, hoping to add an extra class to her schedule. Quickly locking Paige's car, a red Dodge Neon, in the small college parking lot, she stepped down off the curb into what appeared to be a layer of large, multi-colored leaves. Too late she learned that the leaves had covered a puddle of muddy water, and she thoroughly soaked both feet. Disgruntled, she tried to wipe off what she could with a handful of tissue from her backpack. Giving up, she sloshed her way across the street and into the administration building. She waited in the wrong line for several minutes before figuring out where she needed to go. Then, as she approached the Cashier to pay the difference in tuition, discovered she had left her wallet in the car.

Hurriedly retracing her steps, Kate made it a point to avoid the leaf-covered puddle. As she approached Paige's car, she searched her backpack for the keys. Alarmed when she couldn't find them, she went through the pockets of her new jeans, and then hunted through her jacket. A sinking feeling gripped her and was verified when she gazed into the car and saw that the keys were still in the ignition. Stan had already told her it was next to impossible to break into the little car, so Kate reluctantly walked back to the administration building to make a phone call.

Fortunately, Paige was home. Shaking her head as Kate revealed what had happened, Paige patiently assured that she had to come downtown anyway. Nearly forty minutes later, Paige pulled up in the mini-van with an extra set of keys.

"I hurried. The traffic was dreadful, as usual," Paige explained, smiling at Kate.

"I'm just sorry you had to come bail me out," Kate replied.

"No problem. This sort of thing happens to me all the time," Paige tried to soothe, noticing the mud stains on Kate's new shoes. Refraining from asking the obvious question, Paige concentrated instead on unlocking the Neon.

"There you go," she said brightly. Then, touched by the aggravated look on her niece's face, she put an arm around Kate's sagging shoulders. "You're not off to a very good start this morning. Can I do anything else to help?" she offered.

"No," Kate said, pulling away from her aunt to reach for her wallet. "I appreciate what you've already done, but hopefully I can handle things from here."

Smiling, Paige moved back to the mini-van and waved before driving off.

Kate sighed heavily and trudged back to the administration building where she again had to wait in line. By the time she made it to her first class, she was thirty minutes late.

"Late on your first day," the professor observed as Kate breathlessly entered the room. "Don't let it bother you," he said, winking at the class. "It takes a while to learn your way around this large campus."

As the class erupted in laughter, Kate's ears burned with embarrassment. Hurriedly moving to a empty chair, she sat down.

"He's just kidding," a male voice informed her.

Turning slightly, Kate glanced at the young man beside her. She noticed immediately that she was a head taller than he was.

"You'll like this class. This guy's a riot," he continued, pointing to the front of the room at the professor.

"I'm impressed already," Kate grumbled, setting her backpack on the floor.

* * *

Later that afternoon, Kate walked into the computer lab

located in the east wing of the small college. She had hoped to get a head start on some of her homework, but as she glanced around, didn't see a vacant spot. Closing her eyes in frustration, she began offering a silent prayer of protest. She was startled when the same young man who had talked to her in her first class, basic computer accounting, approached her again.

"This has been a lousy day," he commented, echoing Kate's sentiments.

"Oh?" Kate said, opening her eyes to gaze at the young man who had informed her this morning that his name was Joshua. Joshua Mann from Declo, Idaho, an RM with a quest. Just ask him.

"Yeah. I managed to erase a disk I needed for one of my classes tomorrow," Joshua said with a grin, his voice cracking. "Can you believe that could happen to a computer genius like me?"

Fighting the urge to offer a sarcastic reply, Kate tried to appear sympathetic when she said, "You don't have a backup?"

"Nope. I didn't think I'd need one. How about you—did the rest of your day go any better?"

Kate slowly nodded.

"Good. Do you have another class this afternoon?"

"No. I thought I'd get in a little practice time, but things look pretty full in here."

Joshua smiled, his braces gleaming. "It helps if you reserve ahead of time," he suggested. "You can't always find an open computer."

"Could I use the one you just gave up?" she suddenly pleaded, desperate.

"We could share. I've got it for another hour," Joshua suggested, winking at her.

"Maybe another time," Kate responded, unwilling to give Joshua false hope. She had already picked up on his attraction to her in class. After learning her name, he had doodled it all over his notebook. "Actually, I didn't realize it was this late. I've got to head to work," she added, glancing at her watch.

"You're sure?"

Kate vigorously nodded before making her escape.

* * *

"I'm sure it wasn't that bad," Stan said as Kate hung up her jacket.

"Don't even get me started," Kate warned.

"It'll go better tomorrow," he encouraged, smiling.

"It'd better," Kate responded, moving to her desk. "Where's that file of reports you wanted me to type up?" she asked.

Stan pointed it out to her and then retreated to his private office to make a phone call.

"Paige, what's Kate's favorite dish?"

"Lasagna. Why?" Paige asked.

"Remember this morning when you had to bring her that extra set of keys?"

"Yeah?"

"Let's just say that was the bright spot of her day."

CHAPTER TWENTY-SIX

Frustrated, Kate glared at the computer screen. Aunt Paige was right, this wasn't going to be easy. As far as she could tell, there were no more leads. She scowled at the name that refused to reveal past secrets.

"It's a shame to mar such a pretty face with an expression like that," a deep male voice said at her side.

Startled, Kate jumped in her chair. Turning, she found herself face to face with a blonde young man in a wheelchair.

"I didn't mean to scare you," he said, grinning at her.

"I . . . didn't know you were there," Kate stammered, trying not to look at the wheelchair.

"Guess I should've honked or something," he joked, regretting it when he saw the look on her face. "Sorry. I have a warped sense of humor—but I'm harmless." Deciding he was making things worse, he glanced at the monitor. "Looks like you've run into a bit of a roadblock."

"You might say that," Kate answered, grateful for the topic change. "I've been working on this for weeks. I've tried everything I can think of, but I can't get past the third generation on this line."

"Have you tried the IGI?"

Kate nodded. "It goes back to Helen MacOwen, actually, Helen MacOwen Evans, then nothing."

"Helen who?"

"My great-grandmother. Unfortunately, I have no idea who her parents are."

"I assume she was from somewhere in the British Isles, or you wouldn't be down here in the nether regions."

"The nether regions?"

"The basement," he said with a smile. "You know, the lowest level in the building."

"Oh," Kate said, wondering why this guy had wheeled himself into her problem. "Look, uh . . . did you tell me your name?" she asked, feeling slightly embarrassed.

"Ian—Ian Campbell. And you are . . .?"

"Kate . . . Erickson."

"Kate," he repeated, turning the name over in his mind. "That could definitely come from the British Isles, but Erickson, that's Scandinavian, right?"

"My father's family is from Norway. This line," she said, pointing to the screen, "is my mother's side of the family."

"I see. MacOwen—Scotland?"

"Yeah. Mom's quite a mixture. On her father's side, she has Irish blood, and on her mother's, Scottish."

"Oooh, I'll bet she has a temper."

"She does," Kate laughed. "But she's a great lady."

"Glad to hear it. I'm sure her daughter takes after her."

Kate could feel the blush as it spread across her face.

"I have to be honest," Ian said, suddenly determined to make the most of this moment. "I've noticed you in here before. In fact, I've been trying to get up enough courage to talk to you for a couple of weeks."

"Oh," Kate said uneasily.

"It's rare to get someone as young—" It was Ian's turn for discomfort. "I mean, usually the women who come in here are slightly older than you," he stammered with embarrassment.

"Slightly," Kate admitted, enjoying the flushed look on his face.

"Hey, have you tried the source information?" he asked, focusing on the screen.

"No. What's that?"

"F-nine on the Ancestral File," he said, highlighting Helen's name. A name with an address appeared on the screen. With it was the microfilm number of the original submission.

"Who is that?" Kate asked.

"The person who submitted Helen's name," Ian answered.

"I could contact this person to get more information on my great-grandmother?"

"Maybe," Ian replied. "On the other hand, when there's a microfilm number, it probably means this name was submitted years ago. That person might not be living at the same address, or—"

"Or they might be not be living at all," Kate offered, finishing the sentence for him.

"True. But you don't know 'til you try. Here, write this stuff down and we could start wading through the microfilm," he said.

"Why are you helping me?" she asked, obediently writing down the information.

"It's what I do," he responded, moving his wheelchair across the room as Kate followed.

"You work here?"

"Sort of. I volunteer my services. I guess it means the same thing."

"I see," Kate said, watching as he moved with ease among the rows of microfiche. He finally stopped at the section that contained the number they were searching for.

"It should be right here," he announced, pulling out a small white box. Then, carefully turning around, he led Kate to the film readers. Expertly threading the film, he flipped on the machine and began scanning through the entries. "Here we go." He pointed to the same name Kate had found on the Ancestral File. "If it was a longer entry, I'd suggest we take it to the copy center, but I think you can handle copying it by hand."

Lifting an eyebrow, Kate glanced at Ian, then began writing down the information on the lighted screen. "It's the same thing I had," she complained.

"Not quite. Look—there's another name listed."

"You're right. Good. That means I have twice as much chance of running onto something."

"Uh-huh," he agreed, rewinding the film. Stuffing the film back inside the box, he handed it to Kate to put away. When she returned, he glanced at the paper in her hand. "I see that second address is here in Salt Lake."

Kate looked at the address and frowned. "From what my aunt tells me, that's a pretty scary part of town," she commented.

"Depends," Ian replied.

"On what?"

"On the type of escort you bring along. If you come with a couple of friends, gorgeous young ladies like yourself, you're asking for trouble. But if you bring an ugly guy like me along, they'll leave you alone."

Kate studied the paper in her hand. Was he trying to ask her out or what? Either way, she wasn't interested. She had already turned down several eager young men she had met at LDS Business College.

"How about it? Can I help you with your search in our fair city?"

"Ian, I appreciate the offer but—"

"But you don't go out with guys in wheelchairs. That's okay. Some girls aren't comfortable with the fact that I'm physically challenged," he added, gesturing to his legs. "So, I'll understand if you—"

"It's not the wheelchair. Ian, I don't even know you. We barely met a few minutes ago, remember?!"

"Say no more," Ian said, whirling around to leave. "Good luck with your research."

"Just a minute," Kate said sharply, her temper flaring into existence. Ian obediently turned around. "You wheel yourself into my problem, offer help, which I *do* appreciate, ask me out ten minutes after we've met, then come on with this attitude like I've insulted you! I don't need this!"

"You really do take after your mother," Ian said, with a grin. "A regular spitfire."

"I am not!"

"I stand—no, sit corrected," he said, trying to look repentant.

"That's what I mean. What is it with you?"

"Got about a week?" Ian said.

Furious, Kate began to head out of the room.

"Wait, Kate, I'm sorry. I didn't mean to upset you. But I figure

I have about as much chance of going out with someone like you as I do of walking out of here."

Slowing down, Kate turned to glare at him. "I don't know how girls have treated you in the past, but I'd like to think I judge people by what's in here," she said, pointing to her heart, "not by their appearance."

"Ooooh, the lady thinks I'm ugly."

"Stop putting words in my mouth. I don't think you're ugly. In fact, you're very attractive," Kate snapped, instantly turning a deep shade of red.

Ian tried not to grin. "Really?"

Kate's face softened. "Yes, really. I saw you in here the other day and thought you looked . . . nice."

"Nice?" Ian frowned. "How attractive is *nice?*"

"Personality-wise, it's a definite plus," Kate responded.

"If I'm not mistaken, I think I was insulted," Ian said with a smile. "Are you implying I'm not congenial?"

"Something like that, yeah," Kate said, returning his smile.

"I don't suppose it's possible for us to start over?"

"Maybe," she said, glancing around at the people who were staring in their direction.

"Why don't we go up to the snack room on the main floor and discuss this where we can have a little privacy?" Ian suggested.

"Okay," Kate said, reluctantly following Ian across the room. Starting a relationship with another guy was about the last thing she wanted. *You and your ideas, Aunt Paige,* she thought, imagining the lecture she would hit her aunt with later.

Chapter Twenty-Seven

He's a nice guy. A bit confused about life, but a nice guy."

"I see," Paige replied, glancing at Kate. "And when is this nice guy picking you up?"

"In the morning. It's Saturday, I'm off, and I didn't have anything else planned. Ian thought we—"

"Ian, huh? That's a *nice* name," Paige teased.

"You're not even funny," Kate said as she finished setting the table.

"Sure she is," Stan boomed as he walked through on the way to the bathroom. "I changed the oil filter in the van," he added, holding up his greasy hands. "You can cross it off the *"honey-do"* list."

"Thanks, dear," Paige answered.

"You can make it up to me later." Stan winked, then disappeared from sight. Kate rolled her eyes at the same time as her aunt.

"Ian works at the library?" Paige asked, steering back to the subject at hand.

"Sort of. He's actually an accountant for a law firm. When he gets off work there, he heads over to the library to see what he can turn up on his family lines and to offer assistance to those of us who get stuck."

"I see."

"He's also a returned missionary, so he can't be all bad," Kate added, sounding more confident than she felt.

"Maybe. Just because a person's served a mission is no guarantee . . ."

"I know. I've had this lecture from Mom, Lori Blanchard, President Randolph . . ."

"Ah," Paige said with a smile. "Don't get us wrong, Kate. Most RMs are okay, but we want you to be on your toes."

"I'm trying," Kate responded.

"I would like to meet Ian before you two head out tomorrow," Paige said, stepping into the living room to pick up the clutter that had accumulated during the day. Kate followed, absently straightening the magazines on the end table.

"You can meet him in the morning," Kate replied. "He's coming here to pick me up."

"You called to see if this person . . ."

"Sylvia Myers," Kate filled in.

"To see if Sylvia Myers is still living in Salt Lake?"

"We tried. Ian called before I left the library. That number is no longer in service. So we decided to check this address out in the morning," she said, pulling a slip of paper out of her pocket. "With my luck, the house is probably deserted."

"Maybe I ought to go with you. What do I have tomorrow?" Paige muttered, glancing at the address in Kate's hand. "I could get my counselors to handle the visits we'd planned to make. I'm sure they'd understand if I told them—"

"I'll be fine," Kate insisted.

"Kate, Salt Lake isn't like Bozeman."

"Bozeman has its moments," Kate replied.

"True, but Salt Lake is bigger, and there are more people around who aren't exactly . . . nice."

Kate pulled a face.

"Promise me you'll be careful. I would feel horrible if anything happened to you, not to mention what your parents would do to me."

"Aunt Paige," Kate said, "I'm eighteen. In some countries, people are considered to be adults at that age. I'll be fine."

"Okay. But take my pepper spray with you."

"Your what?" Kate asked, puzzled.

"This," Paige said, reaching for her purse. Pulling it off the coffee table, she unzipped it and pulled out a small plastic container. "If you get into trouble, push this small lever over and fire away."

"Is it like mace?" Kate asked, glancing from the spray to her aunt.

Paige nodded. "It'll incapacitate anyone who messes with you."

"I don't know. I'd probably end up hitting myself in the face with it."

"Not if you're careful. Kate, you're going out with somebody we don't know, and on top of that, you're heading into a bad neighborhood. Take this with you. It's the only way I'll let you go," Paige said firmly.

"Kyle was right," Kate mused, thinking of the conversation she'd had with her cousin the summer before. In an attempt to convince Kate that parents usually have good intentions, Kyle had told her that his mother, Paige, could be stubborn if she thought her children were heading for trouble.

"About what?" Paige asked, her eyes twinkling.

"Last summer, he told me . . . never mind. I'll take the spray," Kate said, not wanting to get her cousin in hot water.

"Wise choice," Paige said, smiling at Kate. "Now, as for what my son, the returned missionary said, come here. Let's talk," she added, patting the couch.

Sighing, Kate obediently sat beside her aunt. This place was feeling more like home all the time.

* * *

"We're almost there," Ian announced, glancing at Kate. "Nervous?"

"A little," Kate responded, forcing a smile. Her aunt's warnings had made her uneasy.

Paige had liked Ian immediately, which made her feel a little better. Still, if she wasn't out to prove a point, she would have turned him down. It was important for Ian to know that she wasn't repulsed by him, but she didn't need or want any more complications in her life right now.

"Don't get your hopes up too high," Ian said.

"What?" Kate asked, startled.

"About this visit. You might gain a few leads, or you might turn up nothing."

"I realize that," Kate said quickly, ignoring the funny look Ian was giving her.

"Here we are," he announced, pulling up along the curb.

Kate peered at the tiny brick house nestled back in a group of trees. The small porch was covered with debris; the paint along the edging had peeled away to reveal grey, weathered wood.

"Looks like someone lives here," Ian said, pointing to the tiny Chihuahua who was barking furiously at the van.

"Oh, good," Kate replied, wondering if it was. She let herself out of the van and moved around to the other side. She had already learned in her aunt's driveway that Ian wasn't about to accept help from anyone.

When Ian had picked her up earlier, he had showed her how his Chrysler Caravan had been custom modified. With a remote control in his hand, Ian had demonstrated how the push of a button opened the automated door. At the push of another button, a ramp slid out. Wheeling himself up into the van, he had motioned for Kate to climb in the passenger side. Remaining in the wheelchair, which now doubled as the driver's seat, Ian had strapped himself in, then used the remote to reload the ramp and slide the door shut. All of the controls were accessible from the wheelchair, allowing Ian to use his hands to steer, brake, and travel with ease.

"Wow," Kate had commented, looking around the van. "This is really neat."

"I think so," he had replied with a grin.

"I had no idea something like this was available."

"I didn't either until after the accident." He had frowned slightly. "When I was finally released from the hospital, I was told to contact an agency called UCAT."

Kate looked at Ian curiously. "You-cat?"

"U-C-A-T—the Utah Center for Assistive Technology."

"Oh. I see. And they're the ones who helped you get this?"

"Yes. They showed me what some of my options were, then

helped me get a low-interest loan to pay for the van. They have all kinds of neat gadgets over there. In fact, it's not far from where we're going. Maybe later, I could drive you over for a look."

"Maybe," Kate had said, trying to be polite. Now, as she watched Ian exit the van, she marveled again at how far technology had come. One thing puzzled her though. She knew there were powered wheelchairs available; she had seen other people using them. She wondered why Ian would choose to use one that was manually operated. Summoning her courage, she asked about it as they made their way to the house.

"Ian, I don't mean to pry or make you uncomfortable, but—"

"What? I have pepper between my teeth?" he quipped, opening his mouth to probe inside.

"No," she said, laughing. "I was wondering why you use a manual wheelchair—"

"When I use such an automated van," he said, finishing the sentence for her. He sighed.

"I'm sorry," Kate stammered. "You don't have to answer."

"No, that's a fair question. It's just a little hard to explain. In the beginning, especially after I tried out a powered wheelchair, I thought that would be the way to go. Then, after I talked to some other special people like me, I realized I wanted as much freedom as possible. With this kind of wheelchair, I control where I go and how fast. I don't feel so much like a robot, and, it builds muscle," he added, flexing one arm, "which I'm told impresses the ladies."

"Oh, it does," Kate said with a smile. Her admiration for this young man was growing, despite his quirky sense of humor. She could see that it was his way of coping, something she could relate to. It wasn't always easy, but being able to laugh about life was a definite plus.

"Have you thought about what you're going to say?" Ian interrupted her train of thought.

"Not really," Kate said, trying to avoid stepping on the Chihuahua as it nipped at her Reeboks. When she reached the wooden steps of the porch, she hurried up, leaving the small dog behind. Furious, the Chihuahua concentrated on trying to bite one of Ian's wheels.

"Nice reception committee," Ian commented, glancing down at the dog.

"I hope it's not an indication of things to come."

"Don't worry, I'll keep this feisty creature from attacking you," he added with a grin. Secretly, he was starting to worry about this entire situation. What was he thinking, bringing a beautiful girl like Kate to this kind of neighborhood? "Hey, maybe this isn't such a good idea," Ian started to say as Kate moved to the door.

"We're here. I might as well give it a try," Kate said, sounding braver than she felt. She unzipped her small purse, fingering the pepper spray. Reaching up, she pushed what looked like the doorbell. When there was no response, she rang it again. She waited a few minutes, then hesitantly knocked on the door.

"I don't think anyone's home," Ian said hopefully. "Let's go. We didn't even try that other number we found."

"That number is listed in California," Kate reminded him. "Let's rule this one out first."

"I don't care what you're sellin', we don't want none," a husky voice rasped, startling both Kate and Ian. A tall, skinny blonde glared at them. She began to cough violently and took the cigarette out of her mouth. Cursing when she regained her breath, she focused on Ian who tried not to look at the revealing nightgown she was wearing under her robe. "Let me guess, sweetheart, you want a handout. You're out collectin' for some bleedin'-heart—"

"We're not asking for money. We're looking for a Mrs. Sylvia Myers," Kate said, hoping they hadn't found her.

"Well, you got the wrong woman. There ain't no Sylvia Myers here," the woman snapped.

"Did she used to live here?" Kate asked.

"How would I know? This ain't even my house. It's his," she said, pointing over her shoulder.

"Who's here?" A bearded man wearing boxer shorts suddenly appeared behind the blonde. Kate turned a deep shade of red when he grabbed the woman from behind, his fingers caressing her body as he kissed her neck.

"These two idiots think some woman named Sylvia lives here," the woman purred, leaning back against him.

"Never heard of her," the man said, staring at Kate.

"We've obviously made a mistake. Sorry," Ian said, motioning for Kate to move down off the porch. He didn't like the way the bearded man was looking at her.

"Well, now, let's not get in a hurry," the man said with a leering smile. "Maybe I can still help this little lady out."

"Uh, no thanks. We really should be going," Kate said, moving away from the door.

"That's not very neighborly. C'mere, I think I got something you might like," the man offered, stepping out onto the porch.

Kate flinched as the blonde woman cuffed him on the side of the head. Furious, the man shoved her back inside, slamming the door behind him. They heard her scream, then loud laughter from the man.

"Let's get out of here," Kate said, running to the van. She waited impatiently for Ian to move himself back inside the safety of the van. After what seemed like an eternity, they drove away from the curb.

"Well, that was fun," Ian said, trying to make light of what had happened.

"I don't think so," Kate quietly replied.

"I was kidding. Those two animals belong in Hogle Zoo."

Kate remained silent, trying to block out the appalling way that man had stared at her. It was like running into an older version of Jace. She shuddered, grateful Jace was no longer part of her life.

"Look, we could go back to your aunt's house and try that other number."

"Yeah, I guess."

"Or, better yet, I could take you to a place that would convince you Salt Lake isn't as bad as you think." He waited for a reply. "Kate?"

"Sorry, I wasn't listening. That guy was so gross."

"I should've taught him a few manners," Ian said, flexing one arm as he used the other to control the van.

"It's okay," Kate said with a smile. "But next time I think I'll listen to my aunt. She tried to tell me what that neighborhood would be like."

"Well, as I was saying, before, when you were rudely ignoring me—"

"Ian," Kate started, anxious to not hurt his feelings, yet, eager to end this disastrous outing.

"Hear me out before you shut me down," Ian said with a rueful smile. "There are several places around this valley that are actually quite beautiful, especially in the fall. Would you let me take you to see one?"

"I don't know. I really should get started on a couple of assignments that are due Monday—"

"It might get rid of that bitter aftertaste still rattling around in your head after our adventure this morning."

"Well," Kate said, slowly caving in. She would probably just go home and brood anyway. "Okay. Where are we going?"

"To a park called the International Peace Gardens. You'll love it!" Ian said eagerly.

"The International what?"

"Peace Gardens. Countries from all over the world are represented by beautiful flower gardens."

"I've never heard of it," Kate replied.

"Good. It'll be a new experience."

"Like the one we just had?"

"No. Better," Ian promised. He stayed on Ninth South until reaching Ninth West. Then, turning into a parking lot, he grinned at Kate. "You're going to love this."

A few minutes later, Kate had to admit he was right. "Ian, these flower beds are gorgeous!" she exclaimed, glancing around. "Where do we start?"

"This way," Ian encouraged, leading her to the left. "India's contribution," he explained, pointing to the small plaque.

"Look at those begonias," Kate exclaimed, glancing from the flowers to the monument bearing a preaching Buddha.

"And over here, we have your ancestors' homeland," Ian said, pointing to the display from Ireland.

Kate knelt beside the flower bed that spelled Ireland with green leafy plants. The tall purple lupines accented the greenness. She gazed across the green lawn to the Celtic cross monument, and for a moment, felt a kinship with her fourth great-grandmother, Colleen Mahoney. The feeling of reverence intensified as she closed her eyes, imagining what it would be like to stand on a green hillside, staring off at the ocean, as her grandmother must have done a hundred times.

Ian waited patiently, sensing that this particular garden held special significance for Kate. He was thrilled by her response, for it was here he first began to believe that beauty still existed in a world of disappointment and pain.

"Is there a garden from Scotland?" Kate asked, breaking the silence.

"No—well, it's not labeled Scotland, but there is a garden from Great Britain, so I guess that counts. Scotland is considered part of that country."

"Where is it?"

"Clear over there," Ian said, pointing across the park. "We have a few more countries to explore first."

Kate nodded, amazed at the beauty hidden in this park. Although the garden from Ireland had a special hold on her heart, it was difficult to select a favorite. Each was enchanting, decorated with flowers and colors representing the country responsible for its creation. "How did this all come together?" Kate asked, gazing at a wooden pagoda made up of brilliant colors in the Korean section.

"It began back in 1947. It started out as a way to celebrate the centennial of the Mormon pioneer emigration into Salt Lake City. It's grown since then, thanks to generous people who want to pay tribute to the nationalities that are mixed in this valley." His eyes lit with excitement as he reflected on what that meant. "Can you imagine what it must've been like, people from all over the world uniting here to build Zion?"

"It's amazing," Kate agreed. "What a wonderful way to honor the different cultures," she added, glancing in the distance at a miniature Matterhorn.

"Yeah," Ian said as he studied Kate's face. She was another beautiful way that separate cultures had combined; Scandinavia, Ireland, and Scotland had united to create a lovely, spirited young woman.

Unaware that Ian was staring at her, Kate moved toward the Japanese exhibit. A small wooden bridge beckoned. Ian followed as she ran to it, halting to gaze into the clear creek. She then raced up a small hill, peering down into the Jordan River.

"Oh, Ian, it's all so beautiful—I love it here! Thank you for bringing me."

"You're welcome." Ian grinned at her enthusiasm. He added silently, "But you are easily the most beautiful creation in this park."

Chapter Twenty-Eight

I know we've taken you and your family to the Peace Gardens before," Paige insisted, looking up from the dishwasher.

"I would've remembered a place like that," Kate refuted, handing her aunt a plate she had scraped off into the garbage.

"You have a point," Paige answered. "We try to cram so much into our visits, it must've been overlooked."

"Well, I can't wait to take Mom there sometime."

"Speaking of which, are you sure we can't talk her into coming back with us when we head up for the wedding? She could bring Sabrina—she'll be out for Christmas vacation."

"She said no the last time I asked her," Kate replied, loading a handful of dirty silverware into the dishwasher. She grinned, thinking about Stephen and Marie together at last. Stephen had finally proposed nearly a month after his baptism. "Mom said something about wanting me home for the holidays."

"She'll have you up there after your finals the second week of December until Christmas—nearly three weeks. This would be after Christmas, after the wedding. Four or five days, tops. You go back to school on January second, right?"

Kate nodded, still seeing the colorful flowers of the Peace Gardens.

"Maybe I can talk some sense into her when we're in Bozeman," Paige said, reaching under the sink for the dishwasher detergent. She couldn't help but notice that Kate had glowed with excited joy all evening. Secretly, she hoped Ian Campbell wasn't responsible for the look on her face. He seemed like a nice enough young man, but she felt Kate needed more time before jumping into a serious romance. On the other hand, if love was in the air, there wasn't much she could do about it. She had learned that much from Tami, and from Kyle who at the moment, was rather smitten with a young woman he had met at BYU.

Suddenly Kate asked, "Do you think Uncle Stan would mind if I left work an hour early on Monday?"

Paige lifted an eyebrow. "I suppose something could be worked out. What's up?"

"Ian wants to take me to see *Legacy*. He has tickets for the five-fifteen show."

"Well, I—"

"I know you guys took me to see it last year, but I really didn't pay attention. I'd like to see it again."

"I'll see what I can do with your Uncle Stan."

"Thanks," Kate said, giving her aunt a quick kiss on the cheek. "You're the greatest!" she exclaimed, hurrying out of the kitchen. Paige shook her head and started the dishwasher.

* * *

"Ian's a returned missionary?" Sue repeated, stunned.

"Yes," Paige admitted. Evidently Kate had left that part out.

"She said they were friends. There's never been a word about— I'm not ready for this," Sue sputtered.

"I didn't think I was either when Tami came home with that rock on her finger, but it happens," Paige said ruefully. "That reminds me, did I mention Kyle gave Tina a ring for Christmas?"

Sue was still in a state of shock. "How long have they been going out?" she asked.

"Let's see, they met in September," Paige replied, her mind still on Kyle and Tina. "About three months."

"That's not enough time for them to get acquainted, let alone—"

"Trust me, those two have become very well acquainted. You should've seen them the other night. All I can say is it's a good thing it will be a short engagement."

"But I thought you said . . . Kate's engaged?" Sue asked, turning an odd shade of green.

"Kate?"

"You just said Kate and Ian will be having a short engagement," Sue accused.

Paige burst out laughing. "I was talking about Kyle and Tina, not Kate and Ian."

"This isn't funny!"

"I know." Paige grew sober at the thought. "It means I have to pull an open house together in less than two months. Tina's from California, so the reception—and possibly even the wedding—will take place there. They're already talking about being married in the Los Angeles temple."

Sue blinked, looking confused. "When did the subject change from Kate and Ian?"

"Didn't you hear me say that Kyle and Tina got engaged over Christmas?"

"No," Sue said, breathing out slowly. "Don't ever do that to me again."

"If you'd paid attention to what I was saying—"

"I guess I'm feeling a bit overwhelmed."

"You're feeling overwhelmed?" Paige said dryly. "Sue, to be honest with you, when it comes to Kate and Ian, I don't think there's anything to worry about yet. Ian hasn't even kissed her."

"How do you know?"

"I asked," Paige admitted with a grin. "Do you honestly think I'd let anything get past me? The only thing that has me concerned is the way he looks at her."

"Gee, thanks, I feel much better now," Sue said sarcastically.

"The truth is, Ian adores your daughter. I think he's convinced the sun rises and sets in her eyes."

"Oh, good. You're saying he's in love with her," Sue said, running a hand through the front of her hair.

"I think he's got it pretty bad for her, yes," Paige replied, gazing at her sister-in-law.

"And how does Kate feel about him?"

"I'm not sure. But there's an easy way for you to see what's going on for yourself," Paige suggested. "Come back with us after Marie's wedding. Greg could come down with Tyler in a few days to pick you up. It'd give you and Sabrina a chance to spend some time with Kate before school starts up again."

"Good idea," Sue replied. "I'd like to meet Ian."

"I thought you might," Paige said, trying not to smile.

* * *

". . . and since we're all home for the holidays, Mike thought it would be fun to get together tonight," Kate said as she helped Sandi put the finishing touches on the snowman they were building. She looked around, breathing in the cool, fresh air. It was so good to be back in Bozeman. Salt Lake hadn't had much snow yet; she hadn't realized how much she would miss the powdery stuff. And it was great, spending time with Sandi.

"That's what Keith said when he called last night," Sandi replied. "It was good to hear his voice again," she added. "It's been a while."

"I know," Kate sighed. "I haven't seen Mike in months."

"Have you two kept in touch since we all headed off to college?" Sandi asked, arranging a hat on top of the snowman.

"I get a letter from him about every two or three weeks. Why?"

Sandi shrugged. "Have you ever said anything to Mike about Ian?" She waited for Kate to respond, then poked her friend with a gloved finger. "C'mon, 'fess up. Mike doesn't know, does he?"

Kate slowly shook her head, focusing on the large buttons she had found for the snowman's mid-section.

"Kate, if it's serious, you need to tell him. You know how Mike feels about you. And what about Randy? The poor guy is off serving a mission, thinking all is well at home—"

"I wrote to Randy over a month ago and told him about Ian," Kate sputtered in her defense. "He knows we're good friends."

"What about Mike?"

"I suppose you tell Keith everything," Kate countered.

"As a matter of fact, I do," Sandi informed her.

"Now it's my turn to ask questions. Just how serious is it getting between you two?"

"Not very. We're both planning to serve missions, remember? And we agreed it was okay to date other people."

Kate gazed at Sandi. She knew Keith adored Sandi. Mike had mentioned that Keith would've followed her to BYU if he hadn't been offered a football scholarship at Ricks. "Keith actually agreed to that?"

"I didn't give him a choice. We're good friends, Kate. That's all for now. He writes me when he gets time and I do the same. This date tonight is the first time I've seen him since he left with Mike to head for Ricks College."

"Uh-huh," Kate teased.

"You're the one I'm concerned about. Tell me more about Ian."

"What do you want to know?"

"Everything. He sounds interesting," Sandi said, shading her eyes with a hand.

"He is. We've had a lot of fun together."

"You said he was a returned missionary," Sandi teased, throwing a handful of snow at Kate. "When can I expect a wedding invitation?"

"Not funny," Kate informed her best friend as she wiped the snow from her face.

"I was kidding," Sandi replied.

"I know," Kate responded. "The problem is, I *am* worried about where this is heading. I mean, he's funny, he's nice. We have a good time when we go out, but I'm really not ready for a serious relationship right now."

"And you're afraid he is?"

Kate nodded. "After everything he's been through, I don't want to hurt him."

Sandi gestured to the porch. Wiping off the snow, they sat down next to each other. "You mentioned he was in an accident," she prompted.

"Yeah. He'd only been home from his mission for about a month. He was driving across town and was hit from the side by a man who'd had a heart attack. Ian's spinal cord was damaged. He's paralyzed from the waist down."

"Any chance he'll recover?"

Kate shrugged. "He told me about some new research they're

doing. In some cases, the nerves in the spinal cord can be partially regenerated. And he mentioned something about a stimulator that can help some paraplegics take a few steps. But I don't know if either of these would help Ian."

Sandi shivered.

"Cold?"

"No. I can't imagine how awful it would be to have to spend your life in a wheelchair."

"Ian hasn't let it stop him. He went back to school, got a degree in accounting, and now has a good job with a law firm."

"That's great," Sandi said. "He must have a wonderful attitude."

Kate laughed. "Actually, he's about as feisty as they come. Which is why I went out with him in the first place. He told me I wouldn't because he's 'physically challenged.'"

"You're kidding?" Sandi asked, intrigued.

"No, I'm not. He made me so angry, I had to prove him wrong. The truth is, he's pretty sensitive about what happened. Here's this great-looking guy who has a wonderful personality, but he's scared to death people won't like him because—"

"He's in a wheelchair," Sandi said, finishing the sentence. "Why would he think that?"

"He's been hurt before. The girlfriend he had before the accident broke up with him while he was still in the hospital."

"Ouch," Sandi said softly. "Why?"

"I'm not sure. I'm only hearing one side, and sometimes Ian can be a little biased. He claims she couldn't handle the changes that came into his life because of the accident."

"What do you think?"

"I'm not sure. I've never met Toni, so I hate to judge. Ian told me they were high school sweethearts. He was quite the athlete . . . still is, really. You should see how he maneuvers himself around in that wheelchair. That reminds me, he took me to this place called UCAT—"

"You-cat?"

Kate smiled at Sandi's bewilderment, remembering her own when Ian had first told her about the technology center. "It stands for Utah something or other Technology. Anyway, they have all kinds of demonstration equipment for people with disabilities. Ian talked me into trying out one of their wheelchairs, one like his. I nearly tipped over on my head at first. Then, when I finally got the hang of it, I wore myself out going around the room a couple of times. My arms ached so bad the next day—I don't know how Ian does it."

"Back to the woman who dumped him," Sandi impatiently prompted.

"Toni," Kate informed her. "Like I said, they were quite the item in high school. She was a cheerleader, he was Mr. Athlete. They wrote back and forth while he was on his mission. Everyone figured they'd get married. Then came the accident."

"Has he dated anyone since she broke up with him?"

Kate shook her head. "You understand my problem?"

Sandi offered a low whistle. "How're you going to handle this one?"

"I don't know. I've prayed about it and feel like everything's okay, but I'm still worried. I'm afraid he's getting too serious." She sighed. "I'm not ready to rush into anything. And yet, I feel so comfortable around Ian. We make each other laugh. And he's shown me so many wonderful places around Salt Lake."

"You have fun together," Sandi commented. "You can talk to him."

"Yeah," Kate agreed. "And he's helped me so much with the genealogy I've been working on. We finally found the lady who submitted the information I came across at the Family History Library. She lives in St. George, and she's coming up to Salt Lake during the holidays. We really lucked out. She only comes once a year to visit relatives. When I called, she said she might have something that would help with my research."

"That's great," Sandi said.

"I know. And I have Ian to thank for all of it. If he hadn't tried to help me that day, I might've given up on this line. That's why I keep thinking we were supposed to meet. I'm just not sure how it's all going to turn out."

"Has he said anything to make you think he's getting serious?"

"He doesn't have to," Kate replied. "You should see how he looks at me sometimes."

"And you're sure you don't feel the same way?"

Kate nodded. "It's like hanging around with an older brother, something I've always wanted, actually. Someone to talk to, confide in, someone to—"

"Pull your hair, tickle you until you can't breathe and tease you until you're ready to scream," Sandi added.

"I forgot who I was talking to, Miss-I-Have-Two-Big-Brothers-And-I'm-Going-To-Rub-Your-Nose-In-It!"

Sandi picked up a handful of loose snow and threw it at Kate. "There are times when they're pretty neat."

"So you know what I'm saying," Kate replied as she threw snow at Sandi.

"Sort of," Sandi answered, standing up to reach for more snow. This time she formed a snowball and threw it at Kate. Kate turned her back, catching it in the side. Soon, both girls were busy hurling snowballs at each other. Several minutes later, out of breath and energy, they collapsed together on the porch.

After a moment, Sandi said, "Kate, maybe you're not giving this enough time. Is it possible you could develop stronger feelings for Ian?"

"I don't know. The thing is, I think I'm running out of time. We had a scary conversation during our last . . . date I guess you'd call it."

"About what?" Sandi prompted.

"We were cruisin' around Crossroads Plaza, killing time until the movie started . . ." Kate hesitated.

"And?"

"Some cute little boys ran by, chasing each other."

"What does that have to do with anything?"

"Ian loves kids. He'd like to have a large family someday."

"Is it possible . . . could he have kids of his own?"

"We talked about it."

"Really?"

Kate nodded.

"You two have covered just about everything. What did he say?"

"That there's a chance he could father children—the fertility rate for males with lumbar lesions is higher than for those with cervical injuries."

"Lumbar?"

"Lower back," Kate answered. "That's where most of the damage was done to his spine."

"So he could have children?"

"I hope so. He'd make a wonderful father. He's so patient with kids. He told me his patriarchal blessing states that children will come into his life. He's hoping that pertains to this life."

"Does his blessing say anything about meeting you?" Sandi teased.

"No. I think he's convinced it does. He said his blessing promises that a choice daughter of our Heavenly Father will come into his life."

"And he's convinced it's you?"

"I think so," Kate groaned. "What am I going to do?"

"Give it time, and keep me posted."

"Don't worry," Kate responded. "You'll be one of the first to know if anything happens."

* * *

Later that night, Keith and Mike picked up Sandi and Kate and headed for Tom's Green Grill. A favorite hangout, the restaurant was decorated to resemble a diner from the forties and fifties. As they walked in, Mike wandered over to the restored jukebox and picked out a few hits from the fifties.

"This is great, isn't it?" Keith asked, glancing around. Recognizing someone from his old football team, he waved.

"Yes it is," Sandi agreed, sliding into a booth.

Kate slid into the opposite side, giving Sandi a meaningful look when Mike approached. She had already sworn Sandi to secrecy concerning Ian. "I'll tell Mike if and when I figure things out with Ian," Kate had finally promised earlier that afternoon.

Remembering the conversation, Sandi smiled at Kate, in silent reassurance that she would keep Kate's secret.

"Hello, kids. Everyone want the usual?" a familiar voice asked.

Kate smiled at the waitress, a lady in her mid-forties who had waited on them in the past. "Hi, Liz. I'm not sure. What do you guys want?"

"Cheeseburgers and fries. Thick chocolate malts," Mike insisted.

"For all of you?" Liz asked.

"Yep," Keith answered as Sandi and Kate nodded in agreement.

"Okay, coming right up," Liz said as she moved to the counter with their order.

"This place hasn't changed a bit," Mike commented, glancing around.

"Did you think it would?" Kate teased. "We haven't been gone that long."

"True. Seems like it though," he added, glancing at Kate. Avoiding his gaze, Kate began playing with the salt and pepper shakers. "So, what's new with you?" Mike asked. "Lately, your letters don't say much. Descriptions of places around Salt Lake don't really tell me how you're doing."

Sandi grinned impishly at Kate, wondering how her friend would work her way out of this line of questioning.

"Sorry. I've had a lot of homework this semester. But I'm doing great. Things haven't changed much." Kate kicked Sandi under the table. Sandi quit grinning long enough to give Kate a dirty look. "I work and go to school," Kate said, placing the salt and pepper shakers against the napkin dispenser.

"Do you still like LDS Business College?" Mike asked, watching Kate closely.

"Oh, yeah," Kate said, smiling at Mike. "It's such a small campus, every student gets a lot of personal attention." Regretting her choice of words, she hurried on to change the subject. "You should be proud of me, I finished this quarter with a 3.8 grade point average."

"Glad to hear it," Mike replied. "Wish Keith could say the same thing."

"Now, just a minute," Keith sputtered in his defense. "Who's the one who had to drop physics?"

"No need to get personal," Mike said, reaching across the table to slug Keith in the shoulder.

"You had to drop out of physics?" Kate asked.

Mike nodded. "I guess I should've paid more attention in

Youngston's class last year," he admitted. "I had no idea how tough college would be."

"I know," Sandi admitted. "It seems like all I do is study."

"Well, that part hasn't changed," Keith teased. Now it was Sandi's turn to punch him in the arm.

"How do you put up with him as a roommate?" Sandi asked, glancing at Mike.

Mike laughed. "We compromise. I tolerate his warped sense of humor—"

"And I try to ignore his snoring," Keith said, tipping his head back to imitate Mike's snoring ability.

"Keep it up, you'll find yourself walking back to Rexburg," Mike threatened.

Keith stopped snoring to grin at his friends. "What a guy! The fun never stops," he said, wiggling his eyebrows.

"Tell me about it," Mike agreed, smiling. He turned to look at Kate. "How do you like Salt Lake by now?" he asked as Liz brought them each a glass of ice water.

"It's okay," Kate replied, sipping at her glass. "Noise, pollution, acts of violence, fun stuff like that."

"Oh, c'mon, it can't be all bad," Mike encouraged.

"No, you're right. There's a lot of neat stuff too. Beautiful scenery—"

"I've heard," Mike groaned, pulling a face.

"Not to mention wonderful stores, great places to eat—" Kate said, bravely continuing.

"Getting back to this *personal attention* you mentioned a few minutes ago, were you implying professors, or other students?" Mike asked, reaching for his own glass of water.

"Professors," Kate answered, staring down at her hands. "They're all pretty neat, anyway, the ones I've met." She glanced at Mike. "As for the students, I've made a lot of good friends."

"Friends, huh?! No one's swept you off your feet yet?"

"No," Kate responded, flushing slightly. She avoided the look Sandi was giving her. "How about you?"

"Your turn on the hot seat, roomie," Keith said with a grin. "Mikey's decided it's his own personal quest to take out every girl in our student ward."

Kate lifted an eyebrow and gazed at Mike. "No wonder you had to drop out of physics," she murmured.

"You're making it sound worse than it is," Mike protested. "I figure this way, I get acquainted, and nobody gets hurt because I never go out with the same girl twice. It's perfectly innocent."

"Yeah, I'll bet," Sandi said, glancing from Mike to Kate. It was difficult to tell who was the most uncomfortable with this conversation.

"Back to my original question, Katie dear, how's your social life?" Mike asked.

"Pretty mundane," Kate replied as Sandi struggled to keep a straight face.

"There must be a herd of guys beggin' to take you out," Mike probed.

"Not really," Kate replied, relieved to see that Liz was bringing their order.

The playful banter was kept up most of the evening. After dinner, they hit a movie. All too soon, it was time to head home. Mike drove to Sandi's house first, which gave him a few minutes alone with Kate while Keith walked Sandi to the door.

"Sounds like you're doing all right down south," Mike said, draping his arm around Kate's shoulders. He played with the back of her hair, enjoying its softness.

"I'm getting used to it," Kate replied.

"Have you missed me as much as I've missed you?"

"I didn't think you'd have time to miss me, what with your busy social calendar," Kate sniffed, deliberately giving him a bad time.

"I'll admit, I've dated a lot of different girls, but I've never kissed any of them like this," he said, leaning forward.

Kate shivered as his lips tenderly brushed hers. Pulling back, Mike gazed at her in the darkness. "How about you?"

"No," Kate said breathlessly.

"But you have met somebody."

"I didn't say that."

"But it's true, isn't it?"

Kate reluctantly nodded.

"I knew it," Mike said, sliding back against his seat. "I could tell by the way you kept changing the subject every time I brought it up."

"He's just a friend, Mike. We spend time together, but not like this."

"Yet," Mike said softly, straightening behind the wheel as Keith opened the door on his side. Mike quickly slid out of the car, waiting for Keith to slip into the back seat before sitting back in the car.

"So, did you escort Sister Kearns to safety?" Mike asked, glancing in the rearview mirror.

"Something like that, yeah," Keith said, grinning.

"What I want to know is—"

"Never mind," Keith interrupted. "How I bid my ladies farewell is no concern of yours."

"I'll expect the same courtesy from you," Mike joked as he turned down the street that led to Kate's house. A few minutes later, Mike held onto Kate's hand as they moved up the sidewalk to her front porch.

"I really have missed you," he said softly, brushing her cheek with his hand.

"I've missed you too, Mike," Kate said with emotion, reaching for a hug. They embraced for several seconds before Mike started to disentangle himself.

"Why is it the one lady who can turn my heart to putty is beyond my reach most of the time?" he complained.

"Because you're leaving to serve a mission in a couple of months," Kate replied.

"You really know how to hurt a guy."

"I know how excited you are to go. It's all you talked about tonight—with the exception of your harem."

"Kate, I meant what I said a few minutes ago. You are the only girl I've ever—"

"Shhhhhh," Kate hushed, holding one of her fingers against his lips. "Whatever happens, happens. If we're both still ready, willing, and able when you get back, we'll work something out. Deal?"

"Do I have a choice?"

Kate shook her head.

"Well, alrighty then. Give us a kiss and we'll be on our way." Grabbing her, he dramatically tipped her toward the ground, kissing her soundly. Pulling her back up, he grinned as she gulped for air. "Until we meet again, my lady." Offering a salute, he quickly headed for his car.

"You are coming to my farewell?" he hollered over his shoulder.

"Wouldn't miss it," she yelled in return.

"Remember, you and Sandi promised me a duet," he reminded her.

"We'll sing our little hearts out for you," she replied.

"I could just kiss you," he said, heading back toward the porch.

"Oh, no, you don't," Kate retorted, hurrying inside the house. She grinned, watching through the small window in the door as Mike acted out a painful death scene. Shaking her head, she laughed when he finally retreated to the car.

"Sounds like you had fun tonight," Sue murmured.

Kate jumped, then turned to smile at her mother.

"How would you like some hot chocolate?" Sue asked, tightening the belt around her robe. She had decided the time had come for a serious mother-daughter conversation.

"I think that's a good idea," Kate said, following her mother into the kitchen.

CHAPTER TWENTY-NINE

Kate's eyes filled with tears as she watched Marie exchange rings with Stephen at the front of the Relief Society room. Deciding to get married now in a civil ceremony, Marie had said they would be sealed together next year, to celebrate Stephen's baptism into the Church.

The spirit of love that filled the small room was overwhelming. Marie's sister, Samantha had come with her husband and two teenage daughters. Marie's brother had come with his family as well. The big surprise, however, was the arrival of Marie's father, whom Marie hadn't seen in nearly eighteen years. At first, they stared at each other, until Samantha gave their father a nudge. Stepping forward, he gripped Marie with a bearlike embrace as they both shed tears of pain and joy.

After the ceremony, as everyone moved forward to congratulate the happy couple, Marie gathered Kate up in an intense hug.

"I can't tell you what it means to have you here," Marie said.

Kate found it difficult to breathe. "I think I'm getting a pretty good idea," she wheezed.

"Sorry," Marie said, pulling back. "Thanks for coming."

"I wouldn't have missed it," Kate said with a smile. "I'm so glad you two got together."

"Me too," Marie said, her eyes sparkling with delight. As others moved in to talk to the new bride, Kate drifted to the back of the room.

"I'm glad her family showed up. It means so much to her," Sue said softly.

Kate glanced at her mother and nodded.

"I don't think I've ever seen her this happy. She's beautiful," Sue commented.

"I know. Stephen looks great too," Kate added, glancing at the ecstatic groom.

"They'll have a wonderful life together." Sue dabbed at her eyes with a handkerchief. "They love each other so much. That's how it should be."

Reflecting on what her mother had told her last night, Kate slowly nodded. "It's easy to get caught up in what you think is a serious relationship," Sue had said, "only to discover later on that it was nothing more than a physical or intellectual attraction. If the relationship doesn't include an emotional bond of love and respect, it can lead to disaster."

"This is about Ian, isn't it," Kate had asked.

Sue had slowly nodded. "Honey, I just want you to be careful. I don't want to see you get hurt."

"Mom, to be honest, I'm not sure where things are heading with Ian. And you're right, I am confused. I know I still feel something for Randy, and then there's Mike. Being with him again tonight was great, but it makes things even more complicated."

"Does Mike know about Ian?" Sue had prompted.

"Sort of," Kate admitted. "I didn't give him any details, but he knows I'm seeing someone else right now. He's not exactly happy about it, but I guess he has a right to know." She had then gone on to explain the situation with Ian, telling her mother of their last conversation together.

"You're already talking about having children," Sue had asked, growing pale.

"We didn't really talk about having kids," Kate had replied. "It was more like Ian telling me what his chances are for someday having a family."

"I see. Kate, I have to be honest, it sounds like Ian's getting pretty serious. Are you ready for this, sweetheart?" Sue had asked, searching her daughter's face. "Do you love him?"

"I don't know, Mom. That's what makes this so hard. I don't

know what I'm feeling or what I should do. I don't want to hurt anyone, including me."

Her mind coming back to the present, Kate gazed at Marie and Stephen. It was obvious that what they shared was special. She shifted her gaze to her parents, remembering all that her mother had told her about their courtship. "Be patient, Kate. Don't rush into anything. If it's meant to work out with Ian, things will fall into place," Sue had advised. "Put some prayer time in on this. Choosing an eternal companion is probably one of the most important decisions you'll ever make."

"No kidding," Kate thought to herself, glancing again at Marie and Stephen. They both looked radiant. A lump formed in Kate's throat. Marie had waited a long time to be this happy. Deciding to share in that happiness, Kate blocked out the troubling questions concerning her own future and walked across the room to talk to the newlyweds.

* * *

After Marie and Stephen drove off to start their life together, Kate took a few flowers from one of the bouquets in the Relief Society room and went to talk to an old friend. Bending down, Kate placed two white roses in front of the headstone, then glanced at the sky.

"Linda, I don't know if you can hear me, but I want you to know that your mom had a wonderful day today. She married one heck of a nice guy this afternoon. I think you'd really like him. Please be happy for her." Straightening, Kate leaned against the headstone. "Now for my latest problem. His name is Ian . . . and I don't know what I'm going to do."

CHAPTER THIRTY

Sue gazed around at the busy mall. She had been to Trolley Square before, but today's visit held special significance—she was having lunch with Kate, Sandi, Paige, and Ian. Ian was meeting them here at the Old Spaghetti Factory. He'd had to work today, so to kill time, the four females had spent most of the morning shopping. Tami had offered to watch Sabrina, and deciding the seven-year-old would enjoy spending some time with her cousins, Sue had agreed.

"Maybe we'd better head upstairs," Kate said, looking at her watch. "It's almost noon."

"Shouldn't we wait for Ian . . . you know, in case he needs help?"

Kate smiled at her mother. "He's not helpless, Mom. You'll see," she said, leading the way up the stairs.

"But how is he going to get up here?" Sue persisted.

"There's an elevator over there," Kate responded, pointing down the hall. "He'll be fine, unless we don't get a good table. Let's go save him a place."

Paige glanced at Sue. She had tried to tell her Ian was very independent—something she had learned herself the past few months.

"This is so cool," Sandi bubbled as they stepped inside the restaurant. "This is really where they kept the trolley cars?"

"They were kept in buildings like this one. They were called trolley car barns," Kate answered, pointing to the restored trolley car that was now part of the restaurant. "This complex housed one hundred and forty-four cars and provided transportation for the whole city in the early nineteen hundreds."

Taking in the occupants of the trolley car and the antique-filled room, Sandi noticed that several tables had been converted out of beds and old dining room sets, giving the restaurant an old-world look. She liked it immediately.

They waited until a waitress led them to an antique table with four matching chairs. "I can get another chair," the waitress offered. They had told her a fifth person would be joining them.

"That's okay, he brings his own," Kate responded, looking the table over. It was low enough, Ian would probably be fine in his wheelchair. Besides, she knew he was nervous about this meeting. The less he had to maneuver himself around her mother, the better.

"Would you like to order now, or when the other party arrives?" the tall waitress asked, giving Kate a funny look. She was still trying to figure out why a customer would bring his own chair.

"Could you bring us a couple of orders of garlic cheese bread? We'll nibble on that until Ian arrives, then order," Kate said quickly. "If that's okay with the rest of you." She glanced around the table.

"That would be fine," Paige said with a smile. Obviously her niece had come here before, and more than likely, with Ian.

"Sounds good," Sandi said, enjoying Kate's nervousness. She could hardly wait to meet this guy.

Sue nodded in agreement. After the waitress left, she turned to Kate. "Where are the menus? I don't see anything that mentions garlic bread."

"Here," Kate said, lifting up a folded paper next to her place setting. Unfolding the paper, she showed her mother. "The menu is printed on this side."

"Here he is now," Paige pointed out as Ian wheeled himself into the restaurant.

Sue forced a smile at the handsome young man dressed in an expensive suit. She wondered if that was for her benefit.

Kate began to fidget as she waited for Ian to move to the head of the table.

"Where's my chair?" he asked with a grin. "You did specify 'party of five,' didn't you Kate?"

"Well, yes, I thought maybe . . ." Her voice faltered as the waitress approached their table with the order of garlic bread.

"Just the woman I need to see," Ian said, wiggling his eyebrows. "We need another chair."

"Oh," the waitress answered, giving Kate an annoyed look. "Sorry, I'll be right back."

Wheeling himself closer to the table, Ian eyed the steaming garlic bread. "I guess before we dive in, we ought to have a few introductions," he said, grinning at Kate.

"Oh, yeah, sorry. Uh . . . Mom," Kate said, pointing to her mother, "this is Ian Campbell. Ian, this is my mother, Sue Erickson."

"I'm glad we finally get to meet," Ian said, reaching to shake her hand. "I've heard a lot about you."

"Hope it's all been good," Sue replied, impressed by his firm grip.

"Every bit of it," he answered, releasing her hand. "You must have a wonderful relationship with Kate. She thinks you're pretty great."

Sue glanced at Kate. "We've been through a lot together," she admitted.

"You know Aunt Paige, and this is Sandi Kearns," Kate hurriedly added, anxious to keep things moving along.

"Hi," Sandi said, staring at Ian strangely.

"Hello," he responded politely, a little discomfited by how Kate's best friend was looking at him. He couldn't read the expression on her face. It wasn't pity or repugnance, but it wasn't elation either. Deciding to brush it off as a form of nervousness, he smiled warmly at the attractive young woman, then at Paige, and finally at Sue. These were the women who had the most influence over Kate. It was important for him to make a good impression.

"Here's a chair," the waitress said, waiting as Ian moved out of the way. Setting the chair down, she marveled at the way Ian swung himself up into it. Kate quickly stood to help move his chair closer to the table.

"I've almost got her trained," Ian quipped as Kate folded his wheelchair and leaned it against his chair. A tiny crease appeared between his eyebrows, revealing he wasn't as amused as he had sounded.

"You've had more luck with her than I have," Paige teased. "I'm still trying to convince her the hamper was created for a purpose."

"You too, huh," Sue said, deciding to help Paige keep this as light as possible. She had also caught on that Ian was embarrassed by Kate's assistance. "I want you to know I did try to teach her."

"I don't even want to hear about it," Paige retorted with a grin.

"I pick up after myself," Kate said in her defense. "Most of the time."

"She does," Paige interjected. "I like to give her a bad time."

"Me too," Ian commented.

"Would you like more time before you order?" the waitress politely asked.

"I don't think that'll be necessary," Ian said brightly. "If it's okay with everyone we'll order now. Not only am I starved, but eventually I have to go back to work, unlike you shopaholics," he commented, glancing around at the bags they had already accumulated from the shops at Trolley Square.

"What would you recommend?" Sue asked, glancing at the menu.

"The special looks good, shrimp primavera. Anything they make here is wonderful. But if you order a hamburger, I'm leaving," Ian said, regaining his sense of humor. Reaching across the table, he enfolded Kate's hand inside of his. He knew she had only tried to help.

"I think I'll try the special," Sandi said to the waitress.

"Separate tickets?" the waitress asked.

"No," Sue said. "My treat."

"Well, in that case, I'll have one of everything," Ian said.

"Me too," Paige added.

The waitress rolled her eyes.

"Seriously, I'll have the special," Ian said.

"Same here," Kate agreed, smiling at Ian as she pulled her hand out of his. She didn't want Ian or her mother to get the wrong idea.

"I'll try the spaghetti with white clam sauce," Sue said.

"Well, if everyone else is going to settle for one item, I guess I'll do the same. Bring me the chicken parmigiana," Paige said.

"Anything to drink?" the waitress asked, glancing up.

"Kate's only eighteen, so I guess not," Ian joked. He avoided Kate's glare, focusing on his place setting. "Kidding. I'll settle for ice water." He gave Kate an apologetic smile.

"I'll have a diet Coke," Kate ordered, giving Ian a warning look.

"That'll be fine for me," Sue responded.

"And for me," Paige agreed.

"I'll have a root beer," Sandi said.

"Okay, got it," the waitress said. Paige could have sworn the woman breathed a sigh of relief as she moved away from their table.

* * *

"So, did I pass inspection?" Ian asked later as Kate walked him out to his van.

"They loved you. I'm the one who kept saying or doing all the wrong things."

"Go easy on yourself, kid. It could've happened to anybody," he said, in his best impression of Marlon Brando as the Godfather.

"I guess I was nervous," Kate said with a laugh.

"You're not the only one," Ian said, stopping beside his van.

"You, nervous? I don't believe it," Kate scoffed. "What could you possibly be nervous about?"

"This," Ian said as he brought Kate's face down close to his. Then, before she could argue or squirm away, he kissed her.

* * *

"Did you see that?" Sue demanded, staring out of the window. She was standing with Paige and Sandi near the door at the back of the plaza, waiting for Kate to rejoin them in their quest to explore the rest of the shops.

"Let's give them some privacy," Paige suggested as she attempted to steer her sister-in-law into a nearby shop. She glanced back at Sandi, wondering at the look on the young woman's face.

CHAPTER THIRTY-ONE

After returning to Paige's house, Sandi dragged Kate down to her room for a chat. "So, how was it?" she probed.

"Lunch or shopping? Both were great," Kate answered, purposely avoiding Sandi's question.

"Kate, we all saw him kiss you."

"Oh, nice! No wonder Mom kept giving me funny looks. Wait a minute, how could you have seen anything? You were all inside that boutique when I finally found you."

"Only because your aunt Paige dragged us in there. She thought we should give you two some privacy."

"How considerate of her."

"Again, how was it?"

"Truthfully?"

Sandi nodded.

"I didn't feel anything."

"You're kidding?"

Kate shook her head.

"And Ian?"

"I don't know. We didn't talk about it. He said he'd wanted to do that for a long time, thanked me for lunch, and promised he'd come by tonight for dinner."

"That's right, Paige invited him during lunch."

Kate nodded.

"Now what?"

"I don't know. Somehow we'll get through dinner and I'll try to talk to him later."

* * *

After dinner, Sandi wandered outside. It was chilly, but warmer than Bozeman. Moving to a picnic table in the back yard, she brushed off the light covering of snow and sat down. *Kate's right. You can't see the stars at night, not like at home or even Provo,* she thought to herself. Her breath came out in frosty plumes as she stared at the back of the house. Puzzled by what she was feeling, she reflected on everything that had happened this evening.

Kate had remained fairly quiet through most of the dinner, allowing Ian to be the center of attention. Kate's uncle Stan had fired off several questions concerning Ian's background and future. Ian had handled the questions with ease and humor, as though he did this kind of thing every day. Sandi had noticed how this had impressed Stan, as well as Sue. But what had really caught her eye was the way Ian's face had lit up every time he had looked at Kate. Glancing at Kate, she had seen how uncomfortable her friend was under his scrutiny.

After dinner, they had quickly cleared the table and began a rousing game of Split Second. The word game had put everyone at ease as they competed against each other for the most correct answer to the often ridiculous questions. As the night progressed, Sandi had found herself strangely drawn to Ian, to his easygoing personality and lighthearted laughter. But it was his dark brown eyes that had held her interest—eyes that reflected a poignant depth. Expressive eyes that had twinkled every time he had looked at Kate.

Sandi shivered. Ian had invited Kate to walk him to his van. "He's probably kissing her right now," she said to herself. She stood, trying to clear the image from her mind. "I just met the guy," she said softly. "I don't even know him."

* * *

"But you feel like you do?" Kate asked later as they sat on the bed in Kate's room.

Sandi slowly nodded. "It doesn't make sense. How could I have ever met him before today? We went to different schools, we have nothing in common . . ."

"*Au contraire,*" Kate said, imitating Ian. "You both know me."

"This isn't funny, Kate."

"Tell me about it," Kate sighed.

"Did he kiss you again tonight?" Sandi blurted out. "No, never mind. I don't want to know."

"As a matter of fact, he did."

"And?"

"Same as last time, for me anyway. Ian, on the other hand, looked like he'd floated into the ozone layer. I panicked, thinking he was going to get the wrong idea. I mean, I wouldn't have kissed him at all, but I had to be sure. Maybe this afternoon was a fluke. But when there was nothing again, I decided to be honest with him."

"What did you say?"

"I said, 'Ian, I think we have a problem.' I told him that I liked him . . . a lot . . . but I didn't think a serious relationship between us was going to work."

"Is he okay?"

"I don't know. He made a couple of bad jokes and left."

"He must be devastated," Sandi said, concerned.

"I didn't want to hurt him, but I had to be honest. You saw how he was looking at me tonight. I know he really wanted it to work between us, but it's not happening, not the way he wants it to."

"Can you still be friends?"

"I hope so. Tomorrow we're supposed to go see the lady he helped me find, Sylvia Myers." Kate closed her eyes, then opened them to slap at her pillow. "Dang it! Why did he have to kiss me? It ruins everything!"

"Maybe," Sandi said thoughtfully. "Maybe it had to happen like this."

"What are you saying?"

"I'm not sure. I've felt some really weird things today, feelings that were even stronger tonight."

Kate gazed steadily at Sandi. "Like thinking you've met him before?"

Sandi nodded.

"You really like Ian, don't you," Kate asked, gazing at her friend. She smiled when Sandi blushed.

"I just met him."

"I know. But you're feeling something for him, I can tell."

"I don't think—"

"You're coming with us tomorrow."

"What? I can't. I told my roommates I'd head to Provo tomorrow. I've already made arrangements to catch a ride with two girls from Salt Lake."

"There's the phone. Give 'em a call."

Sandi stared at Kate. "It's too late."

"All right. First thing in the morning."

"We'll see," Sandi said.

"Sandi, it won't hurt anything to have you along tomorrow. In fact, it might help . . . a lot. And it'll give you a chance to spend more time with Ian. Who knows, maybe something could develop with you two," Kate said, a mischievous glint in her eye.

"I could say you're trying to make yourself feel better by brushing your problem off onto me."

"You could," Kate admitted. "But you'd be wrong and we both know it."

"Maybe," Sandi said slowly. "Kate, this is silly."

"Maybe. Then again, maybe not."

CHAPTER THIRTY-TWO

Sandi yawned. She hadn't slept much at all, unlike Kate who had snored softly by her side. Looking in the mirror one final time, she pulled a face. "You look like walking death," she said to herself. Nevertheless, the soft tone of her new pink sweater enhanced her natural coloring and made her skin glow. Combined with the new jeans she had found on sale yesterday, she looked very attractive, in spite of several uncontrollable yawns.

"Are you about ready?" Kate asked, poking her head in the small bathroom. "Ian called from his cellular phone. He'll be here any minute."

"He's still speaking to you?"

"I guess so," Kate said. "He sounded kind of distant."

"Some cellular phones are like that," Sandi replied, smiling in the mirror at Kate.

"You know what I mean. He's more upset than I thought."

"Can't imagine why. A beautiful young woman merely told him that his kiss did nothing for her. Why let a little thing like that mess up your day?!"

"Smart aleck," Kate accused, pushing Sandi out of the bathroom. "Let's grab our coats."

"Kate! Sandi!" Paige called down the stairs. "Ian is here."

"Told you he's prompt," Kate said, collecting her coat from the couch in the family room. "We're coming," she hollered. She raced Sandi up the stairs.

"You two behave yourselves this morning," Sue said, blocking their way out of the house. She was very much aware that something was up, but she hadn't wanted to drag it out of Kate.

"We'll be good," Kate promised. A loud honk emphasized Ian's arrival. "And we'd better go, or we'll miss our ride." She brushed her mother's cheek with a quick kiss before heading out the front door. Sandi followed close behind.

"What's going on with those three?" Sue asked, watching as Kate and Sandi climbed inside Ian's van.

"I'm not sure," Paige admitted. "This isn't like Ian. Usually he comes to the door."

"The way Kate and Sandi hustled downstairs last night after he left, I know something's up," Sue said.

"All we can do is wait. They'll tell us when they're ready," Paige replied.

* * *

The address Kate had been given was in Bountiful, in a subdivision of beautiful homes not far from the new LDS temple. As Ian skillfully followed the curves in the road, Kate and Sandi quietly watched the scenery going by.

"Look at that home," Sandi said, pointing at a grey brick house.

"It's nice," Kate agreed. "What do you think, Ian?"

"Yeah," was the curt reply. Ian hadn't said much since picking up the two friends.

Kate shared a hurt look with Sandi. This wasn't going as well as she had hoped.

"What was that address again?" Ian asked.

Stung by the acidic tone of his voice, Kate handed him the paper it was written on.

Ian saw the pained expression, but refused to acknowledge it, convinced he was the injured party. Silently, he pulled up in the correct driveway. "There you are, ladies," he said sullenly. "Have at it," he added, using the remote control to open the side door.

"Thank you so much," Kate snapped. "C'mon, Sandi," she said as she slipped out of the van.

"You're not coming in?" Sandi asked, distressed by the way Ian was lashing out at Kate.

"No thanks. I've had my fill of stories," he said.

"Stories?" Sandi prompted.

"Fairy tales, happy endings, that kind of thing." He undid the safety straps around his wheelchair and reached down to unlock the wheels. "Never mind me, I got up on the wrong side of the wheelchair this morning," he said, hating the way Sandi was looking at him.

"Ian," Kate said sharply, "if you want to stay out here and pout, that's your choice. And if you want to leave, we can always call Aunt Paige to come get us later." Turning, she moved angrily toward the house.

"Temper, temper," Ian retorted. Then, glancing at Sandi, he forced a smile. "Enjoy your visit."

"You're serious about leaving?"

"Yes. I got her here, just like I promised. Someone else can come get her royal highness!" he added, increasing his volume so Kate could hear. Purposely turning her back to the van, Kate pushed the doorbell. A few seconds later, a small boy let her into the house.

"Better hurry, she'll leave you in the dust too!" Ian snapped.

"Ian, stop it," Sandi said firmly. "This is ridiculous. Especially when you two have been so close."

"Key words: *have been,*" Ian said. "I never should've agreed to drive you two out here this morning. The end in a series of mistakes that began when I thought someone like Kate could care for me."

"She does care for you, and if you weren't feeling so sorry for yourself, you'd see that!"

"That's right. How did she put it last night? She cares for me as a friend. Just what I always wanted."

"She was trying to be honest with you."

"Well, she succeeded. I got the message loud and clear."

"Did you? I don't think so. She has feelings for you, but not like you were hoping. She loves you as a sister would love a brother."

"Isn't that special?" Ian snorted. "I don't want another sister, I want a wife! An eternal companion! Is that too much to ask? Maybe it is, I don't know. First Toni walks away, now Kate, and I can't even follow because I'm stuck in this stupid chair." He turned away from Sandi, knowing his emotions were getting the best of him.

"Ian, I realize it's been rough, but you're not the only one hurting—and you're not the only one who has had to face challenges in this life."

"I don't need a lecture."

"I won't lecture, but there are some things about Kate I think you ought to know."

"Yeah, like what? Let me guess. She once broke a fingernail."

Sandi opened the passenger side of the van and climbed in beside him. "You really don't know Kate, do you?" she asked as she shut the door. "She didn't tell you what she's been through, did she?"

"What are you talking about?"

"Not what, who. I'm talking about Kate, someone you apparently don't know as well as you think you do. Tell me, Ian, during all this time you two have spent together, did you ever once ask her about her life, her trials, her dreams?"

Ian gazed steadily at Sandi. What was she getting at? "We talked . . . we talked a lot . . . about things. Important things."

"Like what?"

"Genealogy. Her schooling. The Church. Our testimonies."

"Did she tell you what she's personally had to face this past year?"

"Well, no," he admitted. "She always seems so happy, so positive about things," he said in his defense. "Except when her eyes flash." Remembering, the corners of his mouth turned up. "I don't think I've ever met a girl with more spunk." Ian glanced at the determined look on Sandi's face. "Then again, I could be wrong about that."

"Thanks," Sandi said dryly. "Ian, the point I'm trying to make is that some trials are more visible than others. Kate has been through more than you could possibly imagine."

Ian self-consciously scratched behind one ear. "If she's had such a hard time of it, why didn't she say anything?"

"Because that's the kind of person she is. She's not one to complain, and when she does, there's usually a good reason for it."

"So, tell me. What challenges has Kate had in her life, besides me?" he asked quietly.

Hoping Kate wouldn't kill her later, Sandi took a deep breath and began with the accident that had happened a year and a half ago in Salt Lake.

"I can't believe she didn't tell me about any of this," Ian said when Sandi finally finished. "How does she deal with all of it?"

"Time, her testimony, and it helps to have friends like you and me—people who can pick her up when life knocks her down." She gazed at Ian. "I'll be honest with you. I was really worried about her coming to Salt Lake. I was afraid if she had too much time on her hands, everything would start getting to her. I kept praying she would find a good friend. When she first told me about you, I knew my prayer had been answered."

"Then I had to go and ruin everything by playing Romeo!" He slapped the armrest of his wheelchair.

"Don't blame yourself, you didn't know."

"She had told me about Mike and Randy. Not a lot of details, just that she was confused about picking between them." He grimaced. "Silly me, I was convinced that was where I came in."

"She never meant to hurt you," Sandi said softly. "We were up half the night talking about it. She was afraid you were reading something into your relationship that wasn't there. And when you kissed her—"

"She figured she better put the brakes on." He stared down at his hands. "I feel like such a jerk. I was so caught up in having someone like her by my side, I was convinced she and I . . ." his voice trailed off.

"It'll happen someday," Sandi soothed.

"Right! And if it does, how am I supposed to tell? I was convinced Kate was the one."

"Did you pray about it?"

"Yeah, sort of."

"Sort of?"

"I already knew the answer I wanted. I didn't wait around for a heavenly reply. Then when I kissed her . . . I don't know. It was nice, but not like I thought it would be. Either time." He sighed thoughtfully. "I think a part of me realized it wasn't right between us—but I didn't want to believe it. Even when Kate tried to tell me."

"Instead, you got angry and tried to hurt her today like you thought she had hurt you last night."

"Go ahead, tell me what a cretin I am."

"Don't be so hard on yourself. I think you're very sweet when you want to be." He looked so dejected, Sandi impulsively leaned forward to kiss his cheek.

Following through on an impulse of his own, Ian mischievously turned his head, his lips brushing Sandi's as Kate came out of the house. Shocked, Kate froze in place. Clutching the package in her hands, she gaped as her two best friends kissed again, then pulled apart to stare at each other.

"I guess my lips aren't defective, after all," Ian said, grinning.

"Guess not," Sandi murmured.

"What was that anyway?" Ian asked, his eyes bright with excitement.

"I'm not sure," Sandi replied, blushing.

"We'd better try it again to see," he said.

"Ian," Sandi warned.

"In the name of science," he said, rolling toward her, "to adequately assess the situation." Sandi sputtered a protest, then gave up as the attraction between them overpowered her sense of propriety.

Kate walked to the van and cleared her throat. "It's nice you two were able to kiss and make up," she said, lifting an eyebrow.

"Isn't it?" Ian sighed as a flustered Sandi quickly pulled away.

"I . . . oh, Kate, uh, hi. How did it go?" Sandi stammered.

"Obviously not as well as things went in here," she said, enjoying Sandi's embarrassment.

"Get in, Kate," Ian said reaching for the remote to close the side door. "I think it's time we took you home."

CHAPTER THIRTY-THREE

L et me get this straight," Sue asked, staring at her daughter. "Ian and Sandi dropped you off so they can spend *quality time alone?*"

"Yes, indeed," Kate said, grinning. "Like two peas in a pod, those two. I even had to ride in the back coming home."

"I don't know about you, but I'm confused," Sue said, exchanging a puzzled look with Paige, who nodded in agreement.

"It's simple. Romantically speaking, things weren't working out with Ian and me. It was pretty obvious after we—" Kate blushed. "When we kissed, it just wasn't there—you know, like we talked about, Mom."

Sue nodded. "I wondered. Yesterday, when you caught up with us at the boutique, you didn't look like someone who was reeling from a passionate farewell."

"That's one way to put it," Paige commented, glancing from her embarrassed niece to her sister-in-law.

Shifting around on the couch, Sue sat at an angle that would allow a clearer view of her daughter's face. "Two things bother me about this."

"What?" Kate asked, settling back against the couch.

"Your reaction, for starters. You're really okay about this?"

"Yes. I'm fine, Mom. Ian and I are friends, nothing more. This is the best possible solution."

"Is it, or is Ian grabbing at Sandi on the rebound?" Sue flushed as Kate winced and Paige muffled a chuckle. "Sorry, poor choice of words. But you know what I'm trying to say."

"Yeah," Kate murmured. "I'll admit, Ian was hurt over what I told him last night—"

"Which was?" Sue probed.

"That a serious relationship wasn't going to work between us."

"No wonder he stayed out in the van and honked this morning," Paige said.

"He was so ornery, I thought I'd made a mistake by dragging Sandi along. But, after what Sandi told me last night, I wanted to give them a chance to get to know each other a little better."

"Sounds like it worked," Paige said with a smile.

"Tell me about it. I still can't believe it happened. Ian was so angry, he wanted to drop us off in Bountiful and let someone else pick us up. How things developed from there into romance, I have no idea. I stormed into the house and Sandi stayed in the van to talk to Ian. When I came out later, they were . . . getting along very well," Kate said, grinning.

"So I gathered," Sue said dryly.

"It'll be okay, Mom, Sandi really likes him. She told me last night that she felt like they'd met somewhere before, which is about next to impossible, at least, in this life. Maybe they were acquainted in the premortal life."

"Maybe," Paige said lightly. "That would explain the look on her face at the Spaghetti Factory, and last night at dinner," Paige observed. "Still, this is happening awfully fast."

"I know, but I feel like it'll work out between them."

Sue shuddered. "Tell me I don't have to break the news to Harriet," she pleaded.

"Aw, c'mon, be a sport," Kate teased. "Ow!" she exclaimed as her mother pinched her leg.

"So, now that Ian has discovered other *interests*, will you start giving those young men from LDS Business College a chance?" Paige asked, hoping her stint as telephone go-between was over. She had lost count of the calls she had taken on Kate's behalf.

"No way," Kate said, rising from the couch. She rubbed at the side of her leg, giving her mother a dirty look. "I'm swearing off men for a while—they're nothing but trouble. Besides, I have more important work to attend to."

"Like what?" Sue asked, secretly relieved.

"Like this journal Mrs. Myers gave me today," Kate said, picking up the package she had set on the coffee table.

"She gave you a journal?" Paige asked, excitedly reaching for the small white sack.

"Ah, ah, ah—this is my little project, right?" Kate said, as she shook her finger at her aunt.

"Okay." Paige sat back in her chair.

"So I get first dibs. I'll catch you guys later," she said, moving to the stairs with her treasured find.

"Remember to come up for air," Paige replied as Kate started to bounce downstairs.

"Will do," Kate responded. "Send food."

"You'll have to come upstairs to eat," Sue countered. "We want to see you at least part of the time we're here."

"Okay," Kate said grudgingly.

"By the way, your Uncle Stan managed to get tickets for that play tonight," Paige reminded her niece. "Are you still planning on going?"

Kate nodded.

"What do we do with Sandi's ticket?"

"I doubt she'll be needing it," Kate laughed. "Call Tami."

"Good idea," Paige answered, watching with amusement as Kate hurried downstairs.

"Do you think she's all right?" Sue worriedly asked.

"Would she be bubbling like that if she wasn't? She told us things weren't working out with her and Ian. I think what's happening between Sandi and Ian is great. Maybe it was supposed to turn out this way. I doubt Sandi would've met Ian without Kate in the picture."

"You're probably right," Sue replied, following her sister-in-law into the kitchen to help fix lunch. "I hope Sandi and Ian know what they're getting into."

"Did we?"

"No." Sue smiled. "I guess that's something we all discover for ourselves."

CHAPTER THIRTY-FOUR

Kate could hardly wait to get her hands on the journal Sylvia Myers had given her. As the older woman had talked to her, she had described a branch of the family tree that was entirely unknown. People who were distantly related, but unfamiliar. Kate gazed at the pedigree chart Sylvia had given her. According to it, Sylvia's husband, John Myers, had been a nephew of Kate's great-grandmother, Helen. John Myers had also been a grandson to John MacOwen, Helen's father. The journal had belonged to Meg Kelly MacOwen, wife of John MacOwen, and mother of Helen.

"There aren't many of us left who know the family legends," Sylvia had told Kate. As such, Kate wanted to get with Sylvia before she went back to St. George to record some of those stories for future reference.

"My hands have been so crippled by arthritis, I haven't been able to do much with John's side of the family. I'm afraid that'll be up to young people like you," Sylvia had said. "This journal was found in Scotland by one of my husband's cousins. When I wrote to them years ago, asking for information about the family, they eventually sent me this and a couple of old photographs." She had sighed, staring into the past. "I thought maybe we'd be able to get going on the temple work that needs to be done. But we moved several times after that and as time went on, I forgot about this journal. That is, until you contacted me." With crooked fingers bent with pain, Sylvia handed Kate the small white sack that contained the journal. "Keep it safe. There may come a time when my grandchildren will want it back. In the meantime, I hope it will help with your research. This family has waited a long time to be joined together."

Kate had solemnly nodded, acutely aware of what she was undertaking. Now as she removed the journal from the sack, she caressed its worn cover. Opening the small book, she began to read.

August 25, 1881

This is the journal of Meg Kelly MacOwen. My current plight has given me cause to finally use this gift from my father. Upon these pages I will record all that does now transpire. I do this in the hopes that my beloved husband, John MacOwen, may soon be guided to my side. On that day, I will present this to him that he may know the suffering I have endured at the hand of his mother.

Kate blinked at this strange inscription. Curious, she turned the page to read the first entry.

August 25, 1881

No one knows the agony I suffer. I tried to speak with the headmaster, but he avoids me as the plague. No one else will listen, so it is to this journal that I reveal my heart. How it aches for you, John. I vow that whatever it takes, I will find my way back to you. As yet, an opportunity has to present itself, but each night I pray to God, trusting He knows of my pain. That it was delivered by your mother, John, has been a bitter blow indeed. How she must hate me to have left me in such dire circumstances.

I will tell you all, knowing you will find it difficult to comprehend. We have both known her feelings toward me, which is why we did not tell her of our secret marriage. It was unbearable, knowing I was your wife, and yet being treated as the lowest form of life imaginable, lower than the cattle that roam your father's land.

In July, nearly a month after we had wed, I sensed a softening in your mother. Instead of the harsh word, kindness. Instead of angry criticism concerning any task I set out to do, compliments. I thought perhaps she had made peace with the thought of a lowly servant girl loving her son. I couldn't have been more wrong. Trusting in her good intentions, I came at her beckoning on this journey, being told nothing save it was to aid me in the service of her household.

She has brought me to a dressmaking school, with promises of an increase in wages for securing this extra training. Fool that I was, I believed her to be sincere when she explained I was to remain for a short time and she would send for me at a later date. She assured me you knew of this arrangement and had approved. Not wanting to reveal the truth of our relationship, I believed all, desiring to stay in her ladyship's good graces.

I have been here for three weeks and nary a word has been sent. Not from you, nor her, and when I was finally permitted to speak to the headmaster, I was informed that I am to remain here until such time as Lady Mary MacOwen deems it is convenient for my return. I have tried to send letters, realizing they are most likely burned. I'm being held here as a prisoner no less. A great deal of money has most likely exchanged hands, money that means more than the life of a servant girl.

Kate breathed out slowly. "I can't believe this," she muttered, skimming through the pages. "How could someone do that . . . and to my great-great-grandmother?" After a moment's pause, Kate continued to read.

October 21, 1881

I wait for you, John. Weeks have gone by and still there is no word. The hours drag into days, my heart aching with despair as I wonder where you are, if you are well, and what you must think of me. I pray you will remember what we have meant to one another, that you will not forget the holy bond between us. Despite what your mother has done, we must find a way to be together. The love we share cannot be ravaged by time nor distance; somehow we will scale the walls hate has placed between us.

The child I carry is growing. Soon those around me will guess this other secret I have guarded. Daily I plead with God to direct you to this place. I cling to that hope, but the days are long and difficult. Tonight, the words to a song my mother used to sing come to mind:

"Ye banks and braes o' bonnie Doon, how can ye bloom sae fresh and fair?

How can ye chant, ye little birds and I sae weary, fu' o' care.

Thou'll break my heart, thou warbling birds, that wantons through the flow'ring thorn,

Thou minds me o' departed joys, departed never to return."

Sniffing, Kate set the journal down. As she reached for a tissue from the box resting on the nightstand, her mother called to her, informing her that lunch was ready.

* * *

"His mother left her there?" Sue asked, staring with disbelief at Kate.

"Yes. Can you imagine how Meg must've felt?" Kate asked, in between mouthfuls of her aunt's homemade clam chowder.

"It must've been difficult," Paige commented, gazing across the bar in the kitchen at her niece. "Did John ever find her?"

"I don't know," Kate answered. "Someone thought I needed to eat."

"It's my job," Sue said, smiling at Kate. Then, as Sabrina tugged on her sleeve, she focused on her younger daughter. "What do you need, honey?"

"More crackers," Sabrina lisped, pointing at the package next to Kate.

"Here you go, Breeny," Kate said, pushing the crackers toward her sister.

"Sabrina," the seven-year-old insisted.

"Sabrina," Kate repeated, trying not to smile. Recently Sabrina had decided Breeny was a baby name.

Paige took a sip of ice water then said, "I have to admit, this is a family story I've never heard before."

"What really gets me, is how John's mother treated Meg," Kate insisted. "Meg loved John. Why couldn't his mother accept that?"

"Well," Paige started, glancing at Sue to see if her sister-in-law wanted to offer insight on the subject. Sue motioned for her to continue. "There used to be a real class distinction between the rich and the poor. It was severely frowned upon if one mingled with the other, especially when it came to marriage. John came from a wealthy family. When he secretly married a servant girl—"

"But they loved each other. I can't believe his own mother would do everything in her power to keep them apart," Kate interrupted.

"She didn't know about the marriage, right?" Sue asked, selecting a slice of homemade bread.

Kate nodded.

"So, she didn't know she'd hauled off her daughter-in-law."

"And grandchild," Kate pointed out.

"True. If she'd known, things might've turned out differently," Sue said.

"I doubt it," Paige countered. "I've read several histories from that era. A lot of cruel things took place when people disagreed, especially when it involved money, or the lack of it."

"I can't believe money meant more than people's lives."

Paige looked thoughtfully at her niece. "The sad thing is, it still does. Watch the news some time."

"That's a depressing thought," Kate said, rising from her stool to carry her bowl to the sink.

"I gather you're heading back down to read more of that journal?"

Kate nodded at her mother. "Holler at me when you're ready to go to the theater."

"Don't you want to eat supper first?" Paige asked.

"Maybe. Depends on what I get into," Kate replied, moving out of the kitchen.

"Stubborn lass," Paige observed.

"Feisty too," Sue added.

"Sounds like someone else I know," Paige said, winking at her sister-in-law.

CHAPTER THIRTY-FIVE

March 8, 1882

*J*ohn, our child—our son, for I am convinced it is a boy who frolics
about beneath my heart—will soon be born, without his father, without
his name. The whispered stories by the other girls have never ceased. It is
rumored I was brought here to hide some lord's shame. I am looked down
upon, scorned as it were by those who have done much worse. There are
days when it is all I can do to hold my tongue. Only the memory of my
sainted mother keeps me from telling all. Always the lady, poor though we
were, she it was who ever reminded me to observe my manners. It was
her insistence that saw me through the few years of schooling granted me.
After her passing, my poor father, in seeking ways to manage, felt it more
important that I find work. So it was that instead of a schoolmate, I
became your servant, John, a maid to those more fortunate than I. I did
not mind it so much, bowing the knee to a laird such as yourself. Those
were moments of sweet joy, unmarred by the bleakness that now fills my
days.

"Why didn't he come for her?" Kate asked, carefully thumbing
through the brittle pages. She paused at an entry in April that
caught her eye.

April 2, 1882

Oh, dear John, why do ye not come? The pain I bear is beyond what I can endure. Our child is no more, passing from this life without so much as a whimper, for he ne'er took a breath. When will the bitter cup pass from me? When will the pain cease to be?

Sucking in sharply, Kate glanced through the entries made on the following pages. A few revealed the despondency Meg had slipped into. Some spoke of the great love she had for John. Others asked why God would permit her to suffer in this manner. Still others radiated a stubborn faith that would see her through to the end. Finally, an entry in June gave Kate the answer she had been seeking.

June 16, 1882

I can scarce believe all that has transpired these past few days. John has come at last! I was by an upstairs window sewing when I heard the sound of a horse approaching. Thinking nothing of it, I continued to work on the garment in my hand. Then it was I heard the bells. Bells that rang out John's presence as nothing else could. Not believing my ears, I stared out the window, my husband riding sure and strong, the bells of his riding outfit singing out in grandeur. Overcome, I fell to the floor. That is how my dear husband found me, lying prostrate, two of the girls trying to bring me 'round. Fearing the worst, he knelt at my side, holding me against him until I regained my senses. At once crying and laughing, we clung to each other, certain we would never let the other go.

John's mother had never told him of my location. He had no knowledge of his mother's role in my disappearance, having been told only that I had left his family's employ. He had spent these many months searching for word of where I had gone and why. Having no way to contact my father or family, as they had all returned to Ireland four years ago to take over my grandfather's small farm, he was beside himself with worry. By chance at the first of this month, he came across my brother, Rupert, who had come back to Campbeltown, Scotland, to attend the horse fairs held the latter part of May. Rupert had been laid low by a vicious bout of pneumonia. I am certain God had a hand in my brother's illness, timing his recovery when my husband would be in town, seeking for signs of his missing wife.

Overjoyed at finding his brother-in-law, John asked if I had returned to Ireland, the place of my birth. Dismayed by my husband's inquiry, Rupert told John of a letter they had received concerning my whereabouts. The letter had stated simply that for a time, I would be continuing my education at a dressmaking school in Lochgilphead, Scotland, this brought about by the kind generosity of the MacOwens.

Puzzled, but not willing to go to his family for an explanation until he had first come to me, John rode from Campbeltown without pausing for food nor rest, save only for the welfare of his horse.

After his arrival, when we were able to talk, it pained me to tell John of our son's death, and his mother's role in my disappearance. Stunned, then angered by her actions, he took me from the school that has been a prison for so long, vowing to have nothing more to do with the MacOwen clan.

We are currently aboard a small vessel that will take us to Ireland. Rupert had told John we would be welcome to join the family there. It is with mixed emotions that I return to my native land. We will make our home in Billy Antrim, among people who will allow our love to thrive.

CHAPTER THIRTY-SIX

The Erickson family was reunited when Greg and Tyler arrived in Salt Lake to join Sue, Kate, and Sabrina at the Mahoney home. Preparations were already underway to see in the new year. Everyone worked together to set the house in order and to fix the trays of food that would feed the invasion of family and friends.

Stan and Paige's oldest daughter, Tami came with her husband, Jason, and their small twin boys, Will and Phil. Kyle came, bringing his fiancée, Tina, who was a tall, attractive blonde. Ian had also been invited to the party, and he had driven to Provo to bring Sandi with him.

The small crowd gathered downstairs in the family room eagerly anticipating the countdown to midnight. When Kate noticed that the supply of hors-d'oeuvres she had helped Paige prepare earlier was disappearing at an alarming rate, she headed upstairs for another tray.

"Kate," Sandi said, following her. "Wait up. Where are you going?"

"To get fresh supplies," Kate replied, grinning down at her friend. "What's a party without food?"

"Good point. Need some help?"

"If it's all right with Ian." Kate glanced down at Ian who was arguing with Tyler and Kyle about an upcoming bowl game. The three of them had become fast friends after Tyler and Kyle had helped Ian maneuver downstairs. "Looks like he's occupied for the moment."

"I know," Sandi said, pushing Kate up the stairs ahead of her. "Besides, who says I have to have his permission?"

"Trouble in paradise already?" Kate quizzed as they walked through the dining room.

"No. It's just . . . let's go into the kitchen."

Kate nodded, leading the way. Once in the kitchen, she opened a cupboard and selected a box of crackers.

"We haven't had a chance to talk since Ian and I—" Sandi stammered.

"Became an item," Kate helpfully suggested, reaching into the refrigerator for a bottle of cheese spread.

Sandi gave Kate a funny look.

"What's up?"

"I'm not sure I can explain."

"Try me. What's eating you?"

"Ian. Kate, I'm so scared," Sandi confessed, climbing onto a bar stool.

"About what?" Kate asked, opening a can of olives. She walked over to the sink to drain them, then handed the can to Sandi. "While you're telling me, make yourself useful. These need to be sliced."

Sandi obediently reached for the cutting board that was still sitting on the bar. Kate handed her a knife.

"What has Ian done now?" Kate asked as she began spreading cheese onto the crackers.

"He thinks we're supposed to get married."

Kate stared at Sandi. "Already?"

Sandi nodded.

"You've been out, what, twice? Three times, counting tonight?"

"I know. The thing is, in a way, I think he's right—but it's happening so fast." She closed her eyes.

"Put the knife down before you cut off a finger," Kate advised.

Sandi opened her eyes, setting the knife on the cutting board.

"He proposed?"

"No, not in so many words," Sandi sighed. "He came down to Provo last night. We went for a drive and ended up near the temple grounds."

"Sounds romantic," Kate said. "Cold, but romantic."

"It was. We left the van and moved around to the front of the temple. It was so beautiful. This time of year, the snow around it looks like a mantle. Combine that with the way the lights contrast with the sky—"

"Uh-oh," Kate commented.

"I know. It was so inspiring, we talked about a lot of serious things, including temple marriage. Ian said that he wants a marriage based on eternal promises."

Kate reached for the olives and began to slice them. "With you?"

"He didn't come right out and say it. But he did tell me that he'd prayed about us."

"And?"

"He's convinced we were supposed to meet."

"How do you feel about that?"

Sandi pulled a face. "I don't know. I like him a lot . . . I might even be falling in love with him, but I don't think I'm ready for this right now. I've only been to college for six months. I want to get my degree. I've always wanted that."

"A lot of people get their degrees after they're married. It's not like you would have to put Ian through school. He's already been there, done that. He could put you through."

"I suppose you're right. The thing is, besides getting a degree, you know I've always planned to serve a mission. If I marry Ian . . ."

"No mission until you're old and grey," Kate said, finishing the sentence. "You could still do a lot of missionary work with the people around you. Remember that lesson Lori taught us when we were Laurels, the one about every member a missionary?"

"I know what you're saying, Kate, but, there's so much to consider, it's overwhelming."

"Like what?" Kate asked, poking the sliced olives on top of the cheese smeared crackers.

"Like kids. I've always wanted a large family, like the one I grew up with. You told me yourself, Ian might not be able—"

"I said there was a chance he could. Think positively."

"And if it doesn't happen?"

"You could adopt. A lot of kids out there need a good home. You and Ian would have one of the best."

"You really think so?" Sandi looked hopefully at Kate, who nodded. "Do you really think it could work?"

"The question is, do you?" Kate countered. "I know things are moving fast with you two, but sometimes, when it's right, it happens that way. That's how it was for my mom and dad."

"Serious?"

Kate nodded. "Mom and I never really talked about it until I went home this last time. I think it scared her when Paige mentioned Ian was a returned missionary. That night you and I went out with Mike and Keith—"

"Yeah?" Sandi impatiently interrupted.

"Mom stayed up till I came home. She had a batch of hot chocolate ready and waiting."

"One of *those* talks."

"Uh-huh. Actually, it was pretty neat. She told me how she and dad had met at Ricks College the first year she was there."

"She went to Ricks?"

"After working for a year to raise the money."

"How did she meet your dad?"

"He was in her bowling class."

"She took bowling?"

"It counted as one of her P.E. credits. Mom wasn't into sports much. She figured bowling would be easier than some of the other choices."

"And?"

"They went out a few times, and Dad proposed."

"So she was what, nineteen when she got married?"

"Twenty. By the time they got everything arranged, she'd had another birthday. But it was only seven months from the time they met until they were married." Kate grinned. "And a year later, they were blessed with me."

"Did your mom ever wonder if she'd made the right choice?"

"Probably several times, especially after I came along."

"Seriously," Sandi said.

"She told me it frightened her when she sensed Dad was getting serious. So, she went home to talk to her mother."

"And?"

"Grandma told her to pray about it, and then asked her a couple of questions."

"What kind of questions?" Sandi asked.

"Like, how would she would feel if my dad— or in your case, Ian, went out with someone else?"

"I'd kill him," Sandi said intensely, then shook her head. "Where did that come from?"

"Your heart. Which pretty much answers my next question. Do you love him?"

Sandi squirmed around on the stool, trying to avoid Kate's probing gaze.

"Well?"

"I . . . think so."

"You think so?"

"That's what's so hard. I've never been in love before. How am I supposed to recognize what I'm feeling?"

"Did Keith or Bill make you feel the same way Ian does?"

Sandi blushed, shaking her head. "This is so complicated."

"I know what you're going through. I had this same conversation with myself several times, especially concerning Ian."

"And we all know how that turned out," Sandi retorted.

"How do you feel when you're with Ian?" Kate asked, ignoring the snide remark.

"That's the problem. I feel so many different things, I don't know what's going on inside of me. I admire his courage. I love the way he laughs, the way he can joke about things that aren't funny. He treats me with such respect, and yet, can tease me until I'm nearly crazy. When he's with me, I feel so alive. When he's not, I feel like a part of me is missing. And when he touches me . . ." Sandi glanced at Kate. "Let's just say, I understand now why you and Mike had to cool things down."

"Hmmm."

"Hmmm—what?"

"I think you've got it pretty bad."

"Got what?" Sandi asked with exasperation.

"What my mom calls twitterpation. You described exactly how she felt when she started going out with Dad. Something that was missing when Ian and I were dating."

"Now what?" Sandi asked. "Kate, this whole thing scares me. I guess that's my problem. I know how I feel about Ian and it frightens me."

"What's that saying Mrs. Marks used to hit us with just before a big test?"

"'There is nothing to fear but fear itself,'" Sandi repeated. "What the heck does that mean anyway?"

Kate shrugged. "Until we figure it out, I guess we go by faith and prayer."

"I definitely need both. Which reminds me, how in the world am I going to tell Mom?"

"Does this mean you're going to take Ian seriously?"

"What makes you think I haven't?"

"If he asked you tonight, you'd say yes?"

"Maybe. On the other hand, can you imagine how Mom is going to react?"

"Sounds like a personal problem," Kate teased, setting the hors d'oeuvres on the tray.

"You're a lot of help!" Sandi said, sliding down off the stool to glare at Kate.

"I'm sure my mother would be happy to talk to your mom about it, after you break the news to Harriet, of course."

"Harriet?"

"I'm sorry, where are my manners? What I meant to say was, Sister Kearns, mother of Sandi, future mother-in-law of—"

"Who's a future mother-in-law?" Sue asked, staring at her daughter as she entered the kitchen. "Sandi, is there something you haven't told us?"

"'Us' meaning me, too," Paige said, walking in behind Sue. "We were beginning to wonder what you two were up to. A certain young man is requesting your presence downstairs," she added, smiling at Sandi. "Maybe now I understand why."

"He didn't . . . we aren't . . . I think I'll go downstairs," Sandi stammered, retreating downstairs.

"What was that all about?" Sue demanded after Sandi had disappeared down the stairs.

"Remember when you volunteered to talk to Sandi's mom

about Ian?" Kate asked.

"I never volunteered—she's engaged?"

"Not yet, but odds are it'll happen in the very near future," Kate said, heading out of the kitchen with the tray of crackers.

"Katherine Colleen Erickson, get back here," Sue commanded.

"Sorry, I have hungry mouths to feed," Kate replied, heading down the stairs.

"Such an obedient child," Paige said as she began to clean up the mess Kate had left behind.

"I keep telling you, she takes after her father," Sue responded, picking up the empty olive can. "If only this can could talk," she sighed, discarding it in the garbage container beneath the sink.

"We'd probably both regret it," Paige said as she wiped up the counter top. "I have a feeling neither of us really wants to know what was said in this room."

"Unfortunately, I already have a pretty good idea," Sue replied. "And let me just say that I am *not* getting involved, especially when it concerns Harriet Kearns."

CHAPTER THIRTY-SEVEN

Sue nervously fingered the cord in her hand. "You owe me, Kate," she murmured under her breath. "Hello, Harriet? This is Sue Erickson . . . I'm fine, how are you? . . . Good, good . . .Yes, we got back late last night . . . The roads were bare most of the way. Say, I was wondering if we could get together for lunch this afternoon . . . my treat." Sue forced a laugh. "No, no, nothing's wrong. Yes, Sandi got back down to Provo without any problem. Sure, one o'clock would be fine. I'll pick you up. See you in a bit." Breathing out slowly, Sue hung up the phone. "Why in the world did I agree to do this?" she moaned. "Stupid, stupid, stupid," she chided herself, banging her forehead against the wall.

* * *

Kate threw off her coat as she hurried downstairs. This quarter her Thursday classes were over by one o'clock. That gave her nearly two hours before she had to go to work. Entering her bedroom, she pulled the door shut and reached for the journal sitting on the dresser. She walked to her bed, stretched across it, and began to read.

October 15, 1882

Months have passed since I last wrote upon these pages. A bittersweet reunion it was with my family. My father was not as favorable as Rupert concerning my marriage, but he is slowly warming up to John. A proud man, my father won't admit it, but he has a grudging admiration for John and his efforts to earn the hard keep of a poor farmer. He called him our "gentleman farmer lad" during our first weeks here. He now refers to my husband as Johnny. Not much in the way of a compliment, but we'll accept it all the same.

John was used to the labor of others providing for his every need. He has done well to master the tilling of ground that doesn't yield easily. Proving himself to be willing no matter what is asked of him, he is also gaining the respect of my brothers.

For me, it has been a blessing to return to my family, to land tamed by my forefathers. It has been a hard thing for my husband. When he thinks I am not watching, he looks away, as if he can see the shores of his beloved Scotland. Other times, I see him caress the scarf that bears his tartan colors, blue plaid upon green, striped with yellow and white, the proud colors of the Campbell clan of Argyll. I know John misses his father, Laird Dougal MacOwen.

"Dougal!" Kate exclaimed. Her patience was paying off. Reaching for a small notebook on her nightstand, she wrote down Dougal MacOwen next to Mary MacOwen. "John's parents," Kate sighed. "Now, if she would only tell me her parents' names." Rupert was the only family member Meg had mentioned by name. Picking up the journal, she continued to read.

Dougal MacOwen is like his son, good and strong, both bearing the traits of their family crest; two lions separated by a royal crown. John and his father are separated by pride and wealth. Separated by a shrew named Mary.

I shouldn't write such things about the woman, but it saddens me to think the child I now carry will never know his grandparents, save my father. I am sure this haunts John. I know he grieves for the heritage he cannot pass on. Dougal will never come seeking John, though I am sure his heart must ache with the loss of his only son. Mary will never permit him to forgive such a trespass. I am sure by now they have learned of our marriage, of our journey to Ireland. Ireland, which is home now and ever more will be.

Kate stifled a yawn. As interested as she was in the journal, the exhaustion she felt was overpowering. Closing her eyes, she decided to rest a few minutes before continuing. Nearly an hour later, Paige came downstairs to shake her awake.

"Kate, I hate to wake you, but your Uncle Stan isn't going to be too happy with either one of us if you show up late for work."

Kate sat up quickly, and the journal fell onto the bed. "Dang it, I must've dozed off. Can I make it?"

"Yes. You still have about twenty minutes. I'm glad I came down to check on you. I was a little worried—you usually come upstairs by two-thirty."

Kate glanced at her watch. It was twenty to three. Traffic didn't start getting ugly until about four. "I'm on my way," she said, grabbing her coat.

"Do you want something to snack on?"

"No thanks. I'll eat when I get home."

"Okay. Drive carefully."

"I will. See you later," Kate hollered as she raced up the stairs and out the front door. Reaching into her coat pocket, she pulled out a set of car keys. Her aunt and uncle were letting her drive an old car Stan had bought for Tami and Kyle to chase around in during high school. Now that they were both off on their own, the rusting Ford Pinto had been left behind. Kate didn't mind driving it. She looked at it this way: people weren't so apt to break into it, and it got her where she needed to go. Better yet, it was possible to get into it with a twisted coat hanger, unlike Paige's Neon.

* * *

"How serious is serious?" Harriet Kearns asked, staring at Sue. Sue pretended to study her soft drink.

"Sue?"

"Harriet, we both know Sandi is very mature for her age."

"She's gone and gotten herself engaged, hasn't she?" Harriet exclaimed. "I told that girl to finish school first. She can always find a husband later."

"Ian is pretty special."

"So is Sandi," Harriet angrily replied. "I knew this would

happen. She wouldn't settle for going to MSU, here in Bozeman. Oh, no, she had to go chasin' off down to Provo to that hotbed of RMs all lookin' for wives! I'm surprised they haven't snapped Sandi up before now!"

"Ian isn't a student," Sue began.

"Oh, that makes it better. She's going to marry someone without an education. They'll have to move in with Fred and me. We'll have to support them while they make goo-goo eyes at each other!"

Sue gazed with disbelief at the woman sitting across the table from her. She was going to have an interesting chat with Kate when this was over. "Ian already has his degree. He's—"

"An older man. Taking advantage of my baby, my poor little Sandi."

"Harriet, your poor little Sandi will be nineteen next month. That's the same age I was when I met Greg."

Harriet refused to comment, jamming a goodly portion of her sandwich into her mouth. She was eager to get out of here and call Sandi. Someone had to set that girl straight.

"How old were you, Harriet?" Sue asked, the question popping into her head.

"How whmmmmph?" Harriet said, trying to chew through what she had bitten off.

"How old were you when you met Fred?"

"I wammmph oldrmmmph thnnn Sannni."

"Run that by again," Sue prompted.

Harriet reached for her glass of water and washed down what was left. "I said, I was older than Sandi."

"How much older?"

Harriet avoided Sue's probing gaze. She glanced at the dessert menu on their table and began to thumb through it, uncomfortably aware that she had only been months older than her daughter.

"Harriet?"

Harriet set the menu down and glared at Sue. "This isn't about me. We're talking about my daughter, someone who has more potential in her big toe than most people have in their entire body."

"I agree with you. Sandi's very gifted. And, from the way she talked, if she and Ian decide to get married, she'll continue going to school."

"They're not engaged yet?" Harriet asked, a gleam in her eye.

"No, but I'd bet it's in the immediate future."

"Sue, I appreciate you telling me this. I want you to know I'd do the same if it was Kate. Thanks for lunch. I'd really better be going."

"Harriet," Sue protested as Harriet stood up to leave. "You haven't heard one word I've said."

"I heard what was important," Harriet countered. Turning around, she hurried out of the restaurant. Groaning, Sue buried her face in her hands.

"Would you like your check now?" the waitress asked.

Sue looked up. "What do you have that's loaded with chocolate?"

* * *

"Whoa, Sandi, calm down. Your mom said what?" Kate pulled a face at her aunt. "My mom said that? Sandi, you know how your mom tends to—I'm positive Mom didn't tell her that. Sandi, don't cry. Look, I'll come down tomorrow after school. We'll talk things over. Don't say that . . . you know your mom loves you. That's why she acts this way. I'm sure this is all just a misunderstanding. I'll call Mom and find out what happened. In the meantime, don't say anything to Ian. Promise? Okay. Hang tight. I'll call you as soon as I get hold of Mom." Kate clicked off her aunt's cordless phone, shifting behind the desk in her uncle's study.

"It sounds pretty bad," Paige said. "What did Sandi's mother say to her?"

Kate grimaced. "You don't want to know." She jumped as the phone rang in her hand. She quickly gave it to her aunt, assuming it would be for Paige.

"Hello? Yes . . . she's sitting right here. Sue, before I hand you over to her, can I ask one tiny question? What happened up there today? I see. Went that well, did it? Here, I'll let you fill your daughter in."

"Hi, Mom," Kate timidly ventured.

"Don't you 'hi, me,' young lady," Sue said. "Having lunch

with Harriet Kearns was one of the biggest mistakes—"

"I heard," Kate said. "I just got off the phone with Sandi. She's so upset."

"She's not the only one," Sue sniffed.

"I'm sorry, Mom. Sandi and I both thought if you could soften Harriet up a little—"

"Not possible, especially when it comes to Sandi. Kate, if I ever act this way with Sabrina, remind me of this wonderful day."

"Deal." Kate frowned. "Now what?"

"I have no idea. I can't believe Harriet would get this upset. They're not even engaged yet. Maybe we should've waited until then."

"Sandi wanted her parents, her mom especially, to be prepared. She thought it would be easier."

"I'd hate to see harder," Sue responded. "Harriet wouldn't even listen to me. She heard one thing and one thing only—her daughter is planning to marry an uneducated, older man."

"Where did that come from, anyway? That's exactly what Harriet told Sandi you'd said."

"I said?! Kate—"

"I know. Harriet probably turned it all around."

"And jumped in with assumptions before I could explain how it really was."

"Why does she do this?" Kate moaned.

"Does Ian know?"

"Not yet. I told Sandi to wait until we sorted everything out. Mom, do you think the real reason Harriet doesn't want them to get together is because Ian's in a wheelchair?"

"She doesn't know," Sue said softly. "Kate, she never gave me a chance to explain about that."

"If she's acting like this without knowing, I don't even want to imagine—"

"Tell you what, let's give it a day or two. And, somehow, we need to keep this from Ian. If he catches wind of how his future mother-in-law is reacting, it wouldn't be good. I don't want to see permanent damage develop in the relationship between Sandi and her mother, or for that matter, between Ian and Harriet."

"That'd be pretty bad," Kate agreed.

"Promise me something," Sue continued.

"What?"

"That you will never involve me in this sort of thing ever again."

Kate smiled. "What are mothers for?"

"Don't even get me started," Sue warned. "Now, back to our plan of action. Try to calm Sandi down and I'll see what I can do with her mother."

"Okay. Good luck."

"That's something I'll definitely need. I'll talk to you in a day or two. In the meantime, try to behave. Keep your grades up, get some rest, and remember I love you," Sue said.

"In spite of this disaster?"

"It's my job, remember? Now, hang up like a good girl so your dad doesn't have a stroke when he gets this phone bill."

"I love you too, Mom," Kate said. "Hang in there." Clicking off the phone, she set it on the desk. "I saw a key chain the other day at the mall. I should've bought it."

"What did it say?"

"'My life is a soap opera.'"

"Sounds appropriate," Paige said, pulling her niece to her feet. "Are you up for a quick trip to Provo?"

"Tonight?"

"Sandi needs you. And if I understand the situation, I don't think she can wait until tomorrow."

"What about your homemaking meeting?"

"People are more important than meetings," Paige said firmly. "You go tell the twins we're leaving and I'll call one of my counselors."

Nodding, Kate hurried out of the study.

CHAPTER THIRTY-EIGHT

Greg pulled on the rope again, wincing when his shoulder reminded him this was the twelfth time he had attempted to fire up the Arctic Cat. "Son, I think it's hopeless," he sighed, releasing the rope to rub his shoulder.

"Try it again," Tyler said, looking up from the engine. "Maybe the choke doesn't need to be all the way open."

"Maybe," Greg replied, partially closing the choke.

"Is the throttle stuck?"

Greg reached for the handlebar closest to him and pushed on the lever. It quickly sprang back into place. "Looks fine on this end of things."

"Try it again."

Greg grabbed the plastic handle and pulled again. The engine sputtered, then died.

"We're so close," Tyler groaned. "Hey, I know. Push in the throttle while you start it."

"And hang on while the stupid thing takes off on its own," Greg grumbled.

"Don't push it in all the way. Just enough to give it a little gas."

"How am I supposed to yank on this," Greg asked, pointing to the rope, "and hold the throttle at the same time?" He was tiring of this father-son bonding moment. Tyler loved to play mechanic. Greg was more into sitting in front of a nice fire with the newspaper, a bowl of his favorite popcorn nearby.

"I'll come hold the throttle while you start it."

"How about I hold the throttle while you start it?" Greg suggested, his shoulder still throbbing from the earlier attempts.

"All right," the fourteen-year-old replied. "It'll start this time, you'll see," he promised, closing the hood.

"Are you taking bets?"

"Sure. How about a chocolate malt?"

"Sounds good," Greg agreed.

"Okay, on the count of three," Tyler began. "One, two, three." He yanked with gusto as Greg held the throttle open. The engine sputtered, then fired. "Give it more gas," Tyler said, thrilled.

Greg pushed the throttle in a little more. As he did, the machine began to move forward.

"All right!" Tyler yelled, quickly jumping onto the snow machine. "Later, Dad," he called back as he sped down the snow-covered street.

"If you get a ticket, I'm not paying for it," Greg hollered. Nevertheless he experienced a surge of pride as he watched his son skillfully handle the Arctic Cat, turning it around to head back toward the Erickson home.

"That was great," Tyler said, as he shut off the engine. "What say we load 'er up in the truck and take 'er out where there's powder? You can buy my malt on the way."

"How convenient," Greg said wryly.

"I'll even volunteer to drive."

"That's okay, son. I'll handle that end of things," Greg said, glancing at his new Chevy truck. It had taken quite a bit of pleading to convince Sue it had been a necessary purchase—the obvious replacement for the Sunbird.

"I'll go grab our snow bibs and important stuff like that," Tyler said, already heading toward the house.

Shaking his head, Greg sat on the seat of the Arctic Cat.

"Going for a ride?" Fred Kearns asked, pulling up in his car. He had rolled down the window after spotting Greg in the driveway.

"Guess so. I told my son if he could get this thing started, we'd take it out for spin."

"Wish I was free this afternoon, I'd invite myself along."

"You're working today?"

"In a manner of speaking. Harriet has a list of things she'd like me to do."

"I know how that goes," Greg sympathized.

"Say, while I'm here, would you mind if I asked you a couple of questions?" Fred killed the engine.

"I can't promise any answers, but I'll give it a try," Greg said, adjusting his glasses.

"What do you know about Ian Campbell?"

Greg glanced down at the snow machine. Sue had explained the situation with Sandi and Harriet; the feud had been going on for over a month. He wanted no part of this conversation.

"I wouldn't ask, but I'm only hearing one side—Harriet's. I tried to call Sandi a couple of times, but she wasn't in. And every time she calls, Harriet's right there to grab the phone out of my hand."

Greg slowly stood up, moving to Fred's car.

"You've met him, right?" Fred asked.

"Yes. He came over to my brother-in-law's place for New Year's Eve with Sandi."

"What did you think?"

Greg rubbed at his chin. "If Kate had fallen for him, I think I might've been worried at first, wondering how he could possibly take care of my daughter." He grinned. "Let's face it, Fred, under the best of circumstances, we fathers tend to be a bit protective when it comes to our little girls, even when they're not so little."

"Harriet said he's in a wheelchair," Fred said, cutting to the heart of the matter.

Greg studied the concerned look on Fred's face. "Yes, but he hasn't let that stop him. He's had challenges in his life, and he's met them head on. In my opinion, he's more of a man than others I've seen. And he treats your daughter like gold, which is definitely something to consider these days. One other thing I might mention, I noticed the way she looked at him. I think it's the real thing."

Fred scowled. "I was afraid you'd say that." He gripped the steering wheel. "If Sandi really loves him, I could probably get used to the idea. I've only been through this four times now—with both of my sons and two of my daughters."

"What's up with Harriet?"

"I'm not sure. She was a real trooper with our other kids. I'll admit, it was rough going with our oldest, but Harriet eventually accepted the inevitable and now she loves our sons and daughters-in-law dearly."

"You think in time she'll be okay with Sandi and Ian?"

Fred chewed his bottom lip. "I don't know what it is about our youngest, but Harriet doesn't want to let go."

"She may not have a choice."

Fred sighed. "Maybe if we could meet Ian, it would make a difference." He gazed at Greg. "I understand that's why Sue went down to Salt Lake after Christmas."

Greg nodded. "We thought things were developing between Kate and Ian."

"Any reason why it didn't work out between them?"

"Kate didn't feel the same way as Ian. And later, when Ian thought about it, he realized that what Kate had tried to tell him was true."

"If you don't mind me asking, what was that?"

"They weren't in love, just very good friends."

"I don't suppose it could turn out like that with Sandi and Ian?"

"I don't think so," Greg said. "Fred, I agree with what you said a few minutes ago. You and Harriet need to meet Ian, see for yourselves who he is."

"If Harriet would bend on this—"

"If she doesn't, you may lose a daughter."

"Don't think that thought hasn't crossed my mind." Fred started his car. "If I manage to check everything off the list Harriet gave me today, maybe I can talk her into taking a jaunt to Utah next weekend."

"Good idea," Greg said, stepping away from the car. "Hope it works," he said under his breath as Fred waved and drove down the street.

CHAPTER THIRTY-NINE

I haven't been this nervous since I tried to kiss my first girl."

"Tried?" Sandi asked, fastening her seat belt.

"I missed," Ian admitted, grinning.

"You missed?"

"Hey, cut me some slack, I was only nine," Ian said as he started his van.

"Nine?"

"We were playing kiss tag. Usually the girls outran us. Trouble was, when I finally caught one, I didn't know what to do with her."

"Kind of like now," Sandi asked, glancing down at the ring on her hand.

"Trust me, when the time comes, I'll know," Ian teased.

Sandi could feel the blush creep into her face. "Ian," she warned.

"I know, I know. None of that," he mimicked, sounding like a female drill sergeant. "I promise to be the gentleman extraordinaire, especially when your parents are watching, *ma cherie*," Ian said, with an exaggerated French accent.

"Ian!"

Sandi stared out the windshield, her stomach twisting into knots she was sure could never be untied.

"Hey, I'm kidding, okay?!" He reached to caress her cheek with his hand. "It's going to be all right. You'll see."

"You don't know my mother," Sandi said, turning to face him.

Tears glistened in her eyes. "This should be the happiest time of my life. Instead, I feel like we're going to face the inquisition."

"What did your mother say to you this afternoon?"

"Let's just say her surprise visit was nothing compared to the surprise on my finger," she replied, holding up her left hand.

"Maybe I should've waited," Ian said quietly.

"No, we both know this is the right thing. I love you so much I can hardly stand it."

"We 'ave a lot in common, *ma petite fille,*" Ian said, reverting to his incredibly bad accent.

"Why can't she be happy for me? Instead, she looked like she was going to faint. If Dad hadn't grabbed her, she probably would've collapsed."

"How did your dad react?"

"He was too busy trying to keep Mom under control. He finally dragged her out to the car and said we'd meet somewhere for dinner."

"Then he called you later?"

"Yes, from their motel room. He sounded calm, but Dad usually is, even when he's upset."

"Is he upset?"

"I don't know," Sandi answered, glancing out her side of the van.

They drove in silence for several minutes until Ian located the Chinese restaurant Sandi's father had suggested. Spotting a parking place with an easy access to the sidewalk, Ian pulled in.

"For once, someone didn't steal my special parking place," he said, shutting off the engine. One of his biggest pet peeves involved people who used parking places reserved for those with disabilities. Several times, he had impatiently waited for the drivers to return to their vehicles, then had slowly wheeled himself within view of the guilty party. He never had to say anything; his point was always very clear.

"There's Dad," Sandi said, saying a silent prayer before opening the door on her side.

Fred hurried toward the van, ignoring the snow flakes that were accumulating on top of his head. "Wait, Sandi, tell Ian to stay put," he said breathlessly as his daughter stepped down to the wet pavement.

"What's wrong?" Sandi asked, gripping her purse.

"We're looking at a thirty-minute wait at least, if we eat here," Fred explained, glancing into the van at Ian.

"Well, I don't mind," Ian said, reaching across the seat to shake Fred's hand.

"Harriet does," Fred replied, amazed at the young man's strength. "Fred Kearns," he said, introducing himself to his prospective son-in-law.

"Ian Campbell."

Fred nodded. "Is there somewhere else we could go?"

"How about the Olive Garden?" Sandi asked.

"Good idea," Ian said. "They have wonderful food."

"Where's Mom?" Sandi asked, shaking the snow out of her hair.

"Waiting in the car," Fred answered. "Where is this place?" he added, stepping back to allow Sandi to move into the shelter of the van.

"Where are you parked?" Ian asked, refastening the safety straps.

"Around the corner," Fred replied.

"The easiest thing would be to have you follow us," Ian suggested and Fred ran back to his car. As he started the van, he turned to Sandi. "He seems like a nice guy."

"Dad's a sweetheart. Mom is too, most of the time. This past year has been interesting, but I know she means well."

"Can't wait to meet her," Ian replied, backing out of the parking space.

Nearly fifteen minutes later, they arrived at the restaurant. Harriet walked with Fred to the entrance, staring at the line that extended outside. People were trying to crowd inside as best they could, out of the storm. When Fred made his way inside to see what was available, he was told it would be at least a forty-minute wait.

"You'd think it was Friday night," Ian quipped when Fred came to the van to report his findings.

"It is Friday night," Harriet said without humor, standing by her husband's side. She avoided looking at Ian, her gaze piercing through Sandi.

"Any other ideas?" Fred asked, brushing the snow from his wife's coat.

"The way things are going, we might be better off to try someplace casual—like the Training Table."

Sandi gave Ian a worried look.

"The Training Table?" Fred asked.

"They make the best hamburgers in town. Any kind you can imagine, patties this thick," Ian said, demonstrating with his hands.

"A hamburger sounds great," Fred said eagerly, before he could stop himself. "What do you think, Harriet?"

"It doesn't really matter what I think," she snapped.

Sandi shifted in her seat, uncomfortably aware of what her mother was implying.

"The Training Table it is then," Ian said brightly. "I'm sure we'll get a seat there."

"Sounds fine," Fred agreed. "We'll follow you," he added, leading Harriet back to their car.

"This was a mistake," Sandi groaned. "Mom is never going to back down."

"Let's give her a chance," Ian said, squeezing her hand to show his support. "I have a good feeling about tonight. I think you'll be surprised how well things are going to go."

"I hope you're right," Sandi sighed. "I can't take much more of Mom's 'guilt gaze'."

"Guilt gaze?"

"It's what my sisters and I call the look Mom gives us when she's upset about something we've done."

"Maybe I'll give her a 'guilt gaze' of my own," Ian said.

"Ian . . ."

"I know, I know. I'll be a good boy, you'll see," he promised, pulling out of the parking place.

True to Ian's word, they had no trouble at their next destination.

"If they serve such good food, why aren't there more people here," Harriet grumbled as they entered the building. "And if we were just going to have a hamburger, why didn't we go to one of those fast food places?"

"Because you haven't eaten a hamburger until you've tried one of these," Ian said, amused by the pained expression on Harriet's face.

They selected a booth near a window. Sandi sat across from her parents while Ian remained on the outside of the table in his wheelchair.

As they studied the menus, Fred whistled. "How does a person choose? This one has bacon and cheese, that one has Swiss cheese and mushrooms. This other one has Santa Fe flavor."

"I'll have a chicken sandwich," Harriet said, cutting him off.

"Same here," Sandi said, smiling at her mother.

Harriet avoided looking at Sandi, concentrating instead on the wall next to her. "Why do we have a phone at our table?"

"Every table has a phone. That's how we order," Ian replied.

"How quaint," Harriet said.

Fred's mouth was already watering at the sight of a hamburger with mushrooms, onions, Swiss cheese, and a special sauce. "I've made my decision," he said.

"I'll stick with the Santa Fe special. I had one of those last week. It was awesome," Ian commented.

"You were here last week?" Fred asked, hoping to cut through the tension with casual conversation.

"Yes, Sandi and I come here all the time."

Harriet's eyes narrowed. "Is this where you proposed?"

Now it was out in the open. Ian unzipped his jacket, then met Harriet's inquiring gaze.

"As a matter of fact, we came here to celebrate, didn't we, Sandi?"

Sandi nodded. "He asked me . . . he proposed while we were in front of the temple."

"Why don't we order?" Fred suggested, giving Harriet a stern look. He had already told her in no uncertain terms that they were to give this young man a fair chance. Harriet wasn't holding up her end of the bargain.

"Mrs. Kearns, would you do the honors?" Ian asked.

"What?"

"Would you please pick up the phone and place our order," he replied.

Harriet was about to tell him he could do it himself, then

caught the warning look on Fred's face. Sighing, she reached for the phone. "Hello," she said, annoyed by this entire setting. "Hello? Nobody's there," she said, glaring at Ian.

"Push that button first," Ian replied. "It lets them know we're ready to order."

Harriet pushed the button. "Hello?" This time a voice responded. Harriet quickly gave their order, then hung up the phone.

"I like this place," Fred said, glancing around. "A person can relax here," he added, removing his tie. Ignoring the look Harriet was giving him, he tucked it in his coat pocket.

"Good idea," Ian said, removing his own tie.

"How long have you two been engaged?" Harriet asked, pretending to study her fingernails.

"Mom," Sandi began, her eyes pleading with her mother.

"Nearly two whole days now. It was murder holding out until Valentine's Day," Ian said with a grin. "But if we'd known you were coming down, I would've waited to pop the question. We could've made a real family affair of the occasion."

"That's okay, Ian," Fred said quickly, hoping to thwart the explosion he sensed was coming from his wife. "Parents aren't usually invited along the night their sons or daughters get engaged."

"Maybe they should be," Harriet said sharply. "We could add helpful insights, things you young people don't consider when you *think* you're in love."

"Well, we have one thing going for us," Ian said brightly. "We *know* we're in love." He winked at Sandi, who was looking about as miserable as he had ever seen her.

Fred tried to defuse the situation. "Good for you. And I understand you've already earned a college degree."

Ian nodded. "I'm an accountant with a law firm," he said, reaching for his wallet. Finding his business card, he handed it to Fred.

"How long has this firm been in business?" Fred asked, trying to sound nonchalant.

"Going on twenty-one years."

"They sound well established."

"They are. And they treat me well. I've already earned myself a raise."

"Ian's the head of his department," Sandi said, eager to impress her parents. "He makes good money."

"What do you consider good money?" Harriet asked, sipping at her ice water.

"The kind I get to spend on Sandi," Ian playfully replied. He wasn't about to back down. He had to win Harriet over; it was crucial to Sandi's well-being.

Fred chuckled. "Son, if you've already learned that, you're way ahead of the rest of us," he said.

Before Harriet could offer a retort, the phone rang, causing her to jump in her seat. Her arm flew out, tipping over her glass of ice water.

"I'll get it, Mom," Sandi offered, handing her mother a handful of napkins from the small dispenser at their booth. She then picked up the phone, learned that their order was ready, and turned to look at Ian.

"We'll pick it up," Ian offered, glancing at Fred. Fred nodded, standing as Ian pushed his wheelchair away from the table. Together they moved to the distant counter.

"This is a sorry mess," Harriet snapped.

"It'll clean up," Sandi said, meekly wiping at the water on her side of the table.

"I'm talking about more than this table," Harriet informed her daughter. "I can't believe you got yourself engaged and didn't even bother to tell us about it."

"I was planning to," Sandi said.

Harriet gave her daughter a long, hard stare.

"Honest, Mom. I didn't think it would go over very well on the phone. We wanted to tell you in person. Ian and I were planning on coming to Bozeman tomorrow. He's off on the weekends, and we thought it would be the best way to break the news. I had no idea you were going to show up today."

"We tried to call. No one was home last night. That's when we started down. We made it to Idaho Falls and stayed the night. Then this morning before we left, we decided it was too early to call. We were trying to be considerate, unlike other people I could mention."

"We never meant to hurt you or Dad."

"That's entirely beside the point," Harriet began. "Sandi, you're too young—"

"I'm only a few months younger than you were," Sandi countered. "I figured it out the other day."

"I'm sure I was better prepared than you could possibly—"

"I love him, Mom. Why can't you accept it? Ian's parents have."

Harriet stared at her daughter. "Ian's parents know?" she asked, her eyes filling with tears.

"Mom—"

"You told them first?" she accused, wiping at her eyes with a napkin.

Sandi slowly nodded. "We went to see them last night. That's why you couldn't reach us. We were in Orem, with his family."

Harriet closed her eyes.

"Ian has a wonderful family. He looks just like his dad. His dad runs a bank. He's the bishop in their ward. His mom works with the Young Women. She's also a registered nurse. Ian's the oldest. He has two younger sisters. They're both still in high school," Sandi said, her words spilling together.

"Do you really think I want to hear all of this?" Harriet's expression revealed the depth of her pain.

"Mom, please," Sandi pleaded. "You don't know how hard it's been. You were the first person I thought of when Ian gave me this ring. But I know how you feel about us getting married. You've made that perfectly clear."

"So, you'll go off and get married anyway, despite what your father or I think and that'll be that. The end of everything we'd planned for you."

"It's not the end," Sandi persisted. "In a lot of ways, it's just the beginning."

"You have no idea what you're getting into," Harriet muttered.

Sandi gazed at her mother. "Maybe not, but when there's a problem, we'll work it out somehow."

"Without anybody's help, I suppose," Harriet snapped. "You always have been too independent for your own good."

"Mom, I know there will be times when I'll . . .when we'll

need help. It would be nice to know we could turn to you."

Harriet wiped at her eyes, then at her nose, avoiding the look on her daughter's face.

"You'll always be an important part of my life," Sandi continued, sensing this was part of the problem. "I will always need you to be there for me. You have to know that's true."

"I have to know one thing," Harriet replied. "Are you sure about this? You're not rushing into something you'll regret later?"

"Ian is the most wonderful man I've ever met," Sandi said softly. "I love him and I know we're supposed to be together."

"I wish I could be as sure about that as you seem to be," Harriet returned. "You know I want nothing but the best for you."

"Ian is what's best for me."

"He'd better be," Harriet said, glancing across the room at Ian. He had wheeled himself over to ketchup dispenser and was filling tiny paper containers with it. "It won't be easy."

"Is it ever?"

"No, but there will be added problems that most don't have to face."

"Maybe, but it's what I want."

"You're sure," Harriet pressed.

"I've never been more sure about anything in my life. I've prayed so much about it, I've nearly worn out the carpet by my bed. I know, Mom. I know this is right."

"I guess if you've made your choice, then it's time I make mine." She forced a small smile. "What can I do to help you?"

Too overwhelmed to answer, Sandi stood, reaching for a hug.

Harriet met her halfway as they stretched across the table, both of them crying as they held onto one another.

Gratefully, Ian and Fred watched from a distance.

"Welcome to the family, Ian," Fred said, carefully balancing the tray he was carrying.

"Thanks," Ian replied, hanging onto a tray with one hand as he moved his wheelchair forward with the other. He set his tray down on the table, and didn't mind a bit when Harriet came forward to smother him with a hug, followed by a sound kiss on the cheek. Tearfully, Sandi watched. She would wait to tell Ian about the bright pink lipstick mark on the side of his face. For now, she would treasure it as a reminder of her mother's acceptance. Sliding out of the booth, she reached for her dad.

CHAPTER FORTY

A couple of nights later, Sandi and Ian dropped in on the Mahoneys and Kate to share their good news. Ecstatic, Kate hugged Sandi, then Ian, congratulating them on their engagement. Paige gave the happy couple a hug, then headed into the kitchen to whip up some refreshments. After a lengthy visit, Ian glanced at his watch and sighed.

"Guess we'd better start back to Provo," he said, nudging Sandi.

"I know. I have an early class in the morning," Sandi replied, slipping into her coat.

Kate followed them to the front door. "You two behave yourselves," she teased.

Sandi's eyes twinkled as she reached for another hug. "Not, you, too," she said accusingly. "We get enough of that from my mom, Ian's dad, my roommates—"

"I get the picture," Kate interrupted, pulling back to gaze at her friend. "I was kidding."

"I know. That's why I'm still smiling," Sandi said, stepping out onto the porch. "See you later."

"I'll call you this weekend," Kate promised. She grinned as she shut the door. "It's about time," she sighed.

"I think so too," Paige agreed. "They make a cute couple."

"I know. And I'm glad Sandi's parents are finally with her on this."

"Have they set a date yet?" Paige asked. She had been in the kitchen when the wedding plans had been discussed.

"June fifteenth."

"They're going to wait until school is out this term," Paige observed. "Probably a wise choice. Let's see, March, April, May, a little over three months to pull off the reception. More time than Kyle and Tina are giving me. Thank heavens I'm the mother of the groom this time," Paige sighed, thinking of the open house she would have to organize in two weeks.

"This too shall pass," Kate said, moving to the stairs. "And now, if you don't mind, I'm going to try to finish Grandma Meg's journal."

"Tonight?"

"This weekend. I forgot to tell you—Sylvia Myers called earlier today. She found something else she wants to send me. In the meantime, I feel like I need to glean as much as possible from this journal. I have a feeling that whatever Sylvia's sending, it will tie everything together."

"Hope so," Paige said. "It would be nice to get going on the temple work."

Nodding, Kate hurried downstairs. Entering her room, she flipped on the light, grabbed the journal, and began to read.

May 28, 1883

I now have a daughter, a sweet bonnie girl we have named for my mother, Kathleen MacOwen, born the twenty-seventh day of May.

"Yes!" Kate exclaimed, reaching for her notebook. "Meg's mother's name was Kathleen Kelly. Don't have her maiden name yet, but it's a start." She made a note beside Meg and John MacOwen. *Daughter born May 27, 1883. Kathleen MacOwen.* Setting the notebook beside her, she continued reading.

Kathleen seems to be thriving, unlike her brother, John. I think of my lost son often, wondering if things would have been different if my circumstances had changed before his birth. Alone as I was with no one to help, I can't help but think that John's mother was indeed responsible for what took place.

Silently agreeing, Kate reached for her notebook and added the name of Meg's infant son.

I'll not spend my life grieving for what could have been. It is enough that John and I are together, our love combining to bring a precious daughter into this world.

The entries that followed were written at irregular intervals, making it clear that Meg's life was busy, as well as full. Several small entries revealed how she and John loved their daughter. In the space of one year, little Kathleen had also stolen her Grandfather Kelly's heart, as well as the hearts of her uncles.

"I'll bet she was spoiled rotten," Kate muttered under her breath. Then, realizing the impoverished state this family had lived in, changed her mind. Skimming through several pages, she stopped at an entry made in 1886.

June 7, 1886

A letter arrived for my husband this day. It bore the MacOwen seal, and as such, I let it be until John came in from the field. It was with great reluctance that I handed it to him. As I feared, the news was not good. John's father has taken ill. John's sister, Kirsty, had sent us word, begging us to return, certain their father is dying.

Kate quickly made a note about John's sister, Kirsty MacOwen, then read carefully through the rest of the entry.

John said not a word. Setting the letter down, he strode from our small cottage, walking down to the pond. I came to him later, shivering with the cool breeze this day has brought.

I know what my husband must do. He would never forgive himself if he did not return to settle things with his father. He wishes me to come as well, but I am certain it would end in disaster. I would never be welcome, and I will not have our child treated as I have been. I will not stand in his way if he decides to heed his family's request. As for myself, I will remain here with Kathleen and my family. John will return to us when he is ready.

Kate continued to read, noting that John did return to Campbeltown, Scotland, to the estate of his father.

July 27, 1886

Your letter arrived today, John. Glad I was to receive it. If I'd known how I would miss you, I would have insisted on coming along, despite your mother. I was sorry to learn that your father is still hovering 'wixt life and death. I know you are doing all that you can to hasten your return home, and until that time comes, I will do what I can to keep our small plot of land from going to waste and weeds.

August 10, 1886

I have never been so ill with child. There are days when it seems I do nothing but lay about. On those days, Kathleen hastens next door for my father. When summoned by his granddaughter, Grandpa Ewan comes running, eager to please his beloved Kathleen.

Kate grabbed for the notebook, eagerly jotting down Ewan Kelly beside his wife, Kathleen. She read for another few minutes, then, unable to keep her eyes open, gave up for the night.

CHAPTER FORTY-ONE

After church, Kate helped her aunt and cousins set the table with the traditional Sunday feast. When they were finished, with most uncomfortably full, Kate began to scrape plates.

"We'll get this," Paige said, nodding to her twin daughters. "Go down and finish that journal."

"I hope I can, I've still got a ways to go." Kate glanced at the less-than-thrilled expressions on her cousins' faces. "But I'll help you clear the table first."

"No, we can get it, right girls?" Paige asked, glancing at Rachel and Renae. They both slowly nodded. "See, I have plenty of help. We'll let you clean up next Sunday."

"By herself," Renae said sullenly, grabbing a handful of silverware on her way to the kitchen.

"Sounds like I need to spend some quality time with my twins," Paige commented, draping an arm around Rachel's sagging shoulders. "Come along, dear," she said leading Rachel into the kitchen. "I'll talk to you later, Kate."

"Okay," Kate grinned, knowing her cousins were in for a fiery lecture. Paige had been grumbling for days about the poor attitude her daughters were developing. They had picked a bad week to get on the wrong side of their mother, with Kyle's wedding looming in the immediate future.

Taking the stairs two at a time, Kate quickly entered her room. She sat on her bed, found her place in the journal, and began to read.

Sept. 12, 1886

I find myself in Scotland, among people I thought I'd never see again. John finally sent for us, as his father's illness continues to take its toll. I must admit, I was indeed leery of coming to this place, fearing what I would say to Mary once I had arrived. But much to my husband's relief, there have been no sharp words spoken—which is due in part to the fact that Mary simply behaves as though I don't exist. She'll have a harder time of it with Kathleen. Already my daughter demands to know why she can't speak to her grandmother. How do I explain to a child no more than three that people are at times separated by circumstances that make no sense at all?

November 18, 1886

John's father appears to be improving. He is still too weak to manage the affairs of the estate, leaving that responsibility to my husband. John spends most of his time out among the laborers, preparing for the harsh winter that is coming. Already we have had small storms. It won't be long before we are beset by snow.

Kathleen finds her way about this large old house with astounding ease. We have been assigned rooms on an upper floor, perhaps to keep us out of sight and out of mind of Mistress Mary. It makes no difference to my young daughter. She babbles constantly about her Grandfather Dougal. At first, I was afraid Kathleen would find herself in trouble because of these visits. But John claims they are raising Dougal's spirits. Mary is not of the same mind, however. She appeared in my bedroom this morning to inform me my child was being a nuisance. That said, she turned to go. They are the first words spoken to me by her ladyship. I was indeed touched by the sentiment.

Kate grinned at her great-great-grandmother's spunk. "At least she kept a sense of humor about the situation," she murmured, rolling over on her side.

December 25, 1886

It seems strange to celebrate the birth of our Lord in a cheerless place such as this. When I recall my father's lively fiddle and the love that flowed among us while I was but a child, I could fair weep for my daughter.

Mary finally permitted a tree to be brought into the sitting room, but the decorations that are usually flaunted about the MacOwen mansion are lacking. John claims it is because of his father's illness. Dougal was the one to always insist upon extravagant decorations and gatherings when it came to the holidays. Now that he is bedridden, Mary does as she pleases and it pleases her to keep things simple and thrifty. Even so, a mysterious package appeared in our rooms Christmas Eve, a box addressed to Kathleen. We allowed her to open it this morning, along with the other gifts from Saint Nicholas. Kathleen squealed with delight at the porcelain doll that lay in the box. Whether it came from both of her grandparents, or Dougal alone, we are not certain, but Kathleen loves it dearly. She went to sleep with the doll in her arms this night.

Feb. 20, 1887

Still we are in Scotland, but it is becoming tolerable. Mary has grudgingly accepted our presence here. I have yet to see the woman smile, but Kathleen is slowly winning her over. A lively sprite of a thing, my daughter has proved to be as stubborn as her grandmother. Perhaps that is why Mary consented to Dougal's request that I escort Kathleen to his room at least twice a day. Dougal adores Kathleen, and is eager for his next grandchild to be born. Certain it is a boy, he fair enjoys badgering me, telling me of his plans for his grandson. A rider he'll be, Dougal assures me, just like John. A true MacOwen. Kathleen, upon hearing this, demanded to know why she could not be a rider as well. It took a bit of doing, but I managed to keep from smiling as Dougal tried to argue with his granddaughter, telling her it would be her role to manage a household and a family, not a horse. In truth, Kathleen excels at managing her grandfather. He finally promised her a pony in the spring.

March 23, 1887

Dougal was correct. He has his grandson. I don't know who was more pleased, John, his father, or Kathleen. I have certainly had a time of it, convincing my daughter that little Dougal John is not to be dragged about.

"Dougal John," Kate murmured, reaching for the notebook. "Quite a list of names we're getting," she said, gazing at the notes she had made on the paper. "Let's see, my great-grandmother wasn't born until 1899. I wonder if they had any other kids between Dougal John and Helen?" Chewing on the end of her pen, Kate picked up the journal again.

April 30, 1887

I write this entry while on the vessel that will carry my children and me back to Ireland. John gave his permission for us to return for a visit with my family. He is still unable to leave, though his father continues to improve. As the weather has tempered, they have started taking him outside to sit for a time in the sun. Dougal is in good spirits, but I fear he will never be the robust man that he was.

Whether John and I will choose to stay is uncertain. I can see the advantages my children would have, should we choose to remain in Scotland. But I will not have them grow up believing money is the only source of happiness in this world.

May 2, 1887

My father was as proud as Dougal concerning his new grandson. And Kathleen squealed with delight at the sight of her beloved Grandpa Kelly. It has been a joyous reunion. If only John were here to enjoy it as well.

Kate carefully read through the following pages, smiling at the mischievous antics of Kathleen. "I'd better not let Mom read this," she murmured. "She'll blame me on the MacOwen side of the family."

May 14, 1887

It won't be long before the children and I must leave for Scotland. I promised John and Dougal we would return in time for Kathleen's birthday. Dougal has a special gift in mind, I'm sure. No doubt the wee pony that's been promised. Kathleen has talked of little else since our arrival in Ireland. My father tries to hide it, but I see the pain in his eyes as his granddaughter describes how we live in Scotland. If he had it to give, Ewan Kelly would no doubt give his grandchildren the world. Papa, how I wish you could know that your love will come to mean so much more to them than the cold touch of silver and gold.

May 27, 1887

A party was held today in Kathleen's honor, a party such as I have never seen before, with gifts, candies, pies of every kind, and children from neighboring homes, all come to share in my daughter's fourth birthday. No expense has been spared, under Dougal's firm instructions. I feared Mary would act as an idjit, but she actually seemed to enjoy the day.

True to Dougal's word, a pony was trotted out in plain view as we gathered in front of the house. Bursting with joy, Kathleen ran first to the pony, then to her grandfather for a kiss, then to her father to plead for a boost upon her sturdy mount. My husband was only too glad to oblige.

June 16, 1887

Dougal is steadily regaining his health. And it is becoming apparent that the MacOwen estate has room for only one master. John has learned of a business opportunity in Glasgow. He refuses to take money from his father, determined to make it on his own. With two small mouths to feed, as well as a wife and himself, I pray John knows what he is doing. I would much prefer to return to Billy Antrim, but John's heart is not in being a farmer nor is it in Ireland. John wishes to establish a fine stable outside of Glasgow, starting with the two sets of matched thoroughbreds he now owns. He claims a true Scot will always be possessed by the love of good horse flesh and as such, there will always be a market for such animals. I pray he is right.

August 8, 1887

It is with heavy heart that I record the death of my daughter, Kathleen MacOwen.

Gripping the journal, Kate sat up and forced herself to read the tragedy that had claimed Kathleen's life.

It has taken me weeks to write of it. Even now, the tears fall. Unbidden they come as I see in my mind's eye, the child that is no more.

Kate gazed at the stained pages, slowly running a finger across paper that had once been soaked by tears. Her own eyes burning, she continued to read.

Hardly a day went by that Kathleen didn't beg for her father to saddle her pony. Following John to the stables, she insisted upon riding beside him as he rode about, surveying the MacOwen land. Each enjoyed the other's company, John slowing his horse's gait to that of the pony's. All was well until July eighth arrived, a day as dark as any I have endured.

Blinking back tears, Kate made a note beside Kathleen's name, adding the date of her death.

It had been a rather sultry day and I tried to talk Kathleen out of being her father's shadow. I sensed a storm was coming, but ne'er imagined the horror that would come of it. John assured me all would be well as he took our daughter by the hand and headed for the stable.

Later, when black clouds filled the sky, even Mary grew concerned. Saddling up her own horse, for she is as agile with a horse as her son, Mary set out after them, fearing John would not have the sense to return ahead of the storm. If only she had reached them before . . .

The words were becoming harder to read. The ink had faded through the years and was hardly legible. Squinting, Kate tried to make out the final words of the entry.

. . . frightened by the thunder, Kathleen's pony shrieked at the lightening, bolting away before John could reach for the reins. He rode hard behind Kathleen, catching up to her as the pony stumbled, throwing our daughter from the saddle. They say she died at once, striking her head upon a rock. Mary later found them, John cradling Kathleen in his arms, sobbing as though his heart would break.

Mary has been a wonder and a blessing. Her strength alone has pulled us through. She it was who made the arrangements for the small graveside ceremony. Somehow she sent word to my father who came at once.

We all blame ourselves. Each day is an agony, but we try to manage as best we can. Little Dougal John clamors for my attention; at times it is he alone who keeps me going. Mary focuses on the duties of the house. John spends his time preparing for our departure to Glasgow. His father suffers in silence, though I was told he walked out to where the pony was being held and shot it. Perhaps it was his way of dealing with what has happened, but taking the life of a pony will not bring back my Kathleen.

CHAPTER FORTY-TWO

Feeling better?" Paige asked, reaching for the empty ice cream dish sitting in front of Kate.

Kate shrugged. "I know it happened a long time ago, but I can see it so clearly in my mind. Maybe it's because of the dream I had when I was in that coma. These people are so real to me."

"They should be. They're your ancestors, and like Sylvia said, they've waited a long time to be sealed together."

"True," Kate sighed. "I guess I'd better get back to the grind then. Thanks for the ice cream . . . and pep talk."

"Anytime. If you can come up with enough dates to go with those names, we'll have no problem at all submitting them for temple work. Reuniting this family for eternity should more than make up for the heartache they experienced."

Nodding, Kate headed back to her room. Picking up the journal, she skimmed through the pages that were left. She learned that John and Meg moved to Glasgow, against his parents' wishes. In Glasgow, John was able to make the connections needed to begin building the stable of his dreams. They were never as prosperous as the MacOwens of Campbeltown, but managed to scrape by until John made a name for himself.

During the years that followed, four more children were born. A daughter named Meg, born a year after Kathleen's death, another son who was named after Meg's father, Ewan, and two more daughters, Janet, and Kate's great-grandmother, Helen.

Shortly after Helen was born, her father's reputation for being a man of integrity encouraged two Mormon missionaries to journey to the MacOwen stables to inquire about a horse.

May 18, 1899

Two young men came home with John today. He invited them to dinner, something he often does with prospective buyers. At least my daughter Meg is old enough now to help with the cooking. There are days when I feel all I do is cook meals for those who crowd around my table, but I wouldn't have it any other way.

I could tell at once that there was something special about these two strangers, their faces seemed to glow as they told us they were missionaries, bearing a special message from God. My husband is a good man, but he has never been one to care for formal religion. His dander was up when he thought these two men had come to preach to us. When Elder Matthews and Elder Daniels, for that is what they call themselves, saw that my husband was upset, they apologized for any offense they might've caused and said they would be on their way.

John followed them outside, making arrangements for them to come back later to pick up the horse they desired to purchase.

June 15, 1899

The Mormon missionaries came again this evening. The more they come around, the more John accepts what it is they have to say. It is a remarkable story they tell, concerning the prophet of their church. And yet, as they speak, my heart whispers they are indeed telling us truths.

Tonight they brought a message of hope and joy. They spoke of eternal families, of death not being the final end. John left the room for a time. The elders feared they had offended him again, but I knew the cause. He too was thinking of our daughter, Kathleen. Kathleen who would have celebrated her sixteenth birthday this year. And John, the child neither of us were given the chance to know.

After nearly an hour, John returned, burning with questions that kept the missionaries here until quite late. John now feels as I do that this church must truly be the church of God. Our hearts burn within as we read and ponder the book left by the elders, a book called simply the Book of Mormon.

There were only a few pages left. Reading through them, Kate felt a tingling along her spine as each entry bore witness of the truthfulness of the gospel. When she came to the last page, Kate sat up to read the final journal entry.

September 8, 1899

What a wondrous day this has been! Today John and I entered the waters of baptism, as did our three oldest children, Dougal who is twelve, Meg who is eleven, and Ewan who is now eight. Deeming our two youngest unable to comprehend what we were doing, we left them with a neighbor and drove our best carriage out to a place the elders had prepared in the River Clyde. Damming it with logs, they had formed a small pool, deep enough for the baptisms to be performed.

I can scarce describe the tender feelings of my heart as I was brought forth from the water. And, as the hands of the elders blessed and confirmed me a member of this church of latter-day saints, I saw an image of my daughter, Kathleen, full grown, dressed in white, hovering near my side. At once crying and laughing for joy, it was near impossible for my family to understand what I had seen. John later said that he too experienced this strange vision. Unashamed, my husband shed tears, vowing that Kathleen would not be forgotten. It is because of her his heart softened toward the Mormon missionaries.

Later, when we asked what was needed for our eternal ordinances to take place, the elders explained that we must journey to a temple of the Lord. At present, there are four such places, all located in America, in a state called Utah. John and I talked long into the night, discussing ways we could somehow journey to America to join the other Saints who have gathered and seal our family with eternal bonds of love.

"That's it?" Kate complained. She thumbed back through the preceding pages to see if she had missed anything. "Guess so, for now." She glanced at the pedigree chart she had been able to fill out. "Soon, Meg," she promised, "I'm not sure why things didn't work out as you had planned, but we'll see to it that your family is sealed."

CHAPTER FORTY-THREE

The next day, as if in response to Kate's promise, a package arrived from Sylvia Myers.

"I've waited all day for you to get home," Paige protested. "Open it. Let's see what she sent."

Eagerly tearing the manila envelope open, Kate pulled out two letters. One of the letters bore Sylvia's name. She reached for it first, carefully tearing it open and withdrawing the folded note. The penmanship was terrible, a spidery scrawl that was difficult to read. Knowing the effort Sylvia had made to write this note, Kate sat down at the dining room table and concentrated to decipher Sylvia's message.

Dear Kate,

By now, you've probably finished reading the journal. As I recall, Meg MacOwen wanted her family to be sealed together. We were never sure if this ever took place. We've searched through records but could never prove anything. Then, about a week ago, my granddaughter was helping me clean out the attic. We came across a box of letters. To make a long story short, Maggie (that's my granddaughter) found a letter that your great-grandmother, Helen, sent to my husband's mother, Janet MacOwen Myers years ago. I hope it will be of help.

Sincerely,
Sylvia Myers

"Well, what does it say?"

Kate smiled at her aunt. "I think we finally found the missing link." Handing Sylvia's note to Paige, Kate eagerly reached for the other letter.

March 1, 1955

Dear Janet,

It hasn't been that long ago since I last wrote, but I feel such a sense of urgency about this matter. You know what I am meaning, the promise that was made to our mother.

I wasn't old enough to remember, being but two years old when she died, but I've heard the stories from the rest of you, enough to know that promise has never been kept.

After joining the Mormon Church, our parents were never able to gain the one thing they wanted most, our family sealed for eternity. Neighbors and friends turned away; the persecution suffered was unbearable. Father lost everything when someone set fire to the stables and there was no way for him to buy us all passage to America. In the city he went to work in the factories, barely making enough to keep bread on the table and a roof over our heads. I don't remember those times, but Ewan told me of the rats and the thin windows that never kept out the cold.

Under those conditions, it was not possible for Mother to regain her health. When she realized she would not live to make the journey to Salt Lake, she gathered the family around her. Do you remember how she made Father promise he would take us to Zion to live among the other saints and seal our family together in God's temple?

After she died, the older children worked in the factories, trying to sustain our family as our passage money slowly accumulated. Father worked night and day. Finally, after seven years, in 1908, with the help of other church members, we were able to book passage for all but Dougal John. When he received word from our grandmother, Mary MacOwen, he threw his lot in with her, deciding wealth was more appealing than the poverty we had endured. We were saddened by his choice, but could do nothing to change his mind.

The rest of us traveled to Liverpool, England, where we boarded the ship that would carry us to America. I wasn't very old, but I remember the excitement as we saw New York harbor.

The train ride seemed to take forever but finally we joined the saints of Zion, the people our mother had so desired to live among. Unfortunately, the journey took its toll on Father. His health had so badly deteriorated in the factories of Glasgow that he succumbed to pneumonia and died before he could keep the promise made to our mother.

That responsibility has fallen to us, but we have all wandered our separate ways. Meg married a nonmember. Ewan died fighting in the first World War. That leaves you and me. Janet, I know the bitterness you've carried all these years. Our family has seemed to suffer endless tragedies, one after the other since joining the Church. But I can promise the sacrifices will be one day be worth it.

I would be willing to see to it that all of the ordinance work is taken care of, but first I need your cooperation. There are several dates I'm not sure of. If you could please send me the missing information, I would be eternally grateful. Remember our mother's dying wish and all it would mean to her.

Your loving sister,
Helen

"Oh, man," Kate breathed.

"What?" Paige asked, glancing up from the note in her hand.

Kate handed the letter to Paige and patiently waited for her aunt to read it.

"This letter was written the year Helen died."

Kate nodded. "No wonder none of this work was ever done."

Paige glanced at the letter again and nodded. "We're still missing a few dates, but I think we have enough information we can go ahead and get started. It's been my experience that once you get the ball rolling, it just keeps picking up speed. We'll eventually put it all together."

"Good," Kate said. "This family has waited long enough."

CHAPTER FORTY-FOUR

Paige waited impatiently for Kate to come home from school. On the kitchen table lay the notification that the names they had submitted to the temple had been accepted and were being stored in a special file under her name. Paige had already called to make arrangements at the Bountiful temple. It was the temple Kate had suggested, explaining that it was in Bountiful she had received Meg MacOwen's journal.

"Finally," Paige exclaimed when Kate came through the door. "Cancel any plans you might have made tomorrow night," she said excitedly.

"Why? What's up?" Kate asked, unbuttoning her jacket.

"We have work to do."

"I know. Uncle Stan said the paper work is piling up."

"Wrong paper work. This has nothing to do with the construction company."

"But—"

"It's okay. I already talked to Stan. He'll be going with us."

"Where?"

"To the Bountiful temple."

"We're set, really?"

Paige nodded. "We're scheduled to take care of the baptisms tomorrow night at 6:30. Then, as soon as we can, we'll arrange for the endowments and the sealings."

"This is so neat," Kate said. "What do I need to do to get

ready?"

"I've already set up an interview for you with our bishop. He'll meet you tonight at eight."

"Interview?"

"For your temporary recommend. You'll need it where we're going," Paige said with a smile. "So if you've got any last minute repenting to do . . ."

"Not this girl. My record is squeaky clean, has been for months."

"I figured as much," Paige replied. "Which reminds me, if I haven't said it lately, I want you to know how proud I am of you. And I'm sure I'm not the only one who feels that way," she continued, drawing Kate into hug.

* * *

Kate wrapped a towel around her hair and walked back into the locker room. The warm feeling that had been with her since coming up out of the baptismal font was still with her. The same shivery sensation she had experienced occasionally while working on this family line had returned with vigor. And for a brief moment, she had felt as though someone's arms had gone around her, flooding her heart with a sense of overwhelming love.

Kate smiled, knowing this was just the beginning. Other ancestors waited, and she sensed their impatience. "We'll find you," she promised. "An eternal chain, one link at a time."

CHAPTER FORTY-FIVE

This has been the greatest day of my life," Sandi whispered, embracing Kate. "I can't believe it finally happened."

"I can," Kate said, pulling back to grin at her friend. "I can barely breathe in this dress you and your mother made me wear. And these shoes—"

"The price you pay for being my maid of honor," Sandi teased.

"Yeah, well, sometime I hope to return the favor," Kate retorted.

"I'm planning on it," Sandi replied.

"Are you two through saying good-bye yet?" Ian asked, pulling his bow tie loose. "I'm ready to get out of this tux."

"Okay," Sandi said, moving to his side. "I'll call you when we get back from our trip," she added, smiling at Kate. "Just think, we get to do this again next weekend in Bozeman!"

"Don't remind me," Kate groaned. The wedding had taken place earlier that morning in the Provo temple. Sandi and Ian had decided it would be simpler to have the reception in Orem. An open house would be held in Bozeman to keep Harriet happy.

"Let's head out," Ian said, reaching for his wife's hand.

"Enjoy California," Kate said, leaning down to kiss Ian's cheek. "And remember your promise," she added softly.

"Mormon's honor," Ian said, holding up two fingers.

"I thought that went with scout's honor," Kate reminded him.

"Do I dare ask what this is all about?" Sandi asked, glancing from her husband to Kate.

"Probably not," Ian said with a grin. "Come, my dear. Adventures await." Releasing her hand, he gripped the wheels of his chair and began to move across the floor.

"Kate?"

"It's okay, Sandi. I made him promise to always treat you—" Her voice broke. "Just be happy, both of you." She reached for another hug.

"Mrs. Campbell?!"

"You're being paged," Kate said, attempting a smile.

"I know," Sandi said tearfully. "See you next weekend."

Kate nodded, watching as Sandi moved across the room in the beaded white gown. Reaching down, she removed her shoes. Holding the shoes in one hand, she picked up the bouquet she had been holding all night with the other. She limped outside into the cool night air.

"How are you holding up?"

Kate glanced around, then saw Keith Taylor leaning against the Orem church house. She had been a little surprised to see him come through the line tonight, assuming he would've waited until next week. She smiled at him now, wondering if he was all right. Except for a few polite words exchanged during the reception, she hadn't talked to him since Christmas vacation when she and Mike had doubled with Keith and Sandi. Keith had understandably quit writing to Sandi when he had learned of the engagement. Mike's letters had assured her that Keith would eventually recover from the shock, but doubts had surfaced when Mike's letters continued to describe the depression Keith had slipped into.

"I knew he liked her, but I didn't realize how bad he had it for her," Mike had written, trying to explain. "He'll get over it, though. Some gorgeous female will come along and make him forget all about Sandi. Besides, maybe it's better this way. Now he can go on his mission not having to worry about the girl he left behind." Kate knew Mike had dropped a less than subtle hint. He hadn't written "unlike me," but the words were there between the lines.

Sighing, Kate gazed now at Keith. He still looked shaken. And, as Mike was off serving his mission in Montreal, Canada, it appeared it would fall to her to cheer up the despondent young man.

"I said, how are you holding up?" Keith repeated, moving closer.

"Fair," she said tiredly. "How about you?"

Keith shrugged, loosening his tie. He had been one of the last to come through the line tonight. "Got a minute?" he asked, reaching for her bouquet.

"Sure," Kate said. "But I need to get off these feet."

"My car is parked around here somewhere," Keith offered. "Or, if you'd rather, we could sit on that bench over there."

"Nothing personal, but I'll take the bench. This fresh air feels pretty good."

"It got a little stuffy in there with that crowd, huh?"

Kate nodded, following him to the wooden bench. She sat, groaning as her feet continued to throb.

"Need a foot massage?" he asked.

Kate lifted an eyebrow. No one had ever offered to do that before.

"You're already waiting for two missionaries, right? I'm not up to anymore competition. I'm harmless."

"Keith, I'm not worried, I just don't—"

"The way you're limping, I'd say you're in quite a bit of pain. Let me help you. My sisters claim I give wonderful foot massages," he added, his eyes pleading with her. Sensing his need to talk, she hesitantly agreed.

"Have you heard from Mike?" she asked as he reached for her nylon-clad feet. He gently helped her swerve around until he could comfortably rub her feet and at the same time allow her to sit modestly in her tight-fitting dress.

"Not lately. How about you?"

Kate shook her head. "I'm sure he's busy. He'll write when he gets the chance," she said, suddenly realizing she had already been through this process with Randy. Would Mike's letters dwindle to short notes, sent whenever a whim possessed him?

"Mike told me how things were left between you," Keith said, making conversation.

"He did?" Kate asked, relaxing against the bench. The more

Keith massaged, the better her feet felt. His sisters were right, Keith had a real talent for this kind of thing.

"Yeah. He said that you're strictly friends for now. Possible pen pals. Nothing more until he gets back, unless of course someone snatches you up while he's gone, like that guy you've been writing."

"Randy?"

"That's the one. Did Mike ever tell you about the target he set up on the door of our room at Ricks?" Kate shook her head and Keith smiled. "Mike found a poster of a guy he assumed looked like that missionary of yours. He glued it to some thick cardboard, then rounded up some darts."

"You're kidding?"

"Nope. It made him feel better. Then for a while, he pretended it was this guy you met in Salt Lake."

"Ian?"

"That's the rat," Keith snarled. "I should've thrown a few darts of my own."

"I'm sure you don't mean that," Kate said softly.

"Maybe," Keith said, his grip tightening on Kate's foot.

"Ow! Gently, Keith, gently."

"Sorry," Keith apologized. "Tell me, Kate, is *Ian* an okay guy?"

"Yes, he is. I was there when Sandi and Ian first met. They're perfectly matched. And they are the most loving couple I've ever seen, with maybe two exceptions," she said, thinking of her parents and Paige and Stan.

"Thanks for making me feel better," Keith accused.

"I'm sorry this has been so hard on you. You have to know that Sandi never meant to hurt you. Things happened so fast—"

"Yeah, I know," he grumbled. "It hasn't been easy, but the past few weeks, I thought I'd learned to accept it. I came down tonight to show what a good sport I was being. I was doing really well, too, until I saw him kiss her." Keith let go of Kate's feet and stood. Finally he turned to face Kate. "Oh well, what's done is done."

"You've sent in your mission papers, right?" Kate asked, changing to a brighter subject.

Keith nodded. "A couple of weeks ago. I've been pretty excited about it too—until tonight."

"Keith, you've known all along that Sandi might not be around after your mission."

"I know. Can't a guy feel sorry for himself once in a while? I believe I'm entitled. The first girl that ever stole my heart gave hers to another guy."

Kate smiled. "Try this one on for size. My two best friends just tied the knot. That makes me a permanent third wheel. No more all night gab sessions with Sandi. No more hanging around with Ian."

"You poor thing," Keith sarcastically replied.

Kate gave Keith a dirty look. "You're too kind." Then, remembering she was trying to comfort Keith, she forced a smile. "We're quite a pair, aren't we—you, the ex-boyfriend and me—"

"A friendless soul?"

"Gee, thanks," Kate said, kicking him in the leg. "Ow. Let me put my shoes on." She looked at the high heels. "On second thought, never mind."

"I have an idea. How about if we go drown our sorrows with the biggest hot fudge sundae we can find?"

"That sounds so good," Kate sighed, "but I have a request."

"Anything," Keith said, bowing gallantly.

"Let me change first. I brought jeans and a sweatshirt to wear back to Salt Lake. If I don't get out of this dress soon, I'm going to scream."

"Consider it done," Keith said, helping her off the bench. Just then a crowd poured out of the building. Ian and Sandi emerged, surrounded by excited family members. "There's the happy couple now."

"Finally," Kate replied, limping beside him. She grinned at the sight of Ian's van. Someone had seen to it that the van was decorated appropriately for the occasion.

"Hey, Mr. and Mrs. . . . ." Keith turned to glance at Kate.

"Campbell," she whispered.

"Campbell," Keith hollered. "Happy trails!"

"Happy trails?" Kate asked, lifting an eyebrow.

"I love westerns. 'Happy trails' means, have a wonderful journey till we meet again."

"Oh. Happy trails," she echoed, waving to Ian and Sandi. Tears filled her eyes as she watched them enter the van.

"I almost forgot," Sandi cried out, moving back to the sidewalk. In her hands was the bridal bouquet. Turning around, she threw it into the air. It landed perfectly on top of Kate.

"You caught the bouquet," Keith exclaimed. "How exciting."

"It was self-defense," Kate protested, waving back to Sandi.

"Well, don't look at me, at least, not for a couple of years."

"Smart aleck," Kate accused. "Let's go get that hot fudge sundae you promised!" Handing him the bridal bouquet, she went back after her own bouquet and shoes and disappeared inside the church. Several minutes later, she reappeared, wearing her sweat-shirts, jeans, and a smile. Keith took the clothes bag from her and escorted her to his car. As she slid in on the passenger side, he set the clothes bag in the back, then handed her Sandi's bridal bouquet.

"I thought you'd like to keep track of this souvenir," he teased, moving out of her reach. Chuckling, he opened the door on the driver's side and slipped behind the wheel. "Where to?"

"Surprise me," Kate answered, dropping the bouquet on the seat behind them.

To Be Continued

ABOUT THE AUTHOR

Music, sports, community and church service, and lots of family time can't seem to keep Cheri Crane from writing. Cheri plays guitar and piano by ear, writes songs, loves racquetball, baseball, and volleyball, and she enjoys cooking. Besides these, she is in a Young Women's presidency and heads a local chapter of the American Diabetes Association.

A former resident of Ashton, Idaho, Cheri Nel Jackson Crane and her husband, Kennon, live in Bennington, Idaho, with their three sons. Cheri is the author of two books, the best-selling *Kate's Turn* and *The Fine Print.*